The
Silent
Songbird

MELANIE
DICKERSON

THOMAS NELSON
Since 1798

Published in Nashville, Tennessee, by Thomas Nelson. Thomas Nelson is a registered trademark of HarperCollins Christian Publishing, Inc.

Thomas Nelson titles may be purchased in bulk for educational, business, fund-raising, or sales promotional use. For information, please e-mail SpecialMarkets@ThomasNelson.com.

Scripture quotations are taken from the Holy Bible, New International Version®, NIV®. Copyright © 1973, 1978, 1984, 2011 by Biblica, Inc.® Used by permission of Zondervan. All rights reserved worldwide. www.zondervan. com. The "NIV" and "New International Version" are trademarks registered in the United States Patent and Trademark Office by Biblica, Inc.®

Publisher's Note: This novel is a work of fiction. Names, characters, places, and incidents are either products of the author's imagination or used fictitiously. All characters are fictional, and any similarity to people living or dead is purely coincidental.

Library of Congress Cataloging-in-Publication Data

Names: Dickerson, Melanie, author.
Title: The silent songbird / Melanie Dickerson.
Description: Nashville, Tennessee: Thomas Nelson, 2016. | Summary: In 1384 England, seventeen-year-old Evangeline, ward and cousin of King Richard II, tries to escape from an arranged marriage, dreaming of a life outside Berkhamsted Castle, where she might be free to marry for love and not politics, but when she runs away and joins a small band of servants on their way back to their home village, she finds herself embroiled in a tangled web that threatens England's monarch.
Identifiers: LCCN 2016022313 | ISBN 9780718026318 (hardback)
Subjects: | CYAC: Love--Fiction. | Arranged marriage--Fiction. | Social classes--Fiction. | Middle Ages--Fiction. | Great Britain--History--Richard II, 1377-1399--Fiction. | Christian life--Fiction.
Classification: LCC PZ7.D5575 Si 2016 | DDC [Fic]--dc23 LC record available at https://lccn.loc.gov/2016022313

Printed in the United States of America

16 17 18 19 20 RRD 5 4 3 2 1

Chapter One

Summer 1384. Berkhamsted Castle, Hertfordshire, England.

"Servants may marry whomever they want, but a king's ward has no freedom at all."

Evangeline broke off the song she was singing. A lump rose in her throat. Through her open window facing the castle bailey she watched the servants talking and laughing and milling about, finishing their morning chores.

A kitchen maid was drawing a bucket of water at the well in the center of the bailey. A young man approached her.

Alma gave him the dipper, and he lifted it to his lips.

The stranger's hair was brown and fell over his brow at an angle. He was tall, and even from Evangeline's bedchamber window on the third level of the castle, she could see he was handsome, with a strong chin and a sturdy stance.

He passed the water around to the other men who had followed him to the well. Evangeline leaned out the window to try to catch what they were saying.

"Thank you," the man said as he handed the dipper back to the servant. He wore the clothing of a peasant—a leather mantle over his long linen tunic.

"Where are you from?" Alma asked.

"Glynval, a little village north . . . brought . . . to sell . . . and wheat flour . . ." Evangeline couldn't make out all the words.

The man wasn't like most peasants. Not that she had seen very many. But this man held himself upright with an air of confidence and ease she had rarely seen before.

Evangeline leaned out a little farther, hanging on to the casement. The man was moving on as the cart started forward, Alma still staring after him. He turned to say something to the other men and suddenly looked up at Evangeline.

"Evangeline!"

She jumped backward, her heart crashing against her chest.

"What are you doing, hanging out the window like a common—? Don't you know better than to behave that way?" Muriel hurried to the open window and peered out, then closed it and clamped her hands on her hips.

"Am I not allowed to look out the window? I'm no better than the prisoners in the dungeon. You know, I feel much pity for them. I daydream sometimes about releasing them and running away with them." She tipped her face to the ceiling as if turning her face to the sun and closed her eyes. "How good it would feel, walking free through the fields of wildflowers I read about in a poem once, breathing the fresh air, free to go wherever I want."

"You think your jests are amusing," Muriel said, "but when the king of England is your guardian and is planning your wedding to a wealthy nobleman, you should not expect pity. Envy is more likely."

"Wedding? What do you mean?" Evangeline's heart seemed to stop beating. "What do you know?"

"It is only gossip, but it is said that the king has promised you to one of his closest advisors."

"Who?"

"The Earl of Shiveley."

Evangeline reached out and placed a hand on the stone wall as the room seemed to teeter from side to side. How could the king betroth her to him? Lord Shiveley was old—almost forty—and Evangeline was barely seventeen. She had only seen Lord Shiveley a few times when he had accompanied the king to Berkhamsted Castle. He stared at her in a way that made her stomach sick, and he always managed to put a hand on her—on her shoulder or her back, and even once at her waist. She would always writhe inwardly and step away from him as quickly as she could.

Besides that, it was rumored that Lord Shiveley's first wife had died under mysterious circumstances.

Evangeline shuddered.

"The king and Lord Shiveley will arrive tonight, and you must be ready to greet them." Muriel bustled over to the wardrobe where Evangeline's best dresses were kept. She opened it and rummaged through her clothing. "You should wash your hair. I have ordered your bath sent up, and I shall—"

"Muriel, stop!" Evangeline stared at the woman who had been her closest companion and confidant for ten years. Though Muriel was nearly old enough to be her mother, she could not be so daft.

Muriel stared back at her with a bland expression. "What is it?"

"Surely you must see that I cannot marry that man." Her voice was a breathy whisper.

"My dear," Muriel said, not unkindly, "you know, you have always known, you must marry whomever the king wishes you to."

Evangeline's throat constricted. "The king does not care a whit about my feelings."

"Careful." Muriel's gaze darted about the room. "You mustn't risk speaking against the king. You never know who might betray you."

"I shall tell the king to his face when he arrives that I shall not marry Lord Shiveley, and it is cruel to ask it of me."

"You know you shall do no such thi—"

"I shall! I shall tell him!"

"Evangeline. You are too old to get in such a passion. Sit down and calm yourself. Breathe."

Evangeline crossed her arms over her chest and ignored Muriel's order. She had to think of some way to escape. Women often married men they did not particularly want to marry, but she could not marry Lord Shiveley. She was not like other women. They might accept unfair treatment, but Evangeline would fight, argue, rebel against injustice. Other women conformed to what was expected of them. Perhaps they did not dream of freedom and a different life.

"You must listen to reason," Muriel said. "Lord Shiveley is rich and can give you your own home. You will finally have the freedom to do whatever you wish. You will have servants and your own gardens and even your own horse. Many ladies enjoy falconry and hunting. You can have as many dresses and as much jewelry, or anything else your heart desires."

Only if her husband allowed it.

Muriel knew her well enough to know what might sway her. But a husband did not give freedom. A husband made rules. He took away his wife's control and replaced it with his own. A wealthy, power-ful husband could order his wife around, beat her, do whatever he wished to her, and she could do naught.

Peasants, if they were not married and were free men and women, might be poor, but was it not a hundred times better to be free than to have fancy clothes and expensive food and servants to do everything for you? Freedom and independence were worth more than all the gold a castle could hold. Freedom to choose whom to marry, freedom to walk about the countryside unhindered, to drink from a cool, clear stream and gaze up into the trees, to ride a horse and eat while standing up. To bathe in the river and laugh and sing at the top of her voice—that was freedom.

And now King Richard was about to force her to marry an old, disgusting man.

"But you said it was gossip." Evangeline began to breathe easier. "Perhaps it was only idle talk."

Or if it was true, once she was able to talk to King Richard, he would understand. They'd been friends since they were very young, being cousins and only six months apart in age. Although she had not seen much of Richard in the past few years, surely he would listen to her pleas.

Her stomach sank. She was fooling herself. Richard would not listen to her if he had made up his mind. His loyalty to his advisors came before any childhood friendship he might still feel for Evangeline.

"At least Lord Shiveley is taller than you are." Muriel arched her brows.

"Just because I am taller than half the men I've ever met doesn't mean I want to marry this man." Evangeline turned away from Muriel and sat on the bench by the window, placing her head in her hands. Perhaps if she were able to cry, it would relieve this terrible ache in her chest.

"There now." Muriel sat beside her and placed a hand on her shoulder. "Do not fret about something that may not even be true. We shall wait until the king arrives and let him tell you why he's here and if he has aught to say to you."

But the gentle warmth of Muriel's hand did not feel comforting. Muriel was fifteen years older than Evangeline, but they were both illegitimate daughters of important men—Evangeline's father was the king's uncle, while Muriel's father was an archbishop. Both of them were dependent on the kindness of King Richard.

Fortunately for Muriel, she was not valued as a pawn in the king's political maneuverings, to be married off to a man the king wanted to please or bribe. It was easy for Muriel to tell Evangeline not to fret about marrying a repulsive man.

A knock came at the door. Muriel opened it to a man wearing the livery of the king.

"A message for Evangeline, ward of the king, daughter of Lionel of Antwerp, Duke of Clarence."

Evangeline stood. Muriel brought her the missive, which had been sealed in dark-red wax with the king's signet ring. She tore it open. The words leapt off the page at her:

> Evangeline, I and the Earl of Shiveley would enjoy hearing you sing for us with that famous, incomparable voice of yours. I believe you are acquainted with my advisor, which is more than most noble brides can boast of their betrothed. He became quite enamored of you the last time he heard you sing.

Betrothed.

The note slipped from her hand and fluttered to the floor.

Muriel snatched it up while Evangeline's whole body went cold. Would her blood congeal from horror? Would she fall to the floor dead? Her throat seemed to close and she was dizzy.

She could not allow herself to be overcome like other women she read about who fainted but then went to their fates like sheep with no compunction or will of their own.

Jesus, is that what You would wish me to do? Comply and submit and allow myself to be married off to someone who makes my stomach churn and my skin crawl? Jesus submitted to a terrible fate for the good of mankind, but Evangeline could not see any good that could come from marrying Lord Shiveley. Except that it would please King Richard.

"Now, my dear." Muriel carefully laid the letter down on a shelf. "I know you think you do not wish to marry Lord Shiveley, but consider some other good things this will bring to you. You will win the king's favor. Your husband may truly love you, and you may get children from the union. Indeed, there are many benefits that will come."

"How can any of that be worth marrying someone I cannot abide? And you know what people say about his first wife." Evangeline spun away from her. Muriel would refuse to listen or understand how Evangeline felt.

"That is only idle gossip. No one pays attention to such talk. And it will be far better if you simply accept that you have no choice and try to make the best of it. What else can you do?"

"What else can I do?" Evangeline's voice rose in near-hysterical tones. "Accept that I have no choice?" Sobs choked off further speech as she kept her back to Muriel. Muriel would think she was selfish not to do as the king asked, and Muriel would stop loving her if she thought she was selfish. But it hurt so much to think of losing any chance of contentment and throwing herself away on Lord Shiveley.

"I shall leave you alone for a while." Muriel turned and her footsteps receded to the door. Then she seemed to hesitate and said, "I am truly sorry, Evangeline. But God will sustain you." The door clicked open, then shut again.

If she were like other women, she would let the king use her as a gift, a favor, a pawn. But she would do something no other noble ladies that she knew of ever did. She would refuse to marry Lord Shiveley. If necessary, she would run away, take on another identity, lose herself in the English countryside. She had imagined it many times, had thought long and hard about the different ways she might escape.

All her life Evangeline had lived in various royal residences—mostly at Berkhamsted Castle—wherever the king sent her to live. The king was so afraid she might be kidnapped and held for ransom he had ordered her to stay inside the walls, only allowed to venture out occasionally when she had guards nearby. Most people in England probably did not even know the Duke of Clarence had a second child or that her name was Evangeline.

When the king visited, he and other special guests would accompany her on a hunt in the adjacent deer park or a walk around the gardens. She obeyed, accepting that she was not the master of her own fate. Evangeline had rarely done anything courageous or unexpected.

Tonight was a good time for a change, to see if she was brave enough to carry out her fantasy of running away.

Westley le Wyse thanked the servant girl for the water.

Above him in the castle window, a young red-haired woman was staring down at him. Was she the one who had been singing just moments before? He had been listening, rapt and still, to that voice, the one singing a rustic ballad with such refinement and grace, until it suddenly went silent. As soon as their eyes met, she disappeared from the window, almost as if someone had snatched her back.

He only glimpsed her, but he got the impression she was not a servant by her clothing and hair, and that she was quite lovely. The rumor was that the king had a ward living at Berkhamsted Castle, a young woman with an ethereally beautiful voice. Some said she was the illegitimate daughter of the king's dead uncle, Lionel of Antwerp, which meant she was the granddaughter of King Edward. But she might be only a myth. Legends often were created from some tidbit of gossip.

"Did you hear the news?"

He shifted around to face the servant girl who lingered in the bailey with her bucket of water.

"King Richard is coming to Berkhamsted Castle tonight."

That would be a sight. Even Westley's father had never seen the king.

"We are all busy with preparations for the king and his retinue. What provisions did you and your men bring for us?" The girl was standing on tiptoe, trying to see over his shoulder.

"Wheat flour, oats, malt, and some large cheeses."

It had been a good year for several crops in Glynval and the surrounding land. Westley had come to Berkhamsted Castle with his father's servants to sell their excess.

"This is my little sister." The servant girl indicated the golden-haired child playing behind her. "I have to watch her today since my mother is sick."

The little girl looked to be about six years old. She was squealing and grunting as she leapt and spun about, trying to catch a bright-yellow butterfly that fluttered just out of her reach.

A horse's angry neigh drew Westley's attention to the other end of the bailey.

"Steady," said a man holding the horse's bridle. Its neigh grew into a high-pitched screech. The horse leapt straight up, snatching the bridle out of the man's hands. The horse's hooves touched the ground and the animal bolted forward. The cart knocked the man to the ground as it jolted past him.

The horse galloped across the bailey—heading straight for the little girl.

"Get out of the way!" Westley pushed the servant aside as he raced toward the little girl, willing her to move out of the path of the horse.

The girl suddenly seemed to hear the noise of the horse's hooves and the clattering cart barreling toward her. She froze and stared, her mouth open.

Westley ran and grabbed her around her middle with one arm, then dove to the side. He held her above him as his shoulder and back collided with the ground.

Chapter Two

When Muriel left her room, Evangeline wandered back to the window that faced the bailey.

While she watched Alma talk with the handsome young man, a horse broke away from its handler and careened toward Alma's little sister.

The child saw the horse coming. Why didn't she run? She seemed frozen.

Evangeline screamed, "Run!"

The young man leapt toward the girl, grabbed her, and pulled her out of the way just in time.

The horse galloped on and crashed the cart into the stone wall around the well. The cart now in pieces, the horse kept going and finally stopped at the opposite wall of the bailey.

Evangeline clutched her chest as air seeped back into her lungs.

The little girl was crying. The young man set her on her feet, and Alma ran to her and hugged her. Was the stranger hurt? He took quite a hard fall as he protected the child in his arms.

He got to his feet as the other men with him rushed to his side. He must have spoken to Alma and the little girl because they turned toward him. How Evangeline wished she could hear what they were saying! She leaned out of the window but couldn't catch their words. She imagined he asked the kitchen maid if the child was uninjured and imagined her replying, "Yes, only frightened," as the child's crying lessened.

The man's friends brushed him off and clapped him on the back, their eyes wide as they seemed to be congratulating him on his act of bravery.

He gave them all a smile, and her stomach flipped at his gentle expression.

After a few moments, he approached the little girl and squatted to look her in the eye. They seemed to be having a quiet conversation, then the child stepped close enough to put her arms around his neck. The man put his arms around her.

Evangeline's heart turned to wax and melted into her stomach.

"If only I were a peasant," she whispered. "I could fall in love with him, someone kind and brave and strong. Though he was poor, if he loved me, I would give him my heart."

He walked away with his friends, and she sighed.

What hope did she have to enjoy such a love as portrayed in the traveling minstrels' ballads? She was a king's granddaughter, even if her birth was illegitimate. She would never be free to go wherever she wanted, to work and play and live in the sunshine. If she ever wanted to be free to marry for love, she had no choice but to run away from Berkhamsted Castle and never return.

After an afternoon of bathing, dressing, being fussed over, and sitting still until her neck ached while a servant prepared her hair in loose curls, Evangeline could feel her self-control slipping. They dressed her in a patterned Flemish cotehardie of pale-green-and-pink flowers with an elaborately embroidered hem. Then they placed a jeweled circlet on her head over a sheer headrail. But every minute, she was thinking of the bag she had begun to fill with necessities—clothing she had taken from the servants' quarters, money, and a pair of sturdy shoes, also pilfered from the storage closet where the head house servant kept a surplus.

She was getting dressed up for the king and Lord Shiveley when she did not even know exactly when they might arrive. The only thing that mattered was pleasing the king and his important guests.

She might as well be that poor horse who had broken away from its owner in the castle bailey earlier. Was he so tired of the bit and bridle that dug into his soft, tender mouth that he could take it no longer? Was he in pain in some other part of his body? Did he want to eat? Sleep? Find his mate? No one knew, no one cared, and the horse had had enough of it.

Evangeline knew just how he felt. But if she bolted, just like that horse, would she also be recaptured? Forced into doing her duty to the king after all?

Muriel burst through the door. "The king is here!" Her voice was brisk and breathless. "He is asking for you, Evangeline, just as I knew he would."

"He wants me to come to the Great Hall for the evening meal?"

"He wants you to come now to the solar."

"To sing for Lord Shiveley." Evangeline's stomach sank to her toes. She sat staring at the door.

"What are you waiting for? Go, Evangeline."

"Will you come with me?"

"Of course."

Evangeline stood. "If you are there as my witness, Lord Shiveley cannot do anything vile." She grabbed Muriel's arm. "Promise me you will not leave my side."

"Very well, I shall try." A flash of sympathy passed over Muriel's face, which only made Evangeline's stomach sink even more.

They made their way through the castle and up the stairs that led to the solar. Evangeline had never noticed before how gray the stones were, gray and hard and cold.

When they reached the room, two guards stood outside the door. The guards opened it, then closed it behind Evangeline and Muriel.

Richard was lounging in the largest chair, leaning back against the cushions. Evangeline and Muriel curtsied, bowing their heads.

"My cousin, little Evangeline! Come here." Richard held out his hand to her.

Her heart beat fast as she approached her childhood friend. But she hardly recognized him anymore. Richard was the same height as Evangeline. His blond hair was darker, less yellow than she remembered. Having just turned eighteen years old, he had lost his soft, childlike facial features. Already he had dealt with killings and uprisings, not to mention he had been married for two and a half years.

There was a hardness around his eyes and mouth. Richard had seen the fighting during the Peasants' Uprising three years before, had actually witnessed some of his close advisors murdered. It must have been very hard for him. He was not without feeling. At least, not when he was a boy.

He squeezed her hand, then motioned to her right. "Lord Shiveley wishes to greet you."

Evangeline barely glanced at Lord Shiveley before sinking into a quick curtsy.

"My dear Evangeline. What a beauty you are, and always have been."

He bowed over her hand. His wet lips touched her skin and her stomach turned. She tried to pull her hand out of his grasp, but he held on.

The Earl of Shiveley had a head full of black hair streaked with white. His lips were thick and shiny.

"My dear," King Richard said, "Lord Shiveley and I are eager to hear you sing. Shiveley especially has told everyone in London about your exceptional voice and ability."

Evangeline glanced at Lord Shiveley and couldn't help but see the predatory look in his dark, deep-set eyes—something between masculine and animalistic. She shuddered.

"And just in time, here are the musicians."

Three men entered the room, one carrying a hurdy-gurdy, another a lute, and another a flute.

"What song do you prefer? They can play anything." Richard was smiling and leaning toward her.

All eyes were on Evangeline. She had sung for the king and his retinue before, but the thought of Lord Shiveley watching her with those squinty black eyes, thinking she was soon to be his bride . . . Her cheeks burned.

Evangeline named a song, and the musicians began to play. She cleared her throat and closed her eyes, willing her voice not to shake, but to be clear, strong, and defiant.

It was a warm day, and the window was open. Evangeline imagined that her voice was carrying straight out that window and into the ears of people who would not only appreciate it, but who did not expect her to be their pawn, plaything, or anything else she did not wish to be.

As she sang several verses, Evangeline kept her eyes focused out the window on the trees well beyond and the sky and clouds above those trees. Singing made her feel free. If she kept her mind on faraway places and people, she couldn't think of Lord Shiveley, so she continued to sing to the trees and the clouds and the birds, to the invisible masses in her mind, her heart swelling with the notes, soaring into freedom.

When the song ended, tears pricked her eyelids. Her heart seized at the way Richard was staring at her, at the thought of facing Lord Shiveley.

"Sing another, if you please, Evangeline," King Richard said.

She gave the musicians the title of another song, grateful for the distraction, even though it would only postpone the inevitable.

Could anyone hear her out that window? Inexplicably, in her mind she saw the young man who saved the little girl from the runaway horse. Could he hear the desperation in her voice? Would he be willing to come to her aid and help her escape from the prison that was her life?

But that was foolish. No one could help her. She had to save herself.

When the song was over, she glanced in Lord Shiveley's direction. He smiled.

King Richard was speaking. "We shall have a short ceremony here tomorrow with my own priest. We will have the banns cried afterward to satisfy the Church, but Lord Shiveley is eager to have the formalities over. I'm sure you cannot mind, since Lord Shiveley is well able to take care of you. His country estate in Yorkshire is even larger than Berkhamsted Castle."

Blessedly, Evangeline's mind went numb. She took the time to swallow. He would not even allow her time to accustom herself to the idea or to try to persuade him not to force her to marry Lord Shiveley. What could she possibly say that would change his mind?

"It is sudden, Your Majesty. You had only mentioned this once before."

Richard's eyes widened, then his brows lowered. "But you have no reason to object." He was not asking her; he was telling her.

Instead of replying, she simply lowered her head, a cross between a bow and a nod. She steeled herself against looking at Lord Shiveley. She did not want to see whatever expression he might have at her reluctance to acquiesce to their wedding on the morrow.

"Very good, my dear cousin. Now tell me how you have fared. Are you in good health? Have the servants been treating you as they should?"

"Yes, I have been in very good health, and the servants have been as dutiful and obliging as they have ever been. And you? How has Your Majesty's health fared?"

"Very well, except for a fever I suffered for a few days. I am quite restored now. Shiveley had some lemons sent to me, and they quite cured me. Lemon juice and honey will cure nearly any ill. I am convinced."

Yes, Lord Shiveley was quite the perfect friend and ally, no doubt. And now he must be rewarded. He must get whatever wife he wished, even though he was old and disgusting and—

"How is the hunting this time of year?" the king asked.

"I do not know. Your steward often provides us with venison and pheasant, so I believe the hunting is good."

"Have you still not taken up falconry and hunting stags, my dear?"

"I do not wish to disappoint you, my king."

Richard laughed. "You always did have a mind of your own. Behind that pretty face, you have the mind of a man—though not a man's taste for hunting, I see."

She cast her gaze down at the floor to hide her rebellious eyes in the hopes of looking demure. "I hunt as often as I am allowed to, Your Majesty."

"Evangeline, if I may ask," Lord Shiveley said, his voice as smooth and oily as his hair. "What do you enjoy doing, if not hunting? I know you sing beautifully. Do you also play an instrument? Or perhaps you prefer painting or embroidery?"

It was probably regular and polite conversation, but somehow Lord Shiveley sounded as if he were placing her beneath him by naming these strictly feminine pursuits.

"I do not paint." She disdained telling him that she rather enjoyed embroidery. "I play the lute, and I sing for the servants every Sunday evening." *Shut away here in this stone prison.* "When I am fortunate enough, the steward allows me to roam the gardens, where I enjoy identifying plants and small animals and insects. Muriel helps me by drawing the specimens, and we have started compiling them into a book."

"I see. That is most interesting."

"But I am planning to start training in sword fighting, archery, and knife throwing." She could not resist the rebellious declaration, even though she knew she should pretend to be demure.

Lord Shiveley peered at her while stroking his thin black goatee.

Richard suddenly laughed. "She has quite the humorous streak, Shiveley. A bit of rebellion, perhaps, but Evangeline is as sweet as honey. Aren't you, my dear?" Richard's lip quirked up in a smirk, but a brittleness shone in his eyes.

Heat rose into Evangeline's cheeks. Thinking of her half-packed bag in the bottom of her trunk allowed her to smile. "I enjoy music, my lord. And decorative sewing and reading. I am afraid I have no other talents."

Lord Shiveley lifted his thick lips in what must have been an attempt at a smile. "Your modesty becomes you. And if you wish to learn archery, I am sure that can be arranged."

How magnanimous of you.

"And His Majesty has graciously agreed to allow you to bring any servants you wish to take, anyone you are attached to, and of course, as your personal companion, Muriel will accompany you."

They carried on a three-way conversation until Richard began talking with Muriel. He had known her since he was a child and always remembered her name. Most of the other servants would have been struck speechless, and possibly senseless, if the king spoke to them. Muriel was amazingly unintimidated by him. She spoke with the confidence of a duchess, and he seemed to like that.

"You will enjoy my country home," Lord Shiveley said quietly, bending his head toward Evangeline. "I will not require you to travel with me when I am with the king, but you may join me at the king's favorite residence, Sheen Palace, when I accompany the king there."

His gaze dipped to her chest. Evangeline cringed and leaned away from him, but he did not seem to be bothered by her reaction. His small, alert eyes did not seem to miss a thing, in spite of how low his eyelids hung.

"I hope you are as eager for the marriage as I am. The king has said no one else has asked for you, no doubt because your birth was illegitimate."

Evangeline's face burned. "I should be thankful you are willing to marry me, then?"

His smile disappeared. "Marriage to me will greatly improve the way you will be remembered. Any woman in England would be glad to marry the king's closest advisor."

"I am surprised you do not marry someone more worthy of your status, then. After all, I am illegitimate and have neither fortune nor title."

Lord Shiveley's nostrils flared. "Be that as it may, you have royal blood, which is what I want, and tomorrow you will be my wife." His voice was low and harsh. "Whether you wish it or not."

Her stomach churned. If only she could wipe the smirk off his face. He must think he had Richard completely within his power, proclaiming himself the king's closest advisor.

"It grows late," King Richard said. "Evangeline, you go on and enjoy yourself. I am too tired from my travels to join you for the feast in the Great Hall, but Lord Shiveley will keep you company."

They all began to take their leave of the king, but Evangeline hung back. "Your Majesty, may I speak to you alone for a moment?"

She sensed Lord Shiveley standing behind her, waiting for the king's answer. Was the king shocked at her boldness?

Richard stared at her for a moment. "Everyone leave us. I will speak with my childhood friend."

The others shuffled out the door as she locked gazes with the king. Finally, all were gone except for two guards who stood discreetly in the corners.

"Now, what is it, Evangeline? You must have something important to say." The warning in his voice was unmistakable. "But before you say anything, I want you to understand that it is quite an honor to *you* that I have granted Lord Shiveley permission to marry you."

"Yes, he has made it clear that I am fortunate to be marrying him, since I am only an illegitimate daughter of the king's dead uncle."

"Who left you without any fortune."

So this was the king's attitude toward her. She needed to be strong, to stand up in dignity to him, even if he thought her selfish. Crying would only confirm to him that she was but a weak female. She bit the inside of her mouth.

"It is true, I have no fortune." She carefully considered what she would say. "But you do not resent allowing me to live here, do you? I have not cost you much, have I? All I ask is that you not force me to marry Lord Shiveley just yet. Delay the wedding." It was all she could possibly hope for.

"What is the matter, Evangeline? You are of age. Seventeen is quite old enough for marriage."

"But I do not wish to marry Lord Shiveley." Her voice sounded so desperate, surely Richard would take pity on her.

"My dear," he said after a short pause, "marriage is nothing to be afraid of. And none of us marry who we wish to or whom we have fallen in love with. Love before marriage is for peasants, a foolish notion invented by poets and minstrels. I was fifteen years old, as was Anne, when we married. Two and a half years later, our marriage is as peaceful and pleasant as anyone could wish. I have no doubt that you and Shiveley will be the same."

This was as she had feared. The king not only would not come to her aid and postpone the marriage—during which Evangeline hoped something might happen to prevent it—but he thought she was selfish and unreasonable for not accepting his will.

"As a king, my situation is always precarious. I must take care to make alliances with the most powerful people I can to preserve our country's well-being, not to mention my own. I married the woman I believed would bring me the most powerful and influential allies in England's struggles against her enemies. And I have my own personal enemies, Evangeline, of which you could know nothing. You are safe here at Berkhamsted Castle, while I am the object of hatred for some, not the least of which is the Duke of Templeton, who is even now trying to turn the opinion of the nobility and parliament against me. He would have me deposed and would set up his own puppet in my place. Even though I despise Templeton and he would stab me through the heart if he could, I would gladly marry off my daughter, if I had one, to his son, simply to ensure that he would not someday put that knife through my heart, either literally or politically."

The king sighed. He shook his head. "As I told you, no one marries for love except peasants or perhaps a merchant or landowner who has no political enemies. But you are the king's close cousin, the granddaughter of a king, and therefore . . . Shiveley is a good man, you will see. Steady and reliable, he is everything you could want in a husband."

"I am very grateful for your kindness, I am sure," she murmured, hoping he would stop talking. But if he stopped talking and sent her away, where could she go except to join Lord Shiveley in the Great Hall for the feast?

"You are pleased, then, with marriage?" Evangeline said the first thing that popped in her head. "What I mean is, marriage is something I have never been near enough to observe. I am very close to Muriel, as we are together every day. I imagine marriage is similar to that—a close sort of depending upon each other. And yet I had hoped marriage could be . . . romantic."

Richard's gaze wandered to the ceiling for a moment as though he was thinking. "You have made a good description of it, a close sort of depending upon each other. Muriel is your companion, more than a servant, but marriage is nothing like the relationship between a servant and master. Or it should not be. It is a bit like two souls becoming connected, a stronger bond, even, than friendship or family. You shall understand the mystery I speak of, my dear, once you and Shiveley have been married for a few months."

Hearing him describe that type of bond was beginning to stir a longing inside her—until he mentioned Shiveley. She had no wish to have that sort of bond with him. In fact, the very thought made her sick in her stomach.

Should she try to convince the king that Lord Shiveley was not as virtuous, perhaps, as he thought? That she sensed an ugliness of character to match his less-than-handsome face? That the thought of kissing the man and becoming his wife made her fear she might never be able to eat again?

"Perhaps I will come with you to the Great Hall after all," the king said. "I am feeling more rested now."

"Very good." Evangeline let out a relieved breath. At least she would not be alone with Shiveley.

They walked down the keep steps to the Great Hall where all the guests were waiting. Lord Shiveley's eyes widened when he saw the king, and he shifted his feet as Evangeline and Richard approached.

"I thought you would eat in your room, Your Majesty." Shiveley stood, waiting for the king to be seated at the end of the table.

"I changed my mind."

They sat at the long table with a few other lords and advisors who had traveled with the king, as well as several knights at a separate table.

Evangeline settled herself a few seats away from Richard, allowing some of the earls and barons to sit between her and their monarch, on the opposite side of the table from Lord Shiveley.

The king caught her eye and motioned to her. "I insist you sit beside your future husband. Come, over here."

Everyone turned to see to whom the king was motioning.

She tried to think of an excuse. Finally, she had no choice but to stand and move to the other side of the table. With as much dignity as she could muster, she sat primly beside Lord Shiveley.

King Richard introduced Evangeline to the nearby guests as Lionel of Antwerp's daughter and the soon-to-be wife of Lord Shiveley. Evangeline barely heard the guests' names as she acknowledged each of them with a nod.

The food began arriving, and thankfully Lord Shiveley and the king were listening to an earl tell about his hunt for a deer earlier that afternoon. She talked with the woman next to her—the only other woman at the table—about her journey. The woman was the wife of one of the courtiers, a baron, and they were traveling with the king but would be separating from his retinue soon to go to their home in Derbyshire.

Evangeline was even able to eat some of the food, as it seemed Lord Shiveley would continue to ignore her through the entire meal.

As she reached for her goblet, her elbow brushed against his arm. She snatched her arm away as if she'd touched a hot ember.

She felt Lord Shiveley's eyes on her, but she refused to look at him. From the corner of her eye, she saw him lean toward her. The urge to lean away from him nearly overwhelmed her, but she controlled it. His voice rumbled near her ear, "You are not afraid of me, are you, Evangeline? I do not want a wife who is afraid of me."

Her spine stiffened and she glanced at him. "Of course I am not afraid of you."

For several moments he said nothing. Then he leaned even closer, so close she felt his hot breath in her ear, as he growled, "You may not care for me, but you will submit to me."

Her cheeks burned. She glanced at the king. He was laughing at something someone on the other side of the table had said. Lord Shiveley's hand pressed against her back. She squirmed, but there was no way to escape the hand without slapping it away or otherwise drawing attention to herself.

Evangeline turned to Lady Pettwood. "Will you walk with me to my room? I am feeling unwell."

"Yes, of course, my dear. I am very tired myself."

Evangeline stood, breaking away from Shiveley's touch. She only had to wait a moment for Lady Pettwood to tell her husband she was leaving, and the two of them took their leave of the king, curtsying and hurrying away.

"Will you be well?" Lady Pettwood seemed genuinely concerned.

"I shall be well in the morning. I only need to go to bed early."

"It is to be your wedding day." Lady Pettwood patted Evangeline's arm. "Do you need me to tell you what to expect? My own daughters are too young yet to need to be told any—"

"No, no, I assure you, I do not need . . . no, though I thank you, Lady Pettwood."

They arrived at Evangeline's door first, but then she had to show Lady Pettwood to her room, as she had lost her way in the corridors of the large building.

When Evangeline arrived back at her room, she closed her door behind her and locked it.

Her heart raced as she ran to the trunk where she had stowed her bag. She drew it out and quickly folded her undergowns and stuffed them into the cloth bag. The servants' clothing she had taken only left enough room for two of her oldest and least fine overgowns if she was to include any books at all. And she simply could not bear the thought of not packing her Psalter and Book of Hours.

She closed the bag and stood staring at the door, her bag clutched to her chest. Should she try to leave now? Or wait until everyone had gone to bed? If she left now, Muriel would surely discover she was gone. Could she trust Muriel not to tell the king?

But she could not wait until morning, as the wedding would take place tomorrow. If she waited, Shiveley and the king would send their guards after her and she would not get far.

Her heart pounding, she went to the window. The castle bailey was deserted except for a servant who was drawing water from the well. But then several men appeared, walking away from the castle and across the bailey toward the gate. They approached the well and refilled their water flasks. They packed away the water on the cart their donkey was pulling and continued toward the gate leading out of the bailey to the road beyond.

The party of travelers was the same group with the kind man who had saved Alma's little sister.

She had to take off her elaborate silk dress. But the neckline was too small to pull over her head, and the dress buttoned down the back.

She took hold of the neckline and jerked with all her strength.

Buttons flew off, pinging against the wall behind her. She pulled it over her head and flung it away. She grabbed one of the gowns she had borrowed from the servants' quarters, then pulled it over her head and over her long white undergown.

She snatched up her bag and ran out the door.

Chapter Three

As she hurried down the darkened corridor lit only by a few torches, Evangeline pulled the metal circlet from her hair, then took it and the veil attached and stuffed them behind a loose stone in the wall. Her hair fell unencumbered down her back, and she ran her hand through the few small braids that had been woven through her hair, unbraiding them and jerking her fingers loose when they became entangled.

No one else met her in the corridor, but once she reached the back stairs, she could hear voices. The servants would be running around tending to their extra duties due to all the guests in the king's retinue—all the extra food to be prepared, extra beds to be readied, as well as the care of the extra horses.

She could only hope they would be too busy to notice her.

Evangeline slipped from the bottom step to the door that led outside. Just as her foot touched the ground, someone grabbed her arm from behind.

Evangeline cried out.

"What are you doing?"

"Muriel!" Evangeline clutched her bag closer to her chest.

"Where are you going?"

"Do not try to stop me. If you do, I shall kill myself before morning. I would rather die than marry Lord Shiveley."

They were whispering as men milled around the inner bailey near where they stood.

"You foolish girl!" Muriel's voice was bitter and her brows drew together, wrinkling her forehead. "Why can you not accept your fate as any other woman would?"

"Let me go." A fierceness rose inside her. Evangeline pulled out of Muriel's grasp.

"I am coming with you, then."

Her words made Evangeline stop and look back. "No, Muriel. You cannot."

"I will not let you get killed out in a world you know nothing of. I am coming."

"You will cause me to be discovered. I can blend in better without you." Evangeline tried to say whatever would be most likely to deter Muriel. Searching the bailey for the man and his companions, she saw some men just passing through the gate over the first moat.

"I must go *now*. I cannot wait for you." She blinked back tears at saying such a thing to her friend, but she was desperate.

Muriel only hesitated for a moment. "Let us go, then."

Would Muriel alert the guard at the gate that the king's ward was escaping? Would she get word back to the king where Evangeline was staying? Short of doing bodily harm to her friend and companion, she had little choice.

"Come then. But do not betray me." Evangeline frightened herself with her passionately whispered words.

Muriel answered in her own harsh whisper, "If I wished to betray you, I would run back into the castle and tell the king what you are doing."

"Hurry." Evangeline hastened across the bailey. Her skirt was a bit too short for her tall legs, but that enabled her to move faster. Soon Muriel, with her shorter, heavier frame, was huffing and puffing behind her. Evangeline pushed forward, as the men had already exited the gate.

The main gate on the other side of the double moat was guarded by four men. Would they demand to know their names and what their business was? Servants rarely left the castle, and they certainly should not be leaving now, while the king was there. What would she and Muriel tell them?

Evangeline slowed her pace and kept her head down as they approached the guards. Muriel walked beside her. Evangeline held her breath. At any moment the guards could command them to halt.

As she and Muriel entered the gate, the guards looked at them but then glanced away without pausing their conversation. None of them said anything to Muriel or Evangeline.

Evangeline hurried on, and after several more yards she bowed her head to speak quietly in Muriel's ear. "I will pretend to be mute so no one will suspect my true identity. You will tell this group of men that we wish to travel with them. You may tell them we are peasants whose lord has died of the plague and we are looking for work."

Muriel's eyes widened. "This is your plan?"

Evangeline straightened. "You may go back to the castle if you wish."

"Very well. I suppose it is a good disguise—for you, at least. I will do the talking."

Muriel's dress was much too fine for a peasant's. What if the men did not believe them? What if they became suspicious and alerted the guards?

And why was Muriel being so helpful? Perhaps she wanted to do her duty and protect Evangeline. She probably thought she could talk her into going back to Berkhamsted Castle later.

The men and their cart were just ahead. When Evangeline and

Muriel had nearly caught up with them, the two men at the rear turned and saw them.

"Good evening," Muriel said to them, a smile on her face.

The men called to the others in the group, who also stopped and stared.

"We are traveling tonight," Muriel said, "and would be very grateful if you would allow us to travel with your group."

"Where are you going?"

The man who had rescued the child from the runaway horse stepped toward them. He was even more handsome close up in the light of the moon and stars.

"We are going . . . in the same direction as you. We are free women servants whose master died in the last outbreak of plague, and we are in search of work. Is there work where you are going?"

Muriel sounded so simple, not like herself at all. Perhaps she truly was trying to help Evangeline escape.

"We can always use more workers in Glynval during harvest-time." A look of suspicion crossed his face. He probably did not believe that their master had died. Muriel once told her that many poor vil-leins claimed to be free, when they were actually legally bound to the land and to their lords and were running away unlawfully from their villages. Since the uprising three years earlier, everyone was even more suspicious of strangers.

"You are welcome to travel with us. You have nothing to fear in our company."

What would she have felt if Richard had asked her to marry this handsome stranger, with his kind face and friendly voice? If Lord Shiveley had looked and behaved like this man, she might not be risking her life to find whatever freedom she could.

"I am Westley le Wyse of Glynval, and these men are Roger, Robert, Piers, and Aldred."

"I am Mildred, and this maiden is Eva. She is mute."

"Mute?" Westley raised his brows.

"Yes, her . . . master's wife beat her and injured her throat, and she has not been able to speak since."

She felt a stab in her middle at the outrageous lies Muriel was telling—lies Evangeline had forced her to tell.

Westley le Wyse's mouth went slack with such a look of compassion, she felt another stab. Compared to the Earl of Shiveley, he had such young, perfect, masculine features. Perhaps she was already falling in love, that contemptible emotion King Richard had spoken of as something only peasants felt before marriage.

They continued on, the rocks on the road cutting into Evangeline's feet. The thin, calfskin indoor slippers would soon wear out, so she needed to change into her sturdier servant's shoes as soon as possible.

Westley said, "I suppose the head house servant asked you to leave, due to the king and all his guests being in the castle."

"Oh yes," Muriel said. "We are not fancy enough and might get in the king's way."

"She told us it was his guards who wanted anyone not of the king's party or of the household servants to leave the castle for the sake of the king's safety."

"Oh yes, that too." Muriel gave Evangeline a quick cringing smile.

The darkness surrounded them like a thick fog, and the moon was a sliver in a sky of tiny stars. The sound of the cart wheels covered the sound of their footsteps so that any number of bandits could have been lurking along the road. Yet Evangeline felt safe in the company of the strange men.

She sighed as she walked along. Her feet hurt from the rocky, uneven road, but she was free from King Richard and Lord Shiveley and their oppressive expectation that she would be wedding that man in several hours.

Muriel scowled. Did she think Evangeline was selfish to leave the castle like this, to put them through this hardship? She should have tried harder to convince Muriel not to come with her. *Please, God, don't let her think I'm selfish.*

After an hour or so, Westley said, "We shall stop here for the night."

Evangeline and Muriel hung back and watched as the men guided the donkey and cart off the road. There was nothing here except grass and a few trees, no inn or structure of any kind, and it suddenly struck Evangeline—they would be sleeping on the ground.

The men went into the woods two or three at a time, no doubt to relieve themselves. Muriel and Evangeline went in the opposite direction to do the same behind some thick bushes.

"I cannot believe we are here, defying the king like this, traveling with these strange peasants," Muriel muttered. "I've never slept on the ground in my life."

"It is an adventure, Muriel," Evangeline whispered back. "And you can return to Berkhamsted Castle anytime you wish."

"And what do you think they will do when they realize you lied to them and you are not mute at all? They'll be furious. They will cast you out of their midst."

Evangeline shook her head. They would not be that angry, surely. Perhaps she would tell them she had been miraculously healed. But that lie seemed worse than one that did not include God.

They went back to where the men were spreading blankets on the ground.

Evangeline sat down several feet away on the grass. She pulled off her thin slippers and shook out the dirt and small rocks from her shoes. Muriel did the same while she huffed her displeasure.

Evangeline lay down on the soft, cool grass, hugging her bag to her chest. Muriel stretched out beside her. "I am dirty and tired and I do not have proper shoes for this kind of walking. I have no way of washing even my face, as we have no water."

"If we ask," Evangeline dared to whisper back, "the men will probably let us share their water."

Muriel huffed again. "I'm too tired tonight. I will ask them in the morning. Are you not sorry yet for what you have done?"

"No."

"Sleeping outside on the ground is not something any lady should be doing. How will either of us get a moment of sleep?"

Evangeline did not answer. Muriel was always prone to complaints. Evangeline would send her back to Berkhamsted as soon as she was settled into a new life. Then Muriel could not complain—and Evangeline would not feel guilty about her not being pleased.

She herself felt quite content on the soft grass, staring up at the peaceful stars. She could imagine God winking down at her. Was God thinking, *My beloved child Evangeline has escaped from Berkhamsted Castle*? She imagined God as the father she had never known, a perfect Father. He was proud of her for not staying and marrying someone she could never love. It was also possible that God was angry with her for not doing as her king had directed her. But she preferred not to believe that.

She closed her eyes, stretching her arms above her head, then pillowed her cheek on her hands. She was free of Berkhamsted Castle and free of her own identity.

The day that had begun as the worst of her life had ended as the best.

Evangeline awoke to a soft light all around her and blue sky above her. She turned her head and saw flattened grass beside her.

It was not a dream. She truly had run away and escaped from the castle, King Richard, Lord Shiveley, and her own wedding. And she had slept all night on the ground.

A smile broke out on her face as she opened her arms up to the sky, barely stifling the giddy laugh that bubbled up inside her.

Evangeline finally sat up and looked around. The men were packing up to leave, and Muriel stood over her.

"Get up. We must go. Though how you could sleep all night and still be sleeping at dawn . . . The ground was so hard I barely slept at all."

Evangeline dug through her bag and pulled out her sturdy shoes. As she put them on, she took a deep breath through her nose. Even the air smelled better away from the castle. All around her was fresh and clean and green with life. Birds sang into the stillness like minstrels with no thought for their audience, singing for their own joy.

Westley, the apparent leader of their little group, approached her with that compassionate look on his face. The sun was rising behind him and illuminating his head like the halos surrounding the saints on the chapel windows at the cathedral she'd visited once as a child. His eyes were the same blue as the sky. His chin was slightly square—a chiseled continuation of his masculine jawline. His slightly parted lips gave him a vulnerable expression.

"Mildred told me you did not have a container for water. I have an extra flask." He held it out to her.

Evangeline opened her mouth to thank him, but her chest emptied itself of air.

She had almost forgotten—*I am supposed to be mute!*

She thought she must seem addled as she gazed up at him, so she changed her expression to a sheepish smile.

"I filled it up for you."

She nodded, enjoying the view of him, his brown hair lying in a perfect tousle across his forehead, framing his matching brown brows and thick lashes.

"May I help you up?" His large hand reached down to her.

The touch of his hand sent a sensation through her fingers and up her arm, and she let him pull her to her feet.

He was a bit taller than she was, and he was staring into her eyes. Did he think she was pretty? Even though she was wearing a plain servant's dress and her hair was hanging down her back, having not been brushed since the day before. But the way he was looking at her . . .

"I did not realize you and your friend did not have a blanket last night. I would have given you one of ours."

He did not expect her to answer him, of course, so she shrugged and kept smiling.

"As soon as you are ready, we will be on our way."

Evangeline bent and picked up her bag. She was ready. Ready to follow him wherever he was going on this beautiful, perfect morning.

Chapter Four

Westley could not help looking at the red-haired beauty every time she came within his view. Her hair was a color that caught the rays of the sun and absorbed them, glowing and triumphant. Her skin was pale and yet vibrant and healthy, with only a sprinkling of freckles across her upper cheeks and nose.

She looked as if she might open her mouth and speak to him at any moment, but then he would remember what her friend had said.

His heart clenched every time he thought about her being hurt so cruelly by her mistress. No one deserved that, and certainly not this gentle, sweet maiden with the loveliest green eyes he'd ever seen. When he'd seen her red hair, he wondered for a moment if she was the woman in the window of the castle, whose heavenly singing voice was burned into his mind. But she was mute, so she couldn't be the same woman.

They walked along the road, picking up another small group of travelers who asked to accompany them. But he made sure to keep watch over Eva and Mildred.

Eva's eyes were wide and alert as she seemed to take in everything with childlike wonder, while Mildred wore a constant frown and grumbled under her breath.

They were passing a fast-moving stream only a few feet from

the road. The bank was steep, and they could hear the rushing of the water as they traversed along the top of the bank.

Mildred suddenly sputtered, "E-E-Eva! You are too close to the edge."

Eva glanced back. Westley's heart stopped for a moment at her look of delight. She took one small step back, but she kept staring down at the water as if she'd never seen a river before.

Mildred marched to her friend and grabbed her by the arm, then returned Eva to the road to walk with the group.

A few minutes later, Eva was standing in front of a bush, staring down at it. She turned her head and motioned frantically to Mildred, who hurried over.

"It's only a butterfly," Mildred said.

Eva continued to watch it until it flew away. Her gaze followed its fluttering until it floated too far off the road to see.

Mildred smiled apologetically. "She was not allowed out of the house very much by her master and mistress."

Perhaps the abuse of her past had addled her mind. But then again, if she had never been able to see these things that he had seen so many times before, her behavior was reasonable.

When they stopped to rest and eat some food, he glanced at Mildred and Eva. They were sitting close together, but they were not eating. And the only reason they would not be eating was if they had no food.

He and his men had plenty of bread and hard-boiled eggs, some nuts and dried fruit, since they had stocked up before leaving the castle. So he went to the cart and retrieved a provision bag and brought it to them.

Mildred's cheeks colored. "We can pay you for it." She motioned to her young companion, who seemed to realize what she was saying and grabbed their bag, rummaging through it.

Westley shook his head. "I do not need to be paid. Here, take the food."

"No, no, we wish to pay. At the next village we can buy food."

Eva held out a handful of coins. Where did two peasant women get so much money?

Mildred grabbed her hand, closed Eva's fingers into a fist, and gave her a scolding look. Then she discreetly took one of the coins and thrust it at Westley.

He took it, sensing her pride would be hurt if he did not. He only hoped no one from the small group that had joined them had seen how much money was in Eva's hand. He did not want her to come to harm, especially while she was under his protection. Several ideas came to mind about where they might have gotten those coins, but none of them were lawful.

But he did not like thinking ill of them. Mildred was dressed quite well, so perhaps she had come about the money honestly. He did not want to judge them guilty, but at the same time, the situation was highly suspicious.

Soon they came to a market town, and his men wished to look over the goods being sold.

"We shall all meet again in one hour," Westley told them, "back at the town gate."

They agreed and went their way toward the marketplace. Not wishing to buy anything himself, Westley followed Mildred and Eva far enough behind that they might not notice him.

They went toward the booths selling clothing and shoes. Eva took out her small purse and bought a pair of sturdier shoes for Mildred, which she needed since they'd be walking for another day and a half. She also bought some more clothes. For herself, she bought a dress and a brightly colored scarf, which she wrapped around her neck instead of around her hair.

Westley couldn't help noticing how often men turned their heads to stare at Eva. A bald, middle-aged man leered at her, showing a couple of missing teeth. He called out to her.

"Hey there, with the red hair!" He added a lewd comment, suggesting she go home with him.

His hands clenching into fists, Westley stepped toward the man.

~ର୍ଥ୍ୟ~

Evangeline's stomach twisted at the sickening words this stranger said about her. Muriel pushed Evangeline behind her and planted her feet wide as she faced the man.

Westley stepped in front of him. "You will not trouble this young maiden. She is with me and my men."

The bald man eyed Westley, who was much taller and broader in the shoulders. He held up his hands. "No one is troubling her."

Evangeline's heart fluttered, a pleasant sensation at Westley's willingness to come to her aid. Holding on to Muriel's arm, she sighed.

Muriel narrowed her eyes at her. Doubtless she would have something to say about Evangeline sighing over the peasant Westley. But such a noble peasant.

The bald man pivoted and walked away, holding his shoulders back as though trying to add to his height.

Westley's scowl changed into a concerned crease in his forehead as his eyes locked on hers. She sighed again.

Muriel nodded to Westley. "We thank you for your intervention."

"Verily, it was my pleasure."

Without saying anything further, Muriel walked in the opposite direction. Evangeline followed her but turned and looked over her shoulder. Westley was staring intently at her. She smiled, hoping he could see how thankful she was.

Later when they were buying some bread and other provisions, Evangeline glanced over her shoulder to see Westley several feet behind them. As she suspected, he was trailing them around the market. She would have to be careful not to even whisper to Muriel and give away her secret.

Pointing at whatever she wanted, nodding for yes, and shaking her head for no worked quite well at the market. But at a bread stall, while Muriel was buying some cheese nearby, Evangeline held up four fingers and pointed at the small oat buns in a large basket.

The woman seller told her companion, "I've been watching her. She's deaf and dumb. She won't know if you ask for double the price."

Evangeline raised her brows at the woman. She pointed at her throat and shook her head, then pointed to her ear and nodded.

The woman's mouth fell open. Her companion laughed uproariously.

"Not only will we not charge her double, Nan, but we shall give her an extra bun. Here." The man handed her five of the small oat buns.

Evangeline smiled and paid him. The woman pursed her lips and Evangeline walked away.

Everything at the market was interesting. There were all kinds of animals for sale, both live and dressed to cook. People were shouting, trying to bring attention to their booths and the goods they were selling. Bright colors and every kind of dress, face, and figure drew Evangeline's eye. The only thing she did not like was the way some of the men stared at her. But Westley was watching out for her, so she felt reasonably safe. Besides, Muriel was quite formidable when she was angry, and any molester would have to go through her.

They bought a wool blanket before making their way back to the town gate to meet the rest of the group. She glanced over her shoulder again. Westley was still there.

Someone tugged at Evangeline's skirt. She shifted and found a young woman sitting on the ground, holding a tiny baby in the crook of her arm.

"Please, miss, can you spare some food for me so I can feed my baby?"

Evangeline's stomach clenched at the sunken cheeks of the emaciated woman who looked no older than herself. Though she had no experience with babies, the baby did not seem well. It lay still, its eyes closed and its lips dry.

"Where is your master?" Muriel asked, staring down at her.

"I have no master."

"Have you run away?"

"No. My . . . my mistress cast me off." The poor young woman's eyes filled with tears. "The baby is her husband's and she sent me away, me and my baby." A tear dripped from her eye.

Evangeline was already digging in her bag for the coin purse. She pulled out several coins and put them in the woman's bony hand. She also gave her three of the buns she had just bought.

More tears ran down her thin cheeks. "Thank you. May God bless you for your mercy." She dropped the buns in her lap and tucked the coins into a tiny bag that hung from her belt. Her hand shook as she brought a bun to her mouth and took a bite.

Tears welled in Evangeline's own eyes as she nodded and walked away.

"This is what I warned you about," Muriel whispered in Evangeline's ear, holding on to her arm. "You should not have given her so much money. She will lose it, or someone will take it from her."

O God, please don't allow that to happen. But Evangeline refused to let Muriel ruin the good feeling of having helped the poor woman.

She wiped away the tear from her eye and sighed. *Thank You, God, that I could help her. Please save her from starvation.*

Inside she felt a peace that God indeed would save the woman and would use Evangeline's offering to do so. She couldn't help smiling and looking up at the sky to share her smile with God.

A commotion came from the other side of the marketplace, sounding like several horses galloping their way. A woman screamed, and a man's deep voice came from the same direction, too far away to make out what he was saying. Dogs barked, a child bawled, and a horse neighed.

Evangeline's stomach clenched. Could it be Lord Shiveley? She and Muriel were only a few steps from the gate where Westley's men and the others were waiting.

The horses' hooves clopped on the packed earth. Several men on horseback approached them, some wearing the livery of the king and some of Lord Shiveley.

Evangeline's heart stumbled and she lost her breath. They were coming for her.

Chapter Five

Westley noted the way Eva's face transformed. All the color drained from her cheeks and her eyes went wide as the men on horseback drew close.

The men wore the livery of noble guardsmen. Five were dressed in one set of colors, and the other five guards were dressed in another. He was not certain, but he believed they were the guards of the Earl of Shiveley and King Richard.

Eva threw the scarf she had bought over her head, stuffed her distinctive red hair inside it, and tied it under her chin. Then she clung to Mildred's forearms and seemed to be staring into her eyes. They huddled together just a few feet from the group by the gate.

The guards headed toward Westley's men. "We are searching for two women. One of them is very tall and has red hair."

Westley hurried forward, but before he could reach them, Roger spoke up.

"Is the woman mute?"

"No, she's not mute." The guard's tone was sneering. He glanced around, then his gaze lingered on Eva and Mildred. Eva must have been squatting, because she appeared even shorter than Mildred and she kept her face toward the ground.

The guard stared at her a few moments, then said, "Move on, men." He motioned forward with his arm, and the ten guards rode out the gate and away from the town.

Westley made his way to the two women. "Is everything all right?"

"Oh yes, very well," Mildred said.

"Eva seems frightened. Does she know who those men are?"

"Oh, she was only startled. She thought they might have been sent by her master. She still has difficulty believing he is dead." Mildred turned to Eva. "He is dead, Eva. We saw him with our own eyes. Dead and cold, and that is the end of his tyranny."

"But did you not say it was her master's wife who beat her and made her lose her voice?"

"Yes, well, they both beat her, and they are both dead now."

Her manner made him wonder if she was lying. It seemed too great a coincidence that King Richard and Lord Shiveley were looking for two women, one of whom was tall with red hair.

Was Mildred lying about their masters being dead? The Peasants' Uprising had ended three years before, but tensions existed between villeins and their lords ever since, and even between servants and their masters. But though he was suspicious of Mildred's story, he hoped it was not Eva and Mildred the king was searching for.

Evangeline's hands were still shaking as she and Muriel walked along the road with Westley and his men. Richard would have been smart enough to send guards who had seen her before and therefore could recognize her. If they had seen her face and her hair, they would have known it was her.

A chill passed over her shoulders and she shuddered. What could she have done if they had seized her, intending to take her back to Berkhamsted Castle? There was nothing she could have done. Even the tall, strong Westley could not have stopped them, and he would not have wanted to defy the king for a mute maiden he had just met.

Clouds overshadowed the road, but she hardly noticed until drops of rain began to fall. The group ran toward a thick stand of trees just off the road. Muriel took her arm and pulled her along.

As they all stood under the trees, which only provided minimal protection from the hard rain, Evangeline and Muriel huddled under the blanket she had just bought at the market.

"I'm going for some privacy," Muriel whispered to her.

Evangeline watched to see which direction she took, then put the blanket over her head again.

She had felt so merry and so free just a few hours before. She had hardly stopped smiling as the warm sun shone on her face. A beautiful blue butterfly unlike anything she'd ever seen before had flitted in front of her, lighting on a flower, mesmerizing and lovely. Trees and grass and fresh air surrounded her and lifted her until she felt as light as one of those butterflies. No one was telling her what to do or think or whom to marry. Life had seemed so full of promise. She was in the company of men who treated her like an equal, one of whom was handsome and smiled more than anyone she had ever met. He made her heart swell when he looked at her. But now . . .

She should have known Richard would chase after her, that Lord Shiveley would not simply let her disappear and not search for her. Of course they would send men after her to bring her back and force her to marry Shiveley. Still, she had not expected them to catch up to her so soon.

Westley's expression told her he did not believe Muriel's blatant lies. But Evangeline's ruse of pretending to be mute had actually worked, and he and his men had not turned them in to the king's and

Lord Shiveley's guards. But was it only a matter of time before she was caught?

"Eva?"

She felt a slight touch to her shoulder and jerked the blanket off her face. Westley was standing beside her.

"Why were you so afraid of those men?"

His brows were drawn together, and his gaze delved into hers. She simply shook her head.

"Is someone looking for you?"

Evangeline could no longer look him in the eye. She had to tell him the lie, or he might tell them they could not travel with him and his group. She did not know much about the world, but she did know that people did not take it lightly when a villein ran away from his or her lord. A villein would be severely punished for running away. So she shook her head no.

Someone cleared their throat behind Westley. He stepped aside, revealing Muriel standing there.

"Do you need something?" Muriel glowered at him.

"Only inquiring after Eva."

Evangeline frowned at Muriel and gave a slight shake of her head. *You're not under the king's protection anymore, Muriel.* They had to pretend to be humble and respectful. After all, they were supposed to be poor servants.

Westley gave Evangeline a questioning but kind look, then he left.

Evangeline scowled at Muriel, who huddled with her under the blanket.

"I don't want that man getting too close to you."

Evangeline dared to whisper back, "Why?"

"We don't want him discovering your secrets."

Westley had been nothing but gracious. And he had risked his life to save a little girl. But if Evangeline knew Muriel, the reason she didn't want him getting too close to her was due to his status as a peasant.

~ово~

Evangeline and Muriel walked until dark, slept on the ground again, then walked all the next day. Evangeline had never walked so much in her entire life. By the time they reached Glynval, it was dark and they were all weary and footsore.

She and Muriel were taken inside the bottom floor of a building where beds were lined up and nearly all occupied. A servant showed them two empty beds against the wall. Evangeline did not even take the time to get undressed but lay down and fell instantly to sleep.

She awoke to find herself in a large rectangular room. Light streamed in through the small windows. Several rows of beds, now empty, met her curious glance around the room.

"Are you finally awake?" Muriel bustled toward her. "Get up and get ready. Mistress Alice is deciding where we shall work today."

Evangeline sat up and rubbed her face.

"Most of the servant girls have gone out to the fields to cut the wheat. Here is your breakfast." Muriel handed her a cloth bundle.

Evangeline unwrapped it and found a bread roll and a piece of cheese. She ate it quickly. Since she had slept in her overdress, she was ready to go as soon as she put on her shoes.

The bright sunlight made her blink as she emerged into a large courtyard of green grass. A young woman was slapping the ground with a stick to keep a gaggle of geese from straying, and a young man was leading a flock of sheep through a gate into a pasture. A wooden platform stood in the middle of the courtyard with a pillory, where a person's head and hands would be imprisoned between two wooden boards for punishment. The steward occasionally used the pillory at Berkhamsted Castle to punish a servant for thievery.

A young woman was operating a windlass at a covered well. Muriel led her toward it. "Can she have a dipper of water?" Muriel said to the maiden raising the bucket.

"Who is this?" The maiden stared at Evangeline's face, then looked her over from head to toe.

At Berkhamsted Castle, if a servant had spoken to Muriel that way, she would have given her quite the tongue-lashing. She squeezed Muriel's arm. *Please remember we are peasants now.* Evangeline held her breath.

"And who are you?" Muriel leaned toward the girl, her hands on her hips.

"I am the girl with the bucket." She smirked.

The girl seemed to be about Evangeline's age. She brought the water bucket the rest of the way up and balanced it on the edge of the wall around the well. She had large blue eyes and blonde hair that came to her waist and was only partially covered with a kerchief. Her beauty was marred only by her smug smile.

Muriel simply scowled at her, a look that would have made Evangeline's heart race if she had ever looked at her that way. The girl stared back at them, then finally dipped up some water and held it out to her.

Evangeline took it and drank the entire contents. The water was cold and pure and tasted wonderful. She hadn't realized how thirsty she was. She wanted to ask for another dipper full, so she handed it back but held on to the handle longer than necessary. Then she nodded while raising her eyebrows.

"She wants another."

Muriel's tone was not very friendly, so Evangeline smiled, hoping to win the girl over.

The girl frowned. "What's the matter with her? Can't she talk for herself?"

"She's mute."

"Oh." The girl's face brightened, though she still had that smug smile, still sizing Evangeline up out of the corner of her eye. She dipped the metal ladle into the bucket and handed over the water. "I heard you came back from Berkhamsted Castle with Westley and the boys." Her tone was friendlier.

Some water dribbled down Evangeline's chin and she wiped it with the back of her hand, just like a real peasant. Evangeline smiled as she handed back the empty dipper. *No one would ever guess I am the ward of the king.*

"And your friend is deaf and dumb?"

"No, not deaf. She is only mute."

A pain, like a pricking in her chest, evidenced the guilt of allowing Muriel to repeat the lie. She needed to confess to the priest. But she could not offer confession if everyone thought she was mute. How would she ever be absolved?

But she would not think about that now.

"My name is Sabina. I am the miller's daughter."

"We are Mildred and Eva. Mistress Alice is waiting for us at the main house. Come, Eva." Muriel turned away from Sabina and started off across the courtyard.

Evangeline glanced backward. Sabina was putting the bucket back into the well. She was the miller's daughter then, not a servant.

Evangeline followed Muriel around a stand of trees. In a clearing a castle appeared—a lovely stone castle with towers and stained glass windows but smaller than the palace building at Berkhamsted Castle.

They walked around to a side door. Muriel knocked and a young woman let them into a room where several women were working— two were clearing a long table of food scraps and throwing them into a bucket, while another woman sat at a smaller table. She was using a pen made out of a hollow reed to write on a piece of parchment.

As they approached, the woman looked them up and down. "What are your names?"

"I am Mildred and this is Eva. She doesn't speak."

"She won't speak, or she can't speak?"

"She cannot speak."

Mistress Alice looked sharply at Evangeline's face. "She is young and tall and strong. She can work in the fields. Mildred, you can churn butter with the milkmaids for now."

Muriel opened her mouth as if to speak, glancing at Evangeline out of the corner of her eye, but she pursed her lips instead, a wrinkle forming above the bridge of her nose.

Soon the two were separated, and another maidservant was taking her to the fields. "Can you understand me when I speak to you?"

Evangeline nodded.

"My name is Nicola. I'm sorry you are being sent to the fields. It's harder than working in the house, but they stop work in the mid-afternoon so no one faints from the heat."

Truthfully, she could hardly wait to begin working out in the warm sunshine with all the other peasants. Perhaps she could make her home here, fall in love with a peasant—preferably Westley— "miraculously" regain her voice, and live out her life in the lovely village of Glynval.

"You traveled with Westley and the other men. Did you think he was handsome?"

Evangeline nodded.

"He and Sabina—that's the miller's daughter—are nearly be-trothed. Everyone expects them to marry, at least. More's the pity, because I don't think she's worthy of him. But they are the wealthiest family in Glynval, besides Westley's."

Westley's family was wealthy? Eva's heart sank.

"Here's your new worker, Reeve Folsham," Nicola said to the man standing at the edge of the field. "Her name is Eva, and she is mute."

"Mute?" The man looked almost insulted.

"She understands what you say but she doesn't speak. Farewell, Eva." Nicola turned and walked back toward the manor house.

Reeve Folsham stared at her. Finally, he frowned and handed her a tool with a long wooden handle and a curved, almost circular blade on the end. The man's skin was dark and leathery, like a horse's saddle. He seemed about Lord Shiveley's age, but his hair was entirely white and his shoulders were wide and muscular.

"What are you waiting for? You can start cutting over there."

A swath of standing grain—perhaps wheat—stretched out to her right, and straight ahead several women bent forward as they used the strange instrument to slice through the stalks. As if by magic, the stalks of grain would fall to the ground in perfect flat swaths.

It looked easy, so Evangeline stepped to the edge of the standing grain, bent, and swung her blade across the bottom of the stalks.

A few stalks bent and broke, but most only waved their heads at her.

She huffed out a breath, blowing a strand of hair that had fallen across her eye. The reeve was watching her. She drew back the instrument, clenching her teeth, and swung with all her might.

The handle slipped out of her grasp and went flying in the direction of the reeve.

Evangeline covered her mouth with her hands as Reeve Folsham leapt to the side when the blade sliced through his tunic.

Evangeline stepped toward him, her stomach twisting.

"What kind of evil is this?" he roared at her. "Are you trying to murder me?"

Chapter Six

Evangeline shook her head vehemently. O God, what have I done?

Two men hurried toward them. One of them was Westley.

"What happened?"

"This mute girl tried to kill me." The reeve lifted his shirt. A long stripe of blood shone across his side.

Evangeline's knees went weak and her heart pounded sickeningly. Was it a serious injury? A trickle of bright-red blood oozed from one end of the cut.

She pressed her hands to her cheeks as Westley stepped closer, bringing his face to within inches of the wound.

"Oh, Folsham, it's only a scratch. What are you shouting about? You've scared the poor girl nearly to death."

Westley was looking at her now. Her face tingled and her knees wobbled.

"She slung the scythe at me!" Reeve Folsham waved his arms, still holding up his tunic. "She looked at it as if she'd never seen a scythe in her life, then she slung it at me."

Evangeline could only shake her head. But even if she could speak, what could she say? How could she explain that she hadn't meant to do it, that she was indeed completely ignorant of a scythe and how to use it, and it had slipped out of her hands—and flew straight for the reeve's rather wide body.

"It was just an accident." Westley smiled, then covered his mouth with his hand as if stifling a laugh.

"She is a menace. Look at me. I'm bleeding. Lord le Wyse, you saw it, did you not?"

Another man standing behind Westley now stepped forward. He was much older than Westley, had darker hair that was beginning to gray, and wore a black leather patch over one eye. He pierced Evangeline with his gaze, then turned to the reeve. "Go on to the house, Folsham. One of the maids can tend to your scratch."

"Scratch. Hmph. I tell you, she could have killed me."

It was true. She could have killed him. The breath went out of her and she covered her face. *What did I almost do?* She breathed in and out as a tear squeezed out of each eye. She kept her eyes covered so no one would see.

Surely everyone in the village would hear of what she had done. Would they force her to leave? Was Westley horrified that he had let her come to his village to work? And was he only making light of the incident in front of the reeve so he would calm down?

When she opened her eyes, Reeve Folsham was stalking toward the castle and Westley and the other man were looking at her.

"Father," Westley said, "I'm sure she did not mean to sling the scythe at Folsham."

Was Westley's father the lord of the village? The older man was wearing finer clothes than the other men she had seen; he had on a fine linen shirt that was so bright white it reflected the light of the sun. He was definitely not a peasant or a servant, or even a tradesman. But along with his eye patch, one of his hands appeared to be afflicted in some way, as he held it against his middle.

Finally, he said, "Did you want to hurt Reeve Folsham?"

Tears welled up in Evangeline's eyes. She shook her head.

"Father, she can't speak. She and her friend traveled with us from Berkhamsted Castle." Westley had the same masculine jawline as the lord and the same thick hair. He took a step toward Evangeline. "Eva, this is my father, Lord le Wyse."

Lord le Wyse was still looking at her. "Can you tie up sheaths?"

Tie up sheaths? What was that? Evangeline shook her head and shrugged.

"Perhaps she is a house servant," Westley offered. "Are you?"

How should she respond? Eva nodded. At least if she worked inside, she couldn't nearly decapitate someone.

"Go with Westley." Lord le Wyse nodded to his son. "Take her to the castle. Let your mother find something for her to do there." He bent to pick up the scythe while Evangeline turned to go with Westley.

She had imagined joy and sunshine and freedom, and instead she had nearly killed a man with her incompetence.

⁓

"Don't feel so bad."

Westley walked toward the house beside Eva. Her head hung low and her shoulders drooped.

"The reeve will be well. He will enjoy the attention of getting bandaged, no doubt."

She glanced up at him with a sad smile, then slowly shook her head.

Truly, she was very pretty. He had never seen hair quite the color of hers. But the way she expressed her feelings through her facial expressions was particularly fascinating—vulnerable and yet unashamed.

How sad that someone had abused her. How unfair that she might never speak again. To think of someone striking her at all, and especially to brutally and intentionally injure such a lovely, gentle maiden . . . It was hard to fathom. He was almost sorry they were dead so he could not exact justice on the maiden's behalf.

He remembered her look of abject horror when she stared at the blood on Reeve Folsham's side. But thank God it was only a scratch. Anything worse and she would have had to stand trial at the next manorial court.

"My mother will take good care of you. She is very kind. You will see. And the other house servants are friendly. They will help you with whatever you need."

She smiled up at him. In truth, she was nearly as tall as he was, but with her head down, the way she looked at him through her lashes made it seem as if she was gazing up at him.

When they reached the house, he said, "Everyone calls it the castle to distinguish it from the manor house. But it is not exactly an impressive fortress such as Berkhamsted Castle." She looked at him with interest, so he went on. "My father had planned to build another wing and a new tower, but after the Peasants' Uprising, he changed his mind."

They climbed the front steps and he opened the door, motioning Eva inside. "Mother!" he called.

"Here I am." With a smile on her face, Mother emerged from the storage rooms at the back of the house. She hurried forward and threw her arms around him. He kissed her on the cheek.

"I missed you while you were gone," she said. "Oh, is this Eva?"

"News travels fast in Glynval."

⁂

"My dear, let me welcome you to our little household."

Lady le Wyse was as beautiful as Lord le Wyse was handsome, in spite of his eye patch. Her hair was blonde, with a braid coiled around her head and other braids caught in a ribbon at the back of her neck. Her smile was her most beautiful feature, however. She took Evangeline's hand and squeezed it. "Do you have any special skills, Eva?"

"Mother, she can't—"

"I am aware that she cannot speak. Eva, do you cook?"

She shook her head.

"Do you sew?"

Evangeline nodded, then shrugged. How could she tell her that she embroidered pictures on tapestries but had never done any mending and did not know how to make even the simplest article of clothing? Evangeline had to shake her head.

"Have you ever worked in a dairy, separating the milk and churning butter?"

Evangeline bit her lip. She had never done anything except read books, hunt, sing, and embroider. What kind of servant would she be? Would they send her away?

"No matter. We will find something for you to do." Lady le Wyse smiled kindly at her.

"I shall see you later, then." Westley stepped forward, bent, and kissed his mother on the cheek. He nodded to Evangeline. "Mother will take care of you." He gave her a reassuring smile and walked away.

"And do not worry about the reeve," she said quietly, for Evangeline's ears only. "We are bandaging the scratch on his side and he should be perfectly well."

Evangeline expelled a breath of gratitude.

They walked through the house and out the back door to a stone kitchen a few feet away. Inside, a woman held a large piece of some kind of bloody raw meat. "Lady le Wyse, good morning to you."

"Golda, this is a new helper, Eva. Eva, this is our head cook, Golda." Two other maidens working in the kitchen turned their attention to Lady le Wyse. "Eva does not speak, but she hears and understands what you say to her. Do you have some work she can do?"

"Can she shell peas?"

Lady le Wyse looked at Evangeline. How difficult could it be? At least she couldn't hurt anyone with a pea pod.

Evangeline smiled and nodded.

After getting Evangeline a basket of peas, Golda cocked her head to one side to indicate the door since her hands were occupied. "Lora, show her where the others are shelling."

A maiden with brown hair tied with a gray piece of wool and small eyes put down her knife and left the vegetables she was chopping. She motioned for Evangeline to follow her outside.

Out in the sun, Lora led Evangeline around the side of the kitchen. "Why can't you talk?"

Evangeline pointed at her throat and shook her head.

"Did you get your tongue cut out?"

Evangeline shook her head.

Lora headed toward a large shaded area. Three maidens, one of whom was Nicola, sat on stools while Sabina hovered nearby, smirking, and eyed Evangeline as they drew closer. Then Sabina drew an unoccupied stool up and sat beside one of the servants. Lora only stared for a moment, then walked back toward the kitchen.

"Everyone, this is Eva. She just arrived last night, and she can't talk. I think she can hear what we say, but she can't say a word." Sabina spoke with a gleam in her eye, as if Evangeline were not even present.

"Westley brought her back with him. I suppose he felt sorry for her." Sabina said the words in a hushed tone.

Evangeline sat on the stool, holding her head up as her spine stiffened. The other girls stared at her with wide eyes. She looked down at the basket of peas in her lap, picked up a pod, and stared at it.

"Should we ask her if she sliced off Reeve Folsham's ear?" a blonde maiden asked.

"It wasn't his ear, Cecily," a dark-haired maiden said, and they laughed raucously.

Evangeline's cheeks burned as she fumbled with a pea pod.

"You are all being rude." Nicola, who sat on the other side of Evangeline, spoke up. "How would you feel if someone was laughing at you while you were sitting there listening?" She turned toward Evangeline. "Don't pay them any attention."

Evangeline gave her a tremulous smile. Her kindness made tears sting her eyes.

"My name is Nicola, in case you don't remember. And that is Sabina, Cecily, and Berta." She pointed to each girl as she said her name.

Evangeline nodded to show she understood.

"I saw Reeve Folsham a few minutes ago walking back out to the field, and he didn't look hurt at all."

Evangeline mouthed, *Thank you.*

Nicola smiled.

The others were silent except for the faint sounds of the pea pods being snapped open and the peas hulled, then the pods thrown into buckets at their feet.

Evangeline surreptitiously watched out of the corner of her eye as Nicola transformed a pea pod into an empty shell that she tossed into her bucket. It happened so quickly, Evangeline had no idea how she did it. She watched again, but Nicola's fingers moved too fast.

"Eva has a friend, Mildred"—Sabina rolled her eyes toward Evangeline's basket—"who's helping in the house."

The other maidens murmured awkwardly, as if unsure what cue Sabina was sending them.

"I could help you with shelling your peas. I used to be the fastest pea sheller in my household."

While Sabina was boasting about her speed and skill, Evangeline concentrated on trying to break the side of the pea pod, but it wouldn't break the way Nicola's had. Out of frustration, she used her thumbnail and tore a hole in the pod. She tried to get the peas out but had to rip the pea pod into shreds. She ended up picking out the bits of hull and throwing them into the bucket she shared with Nicola.

"I see you've never shelled peas before. I'll show you." Sabina stepped over to Evangeline, picked up one of her pea pods, and held it out. "You hold it like this and snap off the end, like this. You hold the broken end in this hand and break it open with this thumb. You push out the peas with your thumb, then throw the pod and the end away."

Sabina picked up another pea pod and did it again, only faster. "Can you do that?"

Evangeline gave a stiff nod. She picked up a pea pod and tried to do what Sabina had just done. Her pod was more crushed than broken, but within a few moments, she had all the peas out of the pod and into her basket.

"It just takes some practice," Sabina said. "I've been shelling peas since I was five years old."

Evangeline nodded to show she was impressed, cautiously eyeing the girl who went from mocking to helpful in less than one minute.

As they sat shelling, Cecily and Berta challenged Sabina to a competition to see who could shell the most peas. They took more pea pods into their baskets. Sabina loaded a basket with peas for herself, then cried, "Ready? Go!"

They shelled furiously, hardly talking as they kept their gazes on their laps and their peas.

A while later, with Sabina and Cecily both crowing that they were winning, Mistress Alice strode toward them. "Girls, when you get those peas shelled, go and get your midday meal at the manor. Then help clean and get ready for the field workers to come in for their meal."

"Are these the last of the peas?" Nicola asked.

"This will be the last big batch. Tomorrow I will only need one of you. Cecily, Sabina, what are you doing?"

"They are trying to see who is the fastest sheller," Berta said.

"Are the ones in your baskets all that's left?"

"Yes, Mistress Alice."

Mistress Alice went to look over Sabina's and Cecily's shoulders.

"Finished!" they both screamed simultaneously.

"Who is the winner, Mistress Alice?" Berta said.

Mistress Alice picked up each basket and examined the contents. Frowning, she selected a few pieces of pea hull from Sabina's basket and a few unshelled pea pods from Cecily's, then said, "Cecily has more."

Cecily laughed so loud, they must have heard her in the farthest field.

"What? No!" Sabina stood and slammed her fists against her hips.

Mistress Alice raised her eyebrows at Sabina, then walked away. She stopped beside Evangeline and looked down at her basket. Evangeline held her breath.

Berta said, "I don't think she's ever shelled peas before. We had to show her how to do it."

Cecily laughed again. Nicola gave both Berta and Cecily a narrow-eyed stare, and Sabina stalked off.

"Get finished with the last few and come to the kitchen." Mistress Alice turned to leave.

Two young women approached, both dressed in patched

woolen kirtles. One of them walked ahead of the other and called out, "Excuse me."

Mistress Alice took notice of them.

The young maiden's face was very pale.

"Are you Mistress Alice?"

"Yes."

"We were wondering if you needed servants. We are hard workers and can work in the fields or inside, whatever you need."

"I've only just taken on two new maidservants. Perhaps I'll have need of you next spring."

The two maidens' shoulders seemed to slump as they thanked her and trudged away.

A pain went through Evangeline's heart as she watched them leave. She and Muriel were taking jobs that these two women obviously needed. *O God, I'm so sorry. Please don't let them go hungry.* But from the looks of their sunken cheeks, they were already going hungry.

Cecily let out a whoop. "Did you see Sabina's face when Mistress Alice said I shelled more peas than she did?"

Nicola said quietly, "Yes, and I saw how unkindly you treated Eva. You would do well to remember what Lady le Wyse said about being kind to each other. We are treated well here, but if she catches anyone being unkind, she will send us home as she did with Anna and Beatrice."

"They were fighting," Berta retorted. "Did you see any of us fighting?"

Nicola didn't answer but continued shelling the peas in her basket.

But Evangeline was paying little heed to the squawking maidservants as she noticed Westley speaking quietly with Mistress Alice. Had he been near enough to hear what the two young maidens had said to her? He suddenly reeled away from Mistress Alice and ran after the two maidens.

She strained to hear what Westley was saying, but he spoke too softly and was too far away. The maidens' faces suddenly spread into smiles. They nodded at him, then they both started walking back to the castle with him.

Evangeline's heart soared. Westley would not let the women go hungry. He would find jobs for them. A lump rose in her throat as she turned back to the circle of servants.

"I'm done with my basket." Cecily got up and left.

A few minutes later, Berta did the same.

Evangeline sighed as she looked into her basket and saw how much more she had left to shell. At the slow rate she was going, it would take her at least an hour.

"I'll help." Nicola took some of Evangeline's pea pods and put them into her own basket. "We'll be done soon."

Evangeline was so slow. Why would anyone want a servant who could not do anything worthwhile? They would surely get rid of her the way they had rid themselves of the two fighting girls Nicola mentioned. But if they forced Evangeline to leave, she would never see Westley again, and that thought was sad indeed, especially since she was more intrigued with him than ever.

Chapter Seven

Evangeline hefted the bucket of water off the edge of the well, and the weight of it pulled the bucket out of her wet hands. It overturned on the ground, and she gasped as the cold water swept over her feet, seeping through her shoes.

It was only midmorning and already she had dropped the basket of eggs she and Cecily had gathered from the hens in the henhouse. A hen had flown at Evangeline's head and scratched her cheek, which still stung.

She sighed and picked up the now-empty bucket and placed it back on the rope, then lowered it into the well. She hauled it up, the bucket dripping. This time she tipped it over and poured some of the water back into the well so it would be easier to carry.

When she arrived at the kitchen, Golda stared down at her bucket of water. "Has the well gone dry? That's not very much water."

Evangeline's cheeks heated—a frequent sensation these days.

Golda frowned on one side of her mouth. "Never mind. Just go get me another bucket of water."

But as Evangeline walked away, the pity in the cook's voice and expression made a lump gather in her throat.

"Wait," Golda called after her, then sighed. "I'll get someone else to fetch the water. You go and . . ." She glanced around until she spotted a couple buckets in the corner. "Take those two buckets of slop to the pigs."

What was slop?

"Do you know where the pigsty is?"

Evangeline shook her head.

"It's to the east of the manor house, across the courtyard and the small meadow. You'll see the fence, and you'll also smell it. Just dump the buckets over the fence and be careful you don't fall in."

Evangeline picked up the two buckets, which were surprisingly light and contained the pea pods from the day before, as well as some scraps from the morning's meal. She carried them out of the kitchen, past the manor house, through the courtyard, and past the girl who was herding a gaggle of geese with a stick.

She kept walking until she smelled something foul. She was nowhere near the privy, but she saw a fence in a low place between the meadow and the woods.

Evangeline set down the buckets, which grew heavier the longer she carried them, to get a better hold on the handles. After flexing her fingers a few times, she picked them back up and finally reached the fence. A long wooden box was on the ground on the inside of the fence, and a wooden step was beside it on the outside. Was this where the slop was supposed to go? Flies buzzed all around it, while the pigs lay in the mud a few feet away.

As soon as she put a foot on the wooden step, the pigs lifted their heads and snorted. There must have been at least a dozen of them, squealing and squirming.

She couldn't dump the buckets as long as she was holding both of them, so she put one on the ground and upended the first bucket into the trough just as the pigs reached it and plowed their faces into it.

Evangeline stepped down, picked up the second bucket, and climbed back up on the step. She tilted the bucket, dumping the contents and trying not to let any of the scraps touch her fingers. But it suddenly slipped from her hand and landed on the head of one of the pigs, making it squeal. But it only paused a moment in its feeding, pushing its snout back into the trough. The bucket rolled to a stop behind the pigs' rumps.

Evangeline moaned. Another thing she did wrong. She climbed down from the step, eyeing the grunting, muddied animals as they used their snouts to root in the scraps as well as to push each other out of the way. The slop was already mostly gone. Perhaps when they had eaten it all, the pudgy animals, some of them bigger than a fully grown sheep, would move away so she could get to the bucket without getting too near them.

What would they do to her? She didn't see any tusks, so they weren't wild boars, but they still looked frightening and wild. At the very least, her feet and skirt hem would get muddy.

The pigs were still rooting around in the trough, grunting, occasionally squealing at each other, ramming each other with their snouts. But the slop appeared to be all gone.

Evangeline unlatched the opening to the pen. She had to lift the wattled gate of small sticks out of the mud to move it open. The pigs did not seem to see her at all. One pig stood between her and the bucket. She could not leave the bucket behind. Golda would surely notice if she did not return it to the kitchen, and Evangeline didn't want to be exposed yet again for her incompetence.

Go on, piggy. Get out of my way so I can get the bucket.

The large swine snorted as it examined the ground, then made its way toward the bucket. It put its snout inside, sniffing and root-ing, pushing the bucket farther away from where Evangeline stood just inside the gate.

She stepped forward, her shoes squishing in the mud as she held up her skirts. Maybe she could grab the bucket and outrun the animal. She walked around the animal, which still did not seem to see her as it moved the bucket with its face inside. She moved closer, finally taking the last step to bring her close enough to grab it. She leaned down and snatched it away. She turned to run, but the pig squealed and ran after her.

The muddy pig snout brushed her ankle as she reached the gate.

Her heart was in her throat. She took hold of the gate, but the pig was so close it was already halfway out. The animal's big body slipped right past her and stopped just outside the gate.

She slapped at the pig's snout with the bucket to drive it back inside, but it only squealed louder. The pig turned its tiny eyes away from her, then ran surprisingly fast toward the trees.

Her stomach sank. She started back to the gate, but several more pigs were rushing toward it. Before she could shut it, they ran right through. Their squeals sounded as if they were laughing at her.

No! What would she do now? Her first inclination was to sit where she was and sob. She couldn't. She had to get those pigs! Everybody already looked at her doubtingly, especially Reeve Folsham after she nearly killed him. If they found out she let out all the pigs . . .

How could she get someone to help her? She couldn't even call out for help.

She ran after them. She *would* get those pigs back in their pen, even if it killed her.

⁓

Westley stared as Eva ran, her red hair streaming behind her, after about half a dozen pigs who had apparently just escaped from their pen. She looked quite distraught.

He threw down his fishing gear and raced to close the gate so the remaining pigs didn't get out, then ran after her.

When she neared the pigs, she slowed as if she was trying to sneak up on them.

He picked up a fallen tree limb as he entered the woods. She hurried toward two of the pigs who seemed to be in the lead, but they were rooting in the dead leaves and ignoring her as she shook her skirt at them and stomped her feet. She looked up and her eyes went wide at seeing him.

He pressed a finger to his lips to show he was being quiet on purpose. She nodded.

He came around the side, and when he and Eva had the pigs trapped between them and their pen, Westley yelled, raised his arms, and shook the tree limb at them.

The larger pigs grunted and barely moved, while the smaller pigs squealed and took a few steps toward the pen.

Eva picked up a smaller tree limb and imitated him, shaking it in the air, but the limb was so rotten it snapped in two and crumbled to the ground. Undeterred, she ran toward the four smaller pigs, chasing them back toward the pen.

Westley prodded the older pigs with his stick, making them grunt louder, but they finally obeyed and started back toward the pen. He overtook them to open the gate while Eva herded them through. Three went in, but the fourth little pig scurried past them and stopped to root on the ground with its snout. Eva pursued it while Westley closed the gate.

"We mustn't chase it," Westley said softly, slowly sneaking up behind it. "Pigs are faster than you might think."

Eva nodded, keeping her gaze on the pig. She got very close, then pounced. The pig squealed as if it were being murdered. Eva had the pig by its hind legs. She dragged it backward as it screeched with every breath. Westley yanked open the gate so she could drag it inside. She let it go and it ran to the back of the pen, still squealing.

Eva was breathing hard as she brushed her hands together, a

triumphant glint in her eye. Her cheeks were pink and her red hair was in disarray, more strands hanging loose than in her braid.

He lost his breath for a moment.

She went out of the gate and he closed it. She was already hurrying into the trees where they had left the two older pigs.

The pigs were rooting around in the leaves, finding acorns and mushrooms. The swineherder sometimes took them out foraging, so they were familiar with the kinds of food they would find. They were reluctant to leave off, as they were ignoring the tall redhead clapping at them and shooing them with her skirts.

She picked up another stick and tapped the boar on the head. It made a warning sound in its throat.

"Be careful! He could hurt you," Westley called out. "Male pigs can be very aggressive."

The large boar lifted his head, possibly preparing to bite her.

Westley let out a loud call similar to what he had heard the swineherder use. To his relief, the pig took a step back. But Eva did not give up, and she came at them both again.

"Chuck-chuck!" Westley imitated the swineherder's call again.

The hogs turned their heads in his direction and began moving slowly but steadily on their short legs, with Eva clapping right behind them.

When they got closer, Westley guided them with his long stick into the pen and closed the gate.

Eva gave him a smile, her cheeks glowing pink and her chest rising and falling with every breath. Her skirt was splattered with mud. She pushed several strands of hair off her face using the back of her hand.

"Are you well?"

She nodded and bent to pick up two buckets off the ground.

"Please, sit down and rest for a while. You look tired."

She sat on the grass. He sat as well, a few feet away.

He started to ask her how the pigs got out of the pen, but it was pretty obvious that she had been feeding them—hence the buckets—and had inadvertently let them out.

"You did a very good job getting the pigs back in their pen."

She frowned slightly, keeping her head down even as she glanced up at him. She shook her head and pointed to him. She smiled and placed a hand on her heart.

"I'm glad I was nearby and was able to help."

She picked at the grass, then lay on her side, propping her head on her arm. She picked a tiny flower and twirled it between her fingers, smiling.

"I wish you could talk."

She shrugged and shook her head, almost as if the subject embarrassed her.

"Did your injury happen before or after the Peasants' Uprising?"

She seemed to think for a moment, then pushed her hand outward.

"After?"

She nodded.

"I'm sorry that happened to you. I think cruelties by masters like that are what caused the people to become violent. My friend John Underhill's father was killed during the uprising."

She gave him a sympathetic look and touched her hand to her heart again.

"John was grieved and angry. He is the lord of the land south of here, adjacent to my father's, the village of Caversdown. He hasn't been the same since."

She stared at him with those pretty green eyes.

"Ever since the uprising, my father has tried to give his servants a fair wage for their work and has given them more time off to tend to their own fields. But John doesn't understand this. He was furious with me for not talking my father out of the changes in their wages and work hours."

He wanted her to know that he felt bad for what she had been through, for the abuse she had suffered. And perhaps he was motivated by the way her sympathetic eyes shone, as if they saw past the outside and into his thoughts, discerning his feelings.

Eva made him think of the girl he had heard singing at Berkhamsted Castle, probably because they both had red hair. His heart quickened at the thought of the mysterious woman and her singing. He thought of her often, wishing he could hear her again, wishing he knew who she was. He'd even dreamed about her.

If only Eva could speak. He imagined she had a beautiful voice as well. But mostly he wanted to know what she was thinking.

"Why do you let them send you to feed the pigs? Why don't you show Golda and Mistress Alice your skills and talents? I'm sure you are good at many things."

She smiled, a genuine smile. Then she shook her head.

"Why are you shaking your head?"

She looked up at the sky and sighed. Then she shrugged.

"I wish you could tell me."

Eva's face suddenly lit up. She held up a finger. She stood and looked all around. Then she motioned with her hand for him to follow her. She walked several feet, back toward the pigpen. When she was in front of the gate, she bent over and started doing something in the bare ground where the grass had been worn away.

He drew closer, then squatted.

She was drawing in the dirt with her finger. No, those were letters.

"I can read and write."

He stared at the words in the dirt. This meant they could

communicate. Just as he suspected, there was much more to this peasant girl than anyone knew.

$$\sim\!\!\mathit{elle}$$

Evangeline nearly laughed with joy at the look of surprise and the smile that spread over Westley's face.

"Where did you learn to read?"

She brushed the dirt with her hand to erase the words and wrote, *"Hard to explain."*

"I've been wanting to ask you, how did you cut Reeve Folsham? Did he get too close? He was so upset he wouldn't tell us."

Evangeline winced. *"No. I lost my grip."* She waited for him to read the words, then erased them and wrote, *"It flew out of my hand."*

Westley laughed, then he pressed his lips together.

"I was very sorry." She erased it. *"I would have died"*—erased—*"if he had been badly hurt."*

"Had you ever used a scythe before?"

Scythe. That was the word they had used for that long, curving blade with the wooden handle. She shook her head.

"What have you done?"

She wrote, *"Embroidery."* Then, *"I can sing."*

She instantly realized her gaffe and her cheeks heated. She erased it and wrote, *"Or I used to sing, before I lost my voice."*

"I am so sorry for what happened to you." His voice was low and kind. "In a small way, I feel responsible for all the terrible things masters have done to their servants and villeins."

"Why?"

"Because my father owns so much land and has so many servants and villeins, not only here, but in three other counties. His stewards could be mistreating people and we would not know it. Besides that, I suppose I feel a bit guilty that my family lives much better than anyone else in Glynval—better food, better house, better everything."

So he felt guilty for having more than everyone else. It had hardly even occurred to her that she had better food and shelter and clothing than other people around her. A stab of guilt went through her middle. She was too busy feeling sorry for herself that she did not have the freedom of a peasant, while Westley felt sorry for her because of a lie.

She was a terrible person. She did not know how to do anything useful. She had nearly killed a man, and she ruined everything she touched. She was deceiving everyone around her by making them think she could not speak, and she and Muriel were taking jobs other people genuinely needed. And the worst thought of all was that Westley would be hurt if he knew the truth.

"The Bible says masters should treat their servants well."

Evangeline brushed out the last words she had written and wrote, *"You have read the Bible?"*

"Yes."

"You own a Bible?"

"Yes. Would you like to read it?"

Evangeline's heart leapt, then sank. *"Does your priest approve?"*

"He does not disapprove. My father has owned a Bible all his life. He commissioned one to be transcribed into English a few years ago."

Evangeline sat back on her heels. She'd never even heard of such a thing. Westley and his family must be terribly powerful to be so unafraid of translating the Bible into the people's base language. Priests she had known only read and quoted it in Latin. Was it wrong to read it in English?

There was a look of peaceful reflection on Westley's face. Could such a person be wrong? Could someone who was wealthy, who had risked his life to save a child from getting injured by a runaway horse, who had helped her get the pigs she had let out back into their pen, could such a person be committing a grievous sin by reading the Holy Writ in the people's language?

"Would you like to read it? The Bible?"

Suddenly she wanted to, more than anything. To be able to read the very words that God spoke, that Jesus said, everything written in that holy book . . . And since she understood Latin . . . *Yes, please. The Latin one.*

"Very well. Come to the castle tonight after your work is done and ask for me."

Her heart thumped. She wrote, *You are very kind.*

"It is nothing. And now I will let you get back to what you were doing. I'm off to see how many fish I can catch." He smiled as he turned away to retrieve his fishing equipment.

His smile might be friendly, but he was not thinking of her as someone he might fall in love with. She was only a servant. When she had thought him a peasant, she hoped that she could get him to marry her. But he was not a peasant. He was the son of the lord of the land. As a servant, was she too lowly for him to fall in love with? And even if he would consider her more than a servant, how would he ever fall in love with her if she had no voice? If he never heard her sing?

Someday, somehow, she might be able to make him think that her throat was gradually healing, and she would begin to speak again. And then, *Please, God,* Westley would fall in love with her, as she was already falling in love with his kindness and good nature.

One day she would tell him the whole truth, because to keep deceiving him would make him hate her so much more if he discovered the truth on his own. Hopefully, if she confessed to him, he would understand why she had played this farce and would forgive her. She could hardly bear to think of him hating her.

Westley was walking back toward home when he heard a commotion in the woods. A woman screamed.

He dropped his catch of fish on the grass and ran toward it.

In a small clearing stood a wattle-and-daub house, and in the doorway, a man held a woman by the hair while he struck her about the head and shoulders with his fist.

Westley ran toward them. "Ho, there! Stop!"

Another man ran toward them from another direction. Together they pulled the man away from the woman, who started alternately sobbing and yelling, "Robert, you surly knave! You evil dog!"

Westley and one of the other villagers took the man by his arms and pulled him several feet away from the house as the woman went inside, her muffled sobs drifting out to them.

"You've done it now, Robert," the other man said gruffly. "Too much ale. What did I tell you? You want your little son and daughter to see you like that, whaling on their mother?"

Westley let him keep speaking to the man. They seemed to know each other well. But all of a sudden the man jerked away from them and glared at Westley.

"What right have you to take hold of me?"

"Hush, Robert. That's the lord's heir, Westley."

"No right!" the inebriated man yelled at Westley. "No right! Go on."

"Forgive him, Lord Westley," the other man said. "He's drunk. He will be meek and mild enough when he's not got the devil drink in his veins."

"He'll answer for his actions at the manorial court."

"Yes, of course, my lord. His Molly will see to that. She has had enough of his rough treatment. It is good of you to come to her aid."

"No right!" The man jabbed his finger at Westley. He growled like an animal, then stumbled away into the woods.

What kind of trouble would this wife-beater make? He had better accept whatever punishment the manorial court doled out to him. Indeed, he had little choice, and hopefully he would get the message that beating one's wife—or anyone else—would not be ignored.

Chapter Eight

Golda met her with a scowl on her face when Evangeline came back from feeding the pigs.

"Where have you been? Dawdling servants have to clean the floors." She had also stared pointedly at Evangeline's skirts, which were covered in dirt from the mud that spattered on her when she had chased the pigs. She sent Evangeline for more water and gave her a block of lye soap and set her to work on the floors.

That evening, when Mistress Alice dismissed Evangeline from her work, she hurried toward the undercroft to change her dress, which was now wet from scrubbing floors all day. Her hands were blistered, cracked, and red, but it had been worth it to spend time talking with Westley.

As she hurriedly pulled on a clean dress, Muriel came up behind her and caught her wrist. "Come outside with me," she whispered.

Evangeline complied and followed her out. It was not dark yet, so they hid among a stand of trees.

Muriel looked hard into her face. "Are you not tired yet of all this nonsense?"

"Nonsense?" Evangeline spoke close to Muriel's ear so she could speak as softly as possible and only be heard by her friend.

"Living like a servant, working harder than either of us were ever meant to work. This is not the kind of life you were born for. Your grandfather was a king!"

"Lower your voice. Someone might hear." Evangeline glanced around, but she did not see anyone.

She grabbed Evangeline's hand and turned up the palm. "Look at this! Red and raw. Blistered and bleeding. Is this what you want?"

Evangeline only stared back at her.

"Listen to me. I understand." Muriel's voice was much softer and kinder. But her eyes still flashed. "You don't want to marry someone you do not feel a courtly love for. But courtly love is for poems and songs. It is not . . ." She sighed. "Romantic love is very well to dream about, to imagine what it might be like to fall in love and marry and live in bliss for the rest of your life." Muriel rolled her eyes at the mention of living in bliss. "But it is not the way of kings and those with royal blood. You have the good fortune of being betrothed to the king's advisor, to an earl. You will be wealthy. You will not have to work or worry about anything. You will be taken care of."

And thereby, Muriel would be taken care of. But perhaps Evangeline was being unkind to her loyal friend.

"I don't mind working." Evangeline stared down at her hands. Some of the blisters were oozing a mixture of blood and clear liquid. The pain would not bother her if she could talk to Westley again tonight and get to read the holy book that he obviously wanted to share with her.

What she did mind was her own incompetence. She cringed inwardly at the thought of there being more incidences such as the ones with the scythe, the water, and the pigs.

Muriel stared hard at her. "What do you think I'm supposed to do? Forget about my life before? I'm thirty-two years old. I have no wish to begin a new life as a servant."

"Are they treating you badly? Is Lady le Wyse cruel to you?"

"No, she is better to me than I ever was to the servants at Berkhamsted Castle, but that does not mean I want to stay here."

"I'm very sorry, Muriel." A fist seemed to pound her chest. "I have been thoughtless. Please forgive me. Perhaps you can return to Berkhamsted Castle without me."

Muriel grunted, then leaned toward Evangeline, her face only inches from hers. "What do you think they will say to me? They know that I left with you. The king's men will force me to tell them where you went. I am trapped here. Trapped." Muriel held out her hands in frustration. "Unless you come back to Berkhamsted Castle with me."

Evangeline's heart twisted inside her. Did Muriel think she was very selfish to want to stay here when Muriel obviously wished to go back to her old life? But if they both went back, Evangeline would be forced to marry Lord Shiveley.

"Lord Shiveley will not give up so easily, Evangeline. His men and King Richard's will find you eventually. You are not far enough away, and your unusual height and red hair will give you away."

If they thought Evangeline was dead, they would stop looking for her. Perhaps Muriel could say she had died, lying to them the same way she was lying to the people of Glynval.

"Please, Muriel. Give me some time to figure out what to do." She clasped her friend's hand. "Please." Evangeline begged with her eyes.

"What choice do I have?"

She squeezed Muriel's hand, but Muriel did not squeeze back. She turned away and began walking back to the undercroft in the bottom floor of the manor house.

Did she think Evangeline was selfish, too selfish to deserve her friendship? The old familiar terror—that she was too selfish to be worthy of love—filled her chest like a full bucket of water.

Evangeline couldn't let Muriel think she was selfish. She needed to think of a plan to get Muriel back to Berkhamsted Castle so she would not lose the one friend she had long depended upon.

Westley was on his way home on a small footpath through the woods when John Underhill rounded the bend just ahead.

"John! I haven't seen you in half a year." A feeling of joy filled his chest at seeing his old friend. But John stepped aside and stood still. Something about the look on his friend's face chased away the joyful feeling and made the hair prickle on the back of Westley's neck. "Come, and you can walk with me."

"You are on your way home, then?" John glanced at Westley out of narrowed eyes. His hand rested on a bundle he carried under his arm.

"Yes. Mother asked me to take some bone broth to a sick family."

"Such benevolence." John's voice was quiet but contained a sneer.

Westley shifted his feet. "You know Mother. She's always wanting to help someone who's sick or hurt."

"Your family always did care too much." John's lip curled. "If it hadn't been for your father making the villeins think they should get such easy treatment, they never would have been bold enough to kill Father."

"John, that's not true."

"Your father gave in to their demands. He—and men like him—are the reason the villeins rose up and killed their lords and masters."

"John, you are not remembering the facts. The two men who killed your father had been beaten the week before, by your father's orders. You said yourself that you would never treat people the way your father did, working them until they passed out and beating them for little or no reason. I'm sorry to say these things to you, John, but it's the truth. Surely you remember—"

"How dare you speak evil of my father! He was a good man. If he beat those men, it was because they deserved it."

"John, I'm sorry, but—"

"You're not sorry." John took a menacing step toward him.

"What's going on here?" Reeve Folsham rounded the bend in the path behind John. "Is there trouble here? Westley?"

John took a step back. "Of course there's no trouble. There's never any trouble in Glynval."

Westley didn't miss the bitterness in his voice, especially when he said *Glynval*.

Westley's heart was heavy as John turned and stalked away, back toward Caversdown.

John's father, Hugh Underhill, had always been a harsh man. He'd even given John a black eye once when John and Westley were just boys of fourteen. It hurt to see his friend have such an unkind father when Westley's own father was so good and wise. Westley had even offered to let John come and live with him, but he had refused.

"Why is John Underhill so angry?"

Westley sighed. "I suppose he doesn't want to think ill of his father, so he's remembering the past differently."

Reeve Folsham nodded and frowned.

⁓⚬⚬⸲

Evangeline waited in the entryway. A pretty blonde maiden a few years younger than she called, "Westley! The new servant is here." She walked away, as if to go find him.

A few moments later, Westley bounded in through the back passageway. "That rude girl was my sister Cate." His brown hair was calmer than usual, as if he had combed it. "I have a place for us to read. Come." He motioned her forward with his hand.

She followed him through the passageway toward the back of the house. They passed through a room where some older children were hunched over a chess game, but they did not look up as she and Westley passed.

Lady le Wyse entered the corridor in front of them. She smiled when she saw them. "Westley."

He kissed her cheek and she patted his.

"Eva. How are you, my dear?"

Evangeline smiled at her.

"How are you doing with your work? I forgot to check on you today. Golda did not work you too hard, I hope?"

Evangeline shrugged and shook her head.

"That is good. Westley tells me you can read and that you wish to read the Bible. It is a noble ambition, to read the Holy Writ."

Her words buoyed Evangeline's spirit and dispelled some of her exhaustion.

The back door opened and Lord le Wyse stepped in.

Lady le Wyse's face lit up as she turned toward him, and Lord le Wyse's attention was immediately caught by her. He stepped toward his wife with a small smile on his lips. He kissed her briefly and she put her arm around him.

The look they gave each other made Evangeline slightly embarrassed, as if she had peeked in on someone when they thought they were alone, but it also pleased her to see a married couple so obviously in love with each other. Had they married for love?

Muriel should see this.

Westley motioned for her to follow him, and they passed by the lord and his lady, who called, "Don't forget supper in an hour."

"Yes, Mother."

"Fine catch of fish," his father told him as he passed.

"Thank you, Father."

Soon Evangeline and Westley were out the back door and standing on a flat expanse of green grass encircled by a low hedge. Beyond the hedge was a beautiful garden that fairly glowed in the light of the late-day summer sun.

"This is a spot where my sisters and I come to read sometimes."

The vulnerable smile on his face seemed to say that he was inviting her to know something personal about himself.

He pointed to the low bench and the cushions on the ground around it, like a comfortable little alcove in the corner against the side of the stone exterior with the bushes juxtaposed against it.

"Here's the Bible, the Latin one." He picked up the large book that lay on the bench and held it reverently.

Evangeline gazed into his eyes. Could he see how grateful she was that he was being so kind to her when she was only a servant girl? How grateful she was for his sharing his family's precious Bible with her? How would he know if she did not speak?

"Sit down, wherever you will be most comfortable, and I'll give you the Bible. It's very heavy."

Evangeline chose a cushion on the ground. *Look at me now, King Richard. Your ward, your pawn, is sitting on the ground about to read the Bible.*

Westley bent and laid the book in her lap. "I also brought these." He picked up a wax board and a stick about five inches long and held them out to her as he knelt beside her.

Evangeline's breath caught in her throat. She had used a wax board when her tutors had taught her to read and write as a child. She took the instruments and immediately wrote in the wax on the small board.

"I am so grateful to you," she wrote. She winced, as the action of writing rubbed against her open blisters on the inside of her thumb. But the pain was nothing compared to the joy of "speaking" with Westley.

"Now, which book of the Bible would you like to read first?"

She held the stick a little awkwardly to try to inflict as little pain as possible on herself. *"I have read the Psalms already,"* she wrote.

Suddenly Westley caught her hand and flipped it palm up.

"How did this happen?" He grabbed her other hand, forcing her to drop the wax tablet into her lap. That hand was equally damaged, her pale, delicate skin red and oozing in several places.

Her cheeks grew warm as he continued to stare at her hands.

"Eva." His voice was breathless as he said her name, making her stomach tumble as he looked into her eyes.

She pulled her hands out of his loose grip and held them close to her chest, hiding her palms.

"Who made you work this hard on your first full day? I shall have them sent away for this."

Evangeline shook her head vehemently. She grabbed the wax tablet and stylus and wrote, *"Please, no. It was my fault. They did not know I had not done this kind of work before."* Was she revealing too much?

Westley handed her another wax tablet, as she had run out of room.

"I could have asked Golda to give me another task. It is all right. Please do not punish her."

He closed his eyes for several moments before opening them, then stood. "Stay here. I shall return."

What was he about to do? Would he bring Golda here and force a confrontation? Her heart pounded. After what she did to the reeve, if she caused their cook to be sent away, everyone would hate her even more than they already did. Should she run after him? What if she couldn't find him and Lord or Lady le Wyse found her wandering around their home?

She had to make him see that it was her fault and the cook was not to blame. If she had to, she would beg him not to punish Golda.

Westley suddenly returned and knelt beside her, holding a small pot, such as one might use for perfume or salve, and in the other hand he held a roll of bandages.

"Give me your hands."

She held them out, and he dipped a finger in the small pottery container.

"This is a healing salve my mother makes for scrapes and minor cuts. It will keep your open blisters from becoming septic." His voice was grim, but his expression softened when he touched her hand, then proceeded to smear the thick, golden salve on her wounds.

"Am I hurting you?"

She shook her head.

"I wish someone had been looking out for you," he said softly.

Her heart trembled. She'd never known a man could be so kind and tender, so compassionate and gentle, and yet so masculine and appealing. His touch sent warmth and pleasant sensations all through her.

Surely if God loved her, He would let her marry this man.

Chapter Nine

Westley's heart turned over at the suffering that had been inflicted on this sweet maiden. When he had mentioned sending away the person who made her work this hard, she was horrified at the thought of causing anyone to be punished. And yet her hands were actually bleeding.

He brushed on the healing salve as carefully as possible so as not to inflict any further pain on her, first on one hand and then the other.

His mother always followed any application of her healing salve on one of her children with a kiss next to the wound. What would it feel like to kiss that delicate spot on the inside of Eva's wrist?

What was he thinking? After all the times his parents had warned him not to take advantage of female servants in any way, he should know better than to allow such a thought into his head.

When he finished applying the salve, she just sat quietly, but he was very aware of her watching him. He picked up the roll and wrapped the cloth bandage around her hand. He cut it and tied it off, then repeated for the other hand.

"Not too tight, is it?"

She shook her head, then picked up the wax tablet and stylus, holding them awkwardly in her bandaged hands. *"Thank you,"* she wrote. *"No other lords in England could be as kind as you."*

"Perhaps it makes up for some of the unkindness done to you."

She nodded and ducked her head. Perhaps she wanted to read.

"I'll let you get started. It's a long book, and you may not be able to finish it before supper."

She seemed to appreciate his weak jest, as she smiled up at him.

She opened the book with great care to the Acts of the Apostles and started reading.

He went for a walk in the garden, examining the rosebushes and tearing the leaves off a small limb that had fallen out of a tree. A butterfly flitted in front of him, and he was reminded of how joyfully Eva had chased the butterflies on their trip from Berkhamsted Castle. He'd thought her so childlike and full of life. But since coming here, she did not seem quite so unbridled in her joy. In fact, she had seemed horrified and sad, more than once. And no wonder, with being forced to work until her hands bled. Perhaps she would hate it here and she and her friend would leave.

That thought made his heart sink. He didn't want her to go. He didn't want anyone mistreating her. He wanted to keep her safe. But perhaps that was foolish. She had only just arrived here. He was not responsible for her. He did care about her, though. No one deserved to be mistreated, least of all someone who had already been so mistreated in her life, someone as innocent and fair of form and face as Eva.

When Evangeline reported for work at the manor house the next morning, Mistress Alice pulled her aside. "Someone told me you were injured. Rest your hands for today and we will examine them again in the morning."

Evangeline worried about not being useful to the household for an entire day, and she ended up wandering through the meadow where some sheep were grazing, past the pigpen.

All day and no work to do. If only she could read some more in the Bible, but she did not have the courage to ask Lord or Lady le Wyse. She might be brave enough to ask Westley if she were to find him, so she walked toward the river. Perhaps he had gone fishing.

She wandered along the bank. She smiled to think that Muriel would warn her away, afraid she would fall in, if she were here. The water made a pleasant rushing sound in the still morning air. Even the birds were quiet here. Trees grew right up to the edge of the bank, and it truly was a peaceful place, more beautiful in its wildness than the cultivated and perfectly trimmed bushes of the gardens of Berkhamsted Castle.

Finding a large, smooth rock, she sat down. Wildflowers grew everywhere in Glynval, around the rocky places as well as the open meadows, a whole new world of beauty and wonder. Such a pity that Muriel wanted to go back to her old life.

Evangeline took a deep breath and let it out slowly. If only Muriel could be content here in Glynval. But it was unfair to expect it of her. Poor Muriel. Evangeline had only been thinking of herself, and now, what would the king do to punish Muriel when she returned to Berkhamsted? Of course he would force her to tell where Evangeline had gone.

How could this adventure end well for either of them?

Something caught her eye. By her foot a small frog crawled forward, then leapt away. An ant walked up a nearby tree trunk. And in the water below her, unseen, swam fish and eels, countless water beings full of life. What was it they wanted? What did Evangeline want?

The memory rushed in, of Lord and Lady le Wyse the previous night, how they had hurried to touch each other, to speak to each other. After all the years they had been together, all their children birthed and nurtured, they still looked at each other with love in their eyes.

"That is what I want," Evangeline whispered.

Her own parents had not been able to enjoy each other like that. Her mother died shortly after she was born, and her father soon after that. She was supposedly born outside of marriage, but she liked to think her parents did end up marrying secretly before she was born. Perhaps they intended to make their union known but died before it was possible.

She had never been privy to a married couple and their relationship. But she very much suspected that true married love looked similar to what she saw between Lord and Lady le Wyse. She closed her eyes, crossed herself, and clasped her hands. *Please give me a love like that, God.*

A sound caught her attention. Not wishing any of the other servants to see her doing nothing, she made her way off the path and hid in the trees and bushes, staring out through the leaves.

Two men walked past. One was carrying a short but heavy-looking block of wood. He was blond and dressed in a fine linen shirt with a finely worked leather sleeveless tunic—much too fine for a servant. She caught a bare glimpse of the other man, noting his dark hair.

Evangeline left her hiding place and followed them from a distance. Ahead, she heard them talking, gradually realizing they were speaking with a third man. As she drew closer, she saw that the third man was Westley.

Suddenly the blond man raised the block of wood and struck Westley in the head, then pushed him off the bank into the river.

Frozen, unable to breathe, Evangeline watched as the two strange men ran in the other direction.

Westley.

She ran as fast as she could, stumbling over her skirt before jerking it up to her knees.

She scrambled down the side of the bank. He was lying facedown in the water a little farther downstream, his body caught on a tree whose roots extended into the river.

Evangeline jumped into the river feet first, water splashing on her face. The water pushed her skirt up to her waist, but she had to get to Westley. He would surely drown. *O God, help me! Please, please.*

Walking through the chest-high water was slow, no matter how hard she pushed her legs to move faster. Her eyes were locked on Westley's body. Every moment his face was under water brought him closer to death.

She finally reached him, grabbed him under his arm, and used her other hand to pull his head up.

He was heavier than she imagined. Using all her strength, she put his arm around her shoulders and held his head out of the water. His eyes were closed, his face pale. A trickle of blood ran down his temple. Was he . . . ?

No. He could not be. She would not believe it.

Stumbling toward the bank, nearly going under herself, she managed to prop his head and shoulders against the side of the steep bank. Her arms under his, climbing up the bank, she pulled as hard as she could. He did not budge. His lower half was still under water.

"Help! Someone, please!" She had to get him out of the water and breathing again. He had to live. Whatever happened to her, she had to save Westley.

She wedged her body underneath his and pushed. She only managed to move him an inch.

"Help! Westley is hurt!" She brushed the trickle of blood away from his closed eye as a sob shook her.

A voice called, indistinguishable in the distance.

"Help! Someone help!" Evangeline screamed.

"Who is that?" the voice called, getting closer.

"Westley is hurt! Please help me!"

Finally, Sabina's face appeared above her.

"Eva!" Her mouth fell open. "You spoke. Is that Westley?"

"Yes, help me, please. He's nearly drowned."

"Maybe I should go get help."

"Just help me drag him to the top of the bank."

Sabina eased herself halfway down the bank. She took one of his arms and Evangeline took the other, and together they managed to pull him to the top as Evangeline dug her toes into the muddy bank and climbed out beside him.

Instinctively Evangeline turned him onto his stomach, holding one shoulder up so his face was not in the dirt, and pounded on his back.

Suddenly he vomited. *Thank You, God, he is alive!*

Sabina screamed. Evangeline kept hold of his shoulder so he was lying on his side and slightly forward.

"I'll get help!" Sabina ran away down the path.

He stopped heaving and lay still. She studied his face. He was pale, but perhaps not as pale as when she first pulled him out of the river. She wished she had a dry cloth to wipe the blood from his temple and the side of his face.

The bandages he had put on her hands were dripping water. She yanked them off and threw them on the ground.

He groaned, then started coughing. Again, he lay still.

"Westley? Are you all right? Please don't die. You are the most beautiful person I've ever met."

His eyelids eased up, as though it hurt to open them. He gazed at her for a moment, a dazed look in his eyes. Then his eyes closed again.

"He's unconscious. But he's alive," she assured herself. "He'll wake up again."

Was he breathing? She laid her cheek over his nose and mouth. She waited, then felt the slight brush of air against her cheek.

The leather bag he often carried with him lay on the ground nearby. Evangeline ran to it and found nothing more helpful than a dry cloth. She carried it back to him.

Gently, she wiped at the blood. She brushed his hair back until she saw the source—a cut at his hairline. She pressed the cloth against the spot while staring down into his face, his perfect features and masculine chin and jaw. But if he never woke up, the heart and mind were what would be missed the most. How could Glynval ever be the same without him?

Who did this to him? Who would want to hurt such a kind and gentle young man?

She heard voices in the distance. Then Sabina's rose above the rest. "He's over here."

Several men appeared, with Sabina leading them. When they saw her kneeling beside Westley on the ground, they ran past Sabina and nudged Evangeline out of the way. They pelted her with questions.

"What happened?"

"Is he alive?"

"Is he breathing?"

Evangeline nodded.

Four of them lifted him and carried him slowly down the path.

Evangeline stood, watching them go, suddenly aware that she was dripping wet from the neck down. Her hands showed smears of blood—Westley's blood—and they were shaking.

God, please let him live.

Chapter Ten

As Muriel left the privy behind the manor house, Evangeline caught her eye and motioned to her. She led her behind some trees and bushes.

"Is Westley well?" Evangeline whispered.

"He has been awake and talking."

"Oh, thank You, God." She let out the breath she was holding. "Will he be all right? Is he in his right mind?"

"I think so. I have not seen him, though. Sabina is crowing to everyone who will listen that she was the one who pulled him out of the river and saved his life."

"What else did she say? Did she tell everyone that I can speak?"

"What do you mean?"

"I was the one who saw the man hit him in the head and throw him in the water. I jumped in and pulled his face out of the water, but I couldn't get him all the way out, so I screamed for help. Sabina came. She heard me talk."

"Be wary of that one," Muriel said softly. "And what do you mean, you saw a man hit him in the head?"

"Doesn't he remember?"

"I don't know. Perhaps you should try to see him yourself."

Would they let her in to see him? "I will try."

Evangeline parted from Muriel and hurried toward the castle. When she was nearly to the front door, someone called her name.

Sabina stood nearby smirking at her, arms crossed in front of her. "You lied about not being able to speak."

"And you lied about saving Westley from the river." Evangeline made her expression emotionless as she stared down at the shorter girl, but inside, her heart was pounding.

Sabina uncrossed her arms and planted her fists on her hips. "Westley is mine. And if you dare to tell him that you were the one who saved him, then I will tell him what a liar you and your friend Mildred are, telling everyone you are mute."

Evangeline's chest rose and fell rapidly. "Westley is a human being. He does not belong to you."

"You stay away from him or I will tell him your secret."

They stared at each other. When a house servant opened the door to throw out a bucket of water, Evangeline darted inside. Sabina made a startled noise and followed on her heels.

Westley's sister Cate stepped into the corridor. "Eva. Did you want to see Westley?"

Evangeline nodded.

"Sabina!" Mistress Alice called. "I need you to give your mother a message . . ." Her voice trailed off as Evangeline hurried after Cate.

Cate turned down one corridor and then another and finally stopped in a doorway.

Inside, Westley was sitting up in a bed propped up with pillows. She drank him in—the healthy color in his face, the blue of his eyes, the movement of his hand as he signaled to her.

"Eva, please come in. I was hoping to see you."

As she drew near to him, he looked almost back to normal, except that his hair was mussed and sticking up over his cut. He also had shadows under his eyes.

"The men told me you were there with me when they arrived. Sabina said you waited with me while she went to get help."

He held out a wax tablet to her. He must not know she could talk.

She scratched her answer, feeling guiltier than usual at her deception. *"I did. I pressed a cloth against your head wound."*

He pointed to his head and winced. "My mother insisted on stitching it up."

Evangeline grimaced back.

"I am glad you came. I wanted to thank you for waiting with me."

She had no real reason to tell him she was actually the one who saved him from drowning. If Sabina would keep her secret, Evangeline might as well let her get the credit for saving him.

"I am grateful you are alive. Do you know who hit you?"

"No one hit me. Sabina said I hit my head when I fell in the river."

"Don't you remember what happened?"

"No. That's the strange thing. All I remember is getting my fishing gear and walking to my favorite fishing spot. And I'm not even sure I'm remembering that from this morning or from another day, since I go fishing so often. All the memories seem jumbled. I don't remember falling in the river at all. I think the head injury has addled my thoughts."

She should tell him the truth, even though Sabina would tell everyone she lied about being mute. But the dangerous man who tried to murder Westley would surely hear that he was not dead after all and would try again to kill him.

But if Westley discovered her lie, he wouldn't trust her. Besides, she did not know who the men were who attacked him and couldn't even describe them very well.

"Perhaps someone pushed you. It seems unlikely that you would fall."

Westley raised his brows. "It does seem strange. I should probably question Sabina a bit more closely."

But before he did, Evangeline needed to tell her what had actually happened. She had to convince Sabina that Westley was in danger so she could warn him. If only Sabina *had* seen who hit him, she might have recognized his attackers. They were strangers to Evangeline.

"Is there someone who might be angry enough to want to kill you?"

"There was a man attacking his wife in the woods just after I helped you get the pigs back in their pen. I heard her scream and helped pull the man away from her. He was very angry. He is the only person I can think of who might have done such a thing."

"Yes, perhaps it was that man. Or a worker who is still dwelling on the Peasants' Uprising?"

"That is possible, I suppose." He looked so troubled. "I told you a little about the uprising."

She nodded.

"My father had experienced something similar years ago, when his villeins had risen up against him and even threatened to kill him, before he and Mother married. Everything quickly settled down and nothing bad happened. But three years ago, some villeins from my friend John Underhill's lands murdered John's father, then came and stirred up our people. My father's villeins started stealing the livestock and tried to set fire to the castle. My father went out and calmed them down, but there was a lot of fear and tension for a while. My father saw the importance of raising the people's wages—as many other landowners around England were doing—and trying to be more fair and generous about how many days' work they owed. In fact, my father was more lenient and generous than any of the other landowners around, including John Underhill, who was the oldest son and had to take over after his father was killed."

Westley gave a slight shake of his head. "John was furious with us."

Her heart clenched to see the pain in his expression and hear it in his voice. No one had ever expressed such feelings so openly with her before. Her heart beat faster. How she wanted this man to think well of her, to see her heart as she was seeing his. But would he see how selfish she was and be disgusted by her? How could he love her if he knew what was in her heart—deception and selfishness?

"But all seems better now." His brows lifted, as did the corners of his mouth. "The anger and bitterness seem to have mostly gone from the people, and I am thankful for that—although I am not so sure about John."

He was almost too good to be real, and yet, here he was, very real and close and with the most beautiful blue eyes.

"What happened to you during that time? Were there any riots where you lived?"

"No, not where I lived," she wrote, which was true. She had thought of the Peasants' Uprising as something that happened a long way away.

"You probably don't want to talk about all those things that happened in the past. It is time for us to read. My mother has ordered me to stay in bed for the rest of the day, so you can keep me company."

"I came because I wanted to know if you were well."

"And I am. Just a small headache." He smiled and her stomach fluttered. "How are your hands? Let me see."

She held them out, palms up. The blisters were still raw but no blood or oozing. She'd cleaned and dried them after her jump into the river.

She picked up the wax tablet again. *"Much better now, as you see."*

"That is very good." He pointed behind her. "I had them bring the Bible in here for you."

Evangeline took the book from the shelf behind her.

She allowed herself to stare at him, at how good it was to see him alive and looking well. Truly, she thanked God she had been able to save him from the river. If she had not followed those two men . . . if she had not been able to pull his head out of the water in time . . . if his body had been carried away by the current . . . A world without a kind young man who wished to help a servant girl read the Bible, who smiled often, and who bandaged a servant's blistered hands would have been a sadder world.

But she put the heavy book down and wrote on the wax tablet, *"I will be back. I must do something first."*

He looked surprised as Evangeline hurried out of the room, out of the house, and into the grassy area behind it. The other servants were folding linens in the bright sunshine, and Evangeline spotted Sabina standing among them, talking and laughing. Evangeline walked past the other servants to Sabina.

"I need to talk to you." Evangeline kept her voice low, looking over her shoulder to make sure no one else was listening.

Sabina walked a few feet away from the others, then turned and pointed her finger in Evangeline's face. "And I told you to stay away from Westley."

"If you care about Westley, you need to tell him that you think two men were trying to kill him."

"Why? What do you mean?"

"I saw a man strike Westley with a block of wood and push him into the river. You have to warn him, so his men can keep him safe."

Sabina stared at her for a moment. "Who? Who struck Westley?"

"I don't know. A man with blond hair. I only saw his face from the side, but I did not know him."

Sabina gave a slow nod. "Very well. I shall tell him." She narrowed her eyes at Evangeline. "Why do you pretend to be mute? Why did you and Mildred lie to everyone?"

"It was a foolish thing to do. But I thank you for not telling anyone." Sensing Sabina was about to say something more, Evangeline fled back to the castle, and back to Westley and the Bible.

That night Evangeline and Muriel kept to the edge of the trees as they made their way to the small glade in the forest to talk.

"I think I will have to tell everyone soon that I am not mute."

"What do you mean?" Muriel's voice was sharp.

"Sabina is likely to tell someone. I don't trust her at all. And for another thing, I don't like pretending." *Especially with Westley.*

"You listen to me." Muriel shook her finger in Evangeline's face. "I am the one who lied. It is more my secret than yours, so if you decide to unburden your conscience, you'll get us both punished. They might throw us out, and then we'll be at the mercy of bandits and wild animals."

"Be calm, Muriel. Nothing like that will happen." Although she was not so sure of that herself. "I was thinking of pretending that my voice was coming back gradually."

Muriel crossed her arms and grunted. "If your conscience is bothering you so much, perhaps it is because you disobeyed your king and ran away from your betrothed."

"We were not betrothed." She stared at her friend. Trying to think of a retort, trying to push down the pain that seemed to boil up in her stomach, Evangeline blinked away the tears. "Perhaps my feelings about who I marry do not matter. They certainly do not matter to the king, nor to you, the best and only friend I've ever had. But they matter to me. I am the one who would have to live as Lord Shiveley's wife—not you and not King Richard."

Muriel pursed her lips and looked away. After an ensuing silence, she finally said, "Do what you think is best. That is all any of us can do."

Muriel's words gave Evangeline an uneasy feeling. Muriel was the only person Evangeline had trusted for a long time. As a lonely girl with no parents and no real friends, she and Muriel had been together since Evangeline was seven years old. But ever since they arrived in Glynval, Muriel had been angry with her. It would have been better if she had not come with her. Perhaps if Evangeline had not been so selfish, thinking solely of herself . . .

But was it wrong of her to run away from Richard and Lord Shiveley? It must be wrong. After all, one did not disobey the king of one's country for one's own comfort or pleasure. And yet she could not bear the thought of going back, of obeying the king and marrying Lord Shiveley, especially now that she knew there was a young man in the world named Westley le Wyse.

If it was a sin, she must somehow find atonement. But how? Should she confess to the priest? How else could she be absolved? She would be risking someone hearing her, but it would be worth it to rid herself of this guilt.

Chapter Eleven

Evangeline reported to the kitchen the next morning.
Mistress Alice was there, and she took Evangeline's hands in hers
and examined them.

"I think you are well enough. Those hands will toughen up soon.
Today I need you to help card and spin. Go to the castle and find the
other maidens. Since it's such a nice day, they'll probably be working
outside in the shady place behind the castle."

Evangeline went out and down the long set of steps outside the
door and past the undercroft where she and the other maidservants
slept. The grassy courtyard lay on one side where a shepherd boy
watched over a small flock of grazing sheep.

She had no idea what it meant to "card and spin," but she hoped
at least it wouldn't be dangerous. They should know by now not to
give her any life-endangering tasks.

She found two servants, Cecily and Nicola, sitting on stools in
the shade of a large oak tree. Cecily was holding a long wooden stick
with a wad of white thread or yarn around the top like a fat cattail.
She held the other end of the thread in her other hand and was spinning it around the top end of the stick. That must be spinning.

Nicola was holding a big, wide brush in each hand. She placed a
large ball of something white and fluffy, probably wool, in between
the two brushes, then pulled the wool in opposite directions with the
brushes. That must be carding.

Cecily saw her first. "If it isn't our mute friend, Eva."

Nicola frowned at Cecily.

Evangeline sat by Nicola and picked up the extra brushes, watching how Nicola was doing it. She took a handful of wool out of the large sack between them and placed it in the hard bristles of one of the brushes. With the other brush she pulled at the coarse wad of wool. Copying Nicola, she pulled and worked it between the two brushes. She was not exactly sure what the purpose of this task was, but when Nicola picked the fluffier, finer wool out of her brushes, she put it in another sack that stood between her and Cecily, who was apparently taking it and spinning it into thread. Evangeline had never seen the process before.

She continued the task, but the wooden brush handles soon rubbed against her still-raw blisters. She did her best to pull with her fingers instead of her hands, but it was impossible to keep all contact off her many blisters. She gritted her teeth and tried to ignore the pain.

Sabina walked toward them with a smirk on her face that was becoming familiar. Evangeline ignored her, tearing at the wool with her two brushes, working into a rhythm.

"If it isn't our mute friend, Eva."

Cecily cackled before saying, "That was what I said!"

Evangeline focused her eyes on her task, never looking up as her face heated.

"You know, Cecily, I am very good at spinning."

"Not as good as I am," Cecily retorted. "And my mother says I am the best at weaving."

"Well, I wove my first tapestry when I was five."

"Ha! I don't believe you!"

"You shan't disbelieve this. When Westley awakened after nearly drowning, he looked deep into my eyes. 'I shall always remember what you did for me, saving my life,' he told me. 'You were so coura-geous.' Those were his very words." Sabina smirked, looking as if she truly felt proud of herself for saving Westley's life single-handedly. "If I had not been there, he would have died."

Evangeline's breath came faster. Even if she told Westley now that she was the one to save him, not Sabina, he probably would not believe her, since it would be her word against Sabina's. But what did it matter, as long as Westley was safe.

She heard the rumbling of cart wheels and some far-off men's voices. As the sounds came closer, Evangeline looked up from her monotonous carding.

Reeve Folsham was walking alongside a cart loaded high with large barrels. She'd seen such barrels filled with ale in the buttery below the ground floor of the castle. Two oxen were pulling the loaded cart, and Reeve Folsham was talking with another man.

Ignoring the chatter between Sabina and Cecily, Evangeline watched as the cart and men drew closer, leaving the dirt ruts to veer off the road toward the back of the castle. She kept her eyes down, only glancing up briefly so the reeve would not see her looking at him.

The ox closest to the reeve seemed to step in a hole and stumble. The cart leaned precariously to one side. The rope holding the sec-ond tier of barrels snapped. The top barrels slowly tipped, falling toward Reeve Folsham's head.

Evangeline gasped and leapt from her stool, throwing down her brushes.

She ran at the reeve, who was still talking. He turned his head and met her eye just as she collided with his shoulder, throwing him off balance. He stumbled backward.

One of the barrels hit her in the back of the leg, knocking her down.

The reeve grabbed her under the arms and snatched her out of the way as a second barrel rolled off the first one and hit the ground where she had just fallen.

Four barrels lay on the ground, one of them smashed and leaking ale. The other man had run around the other side of the cart and halted the oxen.

A man ran toward the reeve. "Are you hurt?"

"No, I'm not hurt! Get these barrels back on the cart! Move those oxen! Don't just stand there gaping."

Reeve Folsham rubbed a hand down his face, staring first at the cart and barrels, then at Evangeline.

"Well then, girlie. You have redeemed yourself now, I trow."

She couldn't help smiling, even though her leg ached where the barrel grazed her.

"Not hurt, are you?"

Evangeline shook her head.

The other man called out, and the reeve went to help him load the barrels back on the cart.

She walked with a slight limp back to her stool to resume her work.

"Well done, Eva," Nicola said. "You saved Reeve Folsham from a grievous injury."

"Yes, after injuring him with the scythe, it was the least she could do." Sabina laughed. "Oh, I'm only jesting, Nicola. You don't have to glare at me like that."

Evangeline was back to carding. She peeked at Nicola out of the corner of her eye and smiled. Nicola smiled back.

On Sunday Evangeline made her way to the church with the rest of the servants and villagers. Muriel was not speaking to her, Evangeline had a long bruise on the back of her lower leg, and the blisters on her hands were bloody and oozing again. But as she considered the previous week, she could be thankful that Westley was alive and well and that no one had been seriously injured when the ale barrels fell.

As she trudged up the slight hill, her mind kept going to what the king was thinking of her, what Lord Shiveley was doing at this moment to try to find her, and her lie to Westley and everyone else that she was mute and a poor, abused servant. By the time she reached the church, her shoulders were heavy and she kept her head down and eyes on the floor.

Everyone was reverent and quiet. The priest and the small choir of boys began the plainsong hymn. Some people sang along. Evangeline tried to follow them. She didn't know the words, so she simply listened. The second hymn she recognized as one of the psalms.

On Sundays, Evangeline always tried to meditate on her own sins from the past week, so she stood thinking: *Lying. Deceiving. But, God, I had to do it to escape Lord Shiveley. Hating Sabina. Imagining throwing Sabina in the river. Forgive me, God. Disobeying the king of the land.*

But somehow she did not imagine God holding against her the fact that she did not want to give herself to the Earl of Shiveley.

During the priest's homily, he spoke a message of "love your neighbor." Several minutes into it, he quoted the verse from the Bible, "'There is neither Jew nor Gentile, neither slave nor free, nor is there male and female, for you are all one in Christ Jesus.'"

This was good news to Evangeline, now that she was a lowly servant, at least in the eyes of everyone in Glynval. But then the priest went on to talk about lying and deceiving spirits "who will say anything to get what they want."

I'm sorry. Evangeline squeezed her eyes tightly shut. *Forgive me, God.*

But the more her mind replayed all her sins, particularly the sin of falsehood and deception, the more she wished she could confess them and somehow get atonement.

Westley and his family stood near the front, listening respectfully to the priest. Saving the life of one like Westley le Wyse, someone who was so obviously adored by his family and his demesne's villeins, would that atone for her sins?

Whether it absolves me of anything or not, God, I will be grateful all my life that You put me there so I could save him.

When the service was over, everyone left the church, filing out slowly and quietly. No one seemed to notice Evangeline lingering behind. When they were all gone, she wandered toward the baptismal font. If the priest came near and asked anything, she might just speak to him, confess everything to him. Perhaps he could tell her what she must do to find favor with God again.

The stone font was ringed with blue and gray tiles with different symbols and pictures. But etched between the tiles, on the bare places, were crude crosses and other pictures. Someone had been trying to get a message to God, to gain the answer to a prayer, perhaps.

On the wall she found more symbols, and even the words, *God save us or we perish*. Next to the words was written, *June 1349*. The Great Pestilence. Someone desperate for God's help and intervention had scratched the words, fearing, no doubt, that the entire village of Glynval, the entire world, might be perishing from the strange sickness that killed so many so quickly. Though no one at Berkhamsted Castle had died, even Evangeline had heard of the terrifying time, of how thousands of people had perished in the large town of London, and many hundreds more in various villages all over England.

Whoever had etched that message into the stone, Evangeline could feel their desperation, their great need to seek God's favor and attention, even as she sought it now. "Thank You, God. You heard this person's cry. Thank You for having mercy and not destroying the village of Glynval."

Finding a smooth place on the stone wall, she took out her table knife, which she carried in her pocket, and started carving. In a few moments she had written, *Absolve me.* Beside it she carved three crosses. "Remember me, Lord," she whispered, "the way You remembered the thief on the cross beside You. I don't want to lie anymore." *Love me. Please love me, in spite of my selfishness.* The lump in her throat moved to her eyes, and tears streamed down her cheeks.

"The Lord is close to the brokenhearted and saves those who are crushed in spirit." The verse from her Psalter invaded her thoughts. For a moment she stood transfixed, letting the words sink into her spirit.

She put her knife back in her pocket. "A contrite heart, O God, You will not despise," she whispered another promise from the Psalter and wiped her face with her hands. And somehow she did feel lighter, better . . . absolved.

After their midday meal, Evangeline found Muriel in the sleeping quarters. She was washing her hair in a pottery basin.

Evangeline visually checked every bed. No one else was in the room. "Muriel, please talk to me. I'll help you with your hair and braid it for you."

Muriel squeezed her hair out into the basin and sighed. "Hand me that towel."

Evangeline gave her the cloth lying on her bed. She wrapped it around her head.

"Let us go outside. Follow me."

They made their way out past the meadow, the pigsty, skirting around the trees, and found a small secluded place next to the river. They both sat on a large fallen tree trunk.

"I'm sorry you are not pleased with being here." Evangeline squeezed out the excess water from Muriel's hair using the cloth. Then she proceeded to braid her hair. "I would never hurt you or want you to be sad."

"I know." But Muriel's voice did sound sad. "I never wanted this life for you. I imagined something better for you."

"Marrying Lord Shiveley would not be better." Evangeline made an effort to calm herself and her voice. "Why did you let me leave Berkhamsted Castle if you thought I'd be better off with Lord Shiveley?"

"The only way I could have stopped you would have been to call out to the guards, who would have dragged you by force back into the castle. You would have hated me forever."

"And now you hate me."

"I don't hate you." Muriel said the words softly, but again, her voice was sad. "To be honest, I miss my life at Berkhamsted. I'm angry I'm not there with the king, enjoying his favor."

Evangeline's fingers stilled in Muriel's hair. That made sense. How often did one get to converse with the king of England? For Muriel, it was only when the king came to Berkhamsted, and Muriel liked it. Almost anyone would.

Evangeline continued braiding, then fastened the end of the braid with a small tie and started on the next braid, unsure of what to say to her friend. "I'm sorry, Muriel."

"When the next group from Glynval travels to Berkhamsted, I shall go with them."

"I understand, but do you think you will be safe? Lord Shiveley might harm you to get you to tell him where I am. If it comes to that, I want you to tell them."

"Let us talk no more of it now. Why don't you sing to me one of your pretty songs?"

Evangeline tried to think of something pleasant, something that would cheer them both up. She thought she heard something moving in the trees between them and the village. She stared but did not see or hear anything else. It must have been only a bird or a hare.

Finally, she started singing a song that she had heard from the minstrels who traveled with King Richard the last time he had visited Berkhamsted, a love ballad about a shepherd boy and a goose girl. Her heart gradually grew lighter as she wove small flowers into Muriel's hair and let the music cheer her heart.

Westley took the dipper from the bucket at the well and drank several deep gulps. Then he stood staring down at the bucket. This water was nice and cool to drink, but water had nearly killed him three days ago.

"What are you thinking about?"

He turned to find Sabina just behind him.

"I was thinking how grateful I am that God put you nearby when I fell into the river yesterday."

Sabina smiled up at him. "And how grateful I am that I could save you."

"Did you see me fall in? Is it possible that someone struck me?"

A hesitant look came over her face. Then she drew her brows down in a thoughtful squint. "Now that you say that, and after thinking about it, I believe I did see someone running away when you fell into the river. I think it very likely that person struck you. Truly, you should be careful and not allow yourself to be alone, my lord."

Sabina was one of the few people who called him "my lord." At some point, if something happened to his father, everyone would call him that. Normally he didn't like to be reminded that someday he would take his father's place. But something about the way Sabina said the words, so admiring, made him feel . . . taller.

"Thank you for your concern, Sabina. Perhaps you are right." He remembered what Evangeline had said, how it was strange that he would simply fall in. "What did this person who was running away look like?"

"It may have actually been two men, but definitely one man. I did not see his face, so I cannot say what he looked like. I'm very sorry." She spoke as if slightly breathless. "I would do anything to protect you. I only wish I had seen him."

She was standing quite close to him, peering into his eyes. Truly, she was looking particularly fair today, with her blonde hair dangling in loose curls around her jawline, in addition to the adoring expression on her face. Her lips were slightly parted, and she was staring at his mouth.

Someone had asked him a few days before if he would marry Sabina. "You are the lord's oldest son," his father had said when he complained about the question, "so everyone naturally wonders." And Sabina's father was the miller. He was wealthy compared to the other villagers in Glynval. Sabina was fairly well educated, and she had apparently made no secret of the fact that she hoped to marry him. She was always milling about near his house or the well, where she would often see him.

Should he marry Sabina? It was not the first time he had asked himself that question. He must marry someone, after all. Why not Sabina? She seemed to adore him. What man wouldn't want a wife who adored him?

None of the other Glynval maidens interested him. His father and mother had offered to take him to Lincolnshire where his father had grown up and find him a bride from among his relatives' friends, but he had declined. But now that he was twenty-one, he seemed to be thinking more about who he might marry.

For some reason, this thought pattern brought to mind the new maiden, Eva, with the vibrant red hair and the thoughtful green eyes. Sometimes the way she looked at him . . . It was not the same as Sabina, but it was wistful, sweet. And knowing she had been so mistreated made him want to protect her.

"Westley." Sabina leaned even closer, so close her shoulder was pressed against his arm. "I don't think I could bear it if someone hurt you. When I think about it . . ."—tears welled up in her eyes—"my heart breaks in two."

Westley realized he was leaning away from her. But what if he did allow her to kiss him? What if he put his arms around her and kissed her? He cleared his throat instead.

"Perhaps if we went to the place," Sabina said, also leaning away, "where I saw you fall in, one of us would remember some detail about what happened. Perhaps your memory would return."

"That is a good idea." Westley pushed himself away from the stone wall around the well. He allowed her to hold on to his arm while they walked down the path toward the river.

Sabina chattered on about the upcoming harvest festival that would take place soon, about how much she looked forward to it every year. It was rather pleasant to listen to her cheerful voice.

Suddenly he heard another voice, and this new voice was singing.

"I think I hear something." Sabina turned her head, as if listening. "It's coming from over there."

The closer they got, the more beautiful the voice sounded. So pure and lovely. It made a warm feeling sweep over him. He recognized the song—a ballad about a shepherd boy and a goose girl.

His mother used to sing it to him. And the voice sounded somehow familiar, as if he had heard it before but indistinctly.

Then he remembered—the voice at Berkhamsted Castle, the one he'd been dreaming of hearing again. But how could that be?

Sabina pulled on his arm, urging him forward. They moved through the trees and ferns, then finally came to the tiny glade. Two women sat on the ground—Mildred and Eva. He stared. Mildred's mouth was not moving. It was Eva's voice he was hearing. Eva was singing.

Chapter Twelve

She lied. A sharp pain went through his chest. But why would she pretend to be mute? Had her voice come back all of a sudden? No, she had been making a fool of him.

He walked away, his hands curling into fists. If he confronted her now . . . Heat welled inside him.

"Where are you going?" Sabina came from behind and caught his arm.

"Did you know Eva could speak?" When they were back on the open path near the river, he stared Sabina in the eye.

"I thought she was mute. We all did." Her eyes were wide and she placed her hand over her chest. "Could she have lied to us? Could she have been deceiving us all this time?"

Mildred had said she had been beaten, that her throat had been severely injured.

Westley turned and went back through the trees.

"Where are you going?"

"To confront her."

He made his way back and burst into the small clearing, abruptly bringing an end to the singing.

Mildred and Eva both stared at him with their eyes wide and their mouths open.

Westley stomped toward her. He wanted to demand answers. Had she lied to him? But he read the answer on her face, and it made his heart sick.

~✤~

Evangeline jumped to her feet, her heart dropping. Westley had heard her singing. How could she possibly explain? Her cheeks tingled. She should say something, beg for forgiveness, but somehow she couldn't speak.

"Was it all a lie? Were you not ever mute?"

Evangeline could not allow Muriel to lie for her any longer, and she could not lie to Westley either. "Please forgive me. I never meant to hurt anyone."

"So you were never mute." His face was turning red, his eyes accusatory.

Evangeline shook her head. The look on his face twisted her insides.

"Why did you lie?" A coldness infused his voice.

"I . . . I wanted to get away . . . from someone. It was the only way I could think of to disguise myself."

He just stared, not saying anything.

Sabina was standing just behind him. She took hold of his arm. "Let's go, Westley." Her voice had a distinct note of disgust. "You don't deserve to be lied to."

Sabina tugged on his arm, and he walked away with her.

Evangeline sank down on the ground and put her head in her hands.

"Now do you think it's time to go back to Berkhamsted? Now that you know Westley le Wyse is not going to marry you? Sabina will have dragged him to the church altar to say his vows before you can even speak another word to him." Muriel's arms were crossed over her chest, looking down at her.

"Do you hate me so much?" Evangeline was too miserable to even cry.

"I don't hate you, as I told you before, but I am worried about you." Muriel knelt beside her. "You are a gentle-hearted maiden who has never had to live in the world. I underestimated you, though."

"What do you mean?"

"I thought you would hate the hard work. I thought you would work half a day and beg me to take you back to Berkhamsted. In fact, I did not imagine you would walk so far. But you've worked hard, taken your blisters, and hardly complained." A wistful smile quirked the corners of her mouth. "But you still don't want to leave Glynval, do you?"

Evangeline shook her head.

"What are you planning to do?"

"I don't know."

Seeing Westley walk away from her with Sabina . . . Was there any way Evangeline could get forgiveness from Westley and show him that she was not a bad person? For a long moment Muriel said nothing. Then, "I will help you fight for him, if it's him you want."

"Fight for him?" Evangeline shook her head. "He is not a laurel wreath or a piece of money. He is a human being."

Muriel shrugged. "If you want to let Sabina have him, that is all very well. Just as you choose."

She certainly did not want Sabina to have him. And she certainly did want to marry him herself. But the thought of "fighting for him" did not feel right either. "I don't plan to ever go back to Berkhamsted, Muriel. I'll do anything to keep Richard from finding me and forcing me to marry Shiveley. But to marry Westley, a good and noble person who could choose anyone as his wife . . . Well, if that were to happen, I would believe anything in life was possible, and that God was on His throne, granting miracles to His children."

Muriel sighed. "And if you don't get what you want? Does that mean God is not on His throne and that He is not granting miracles to His children?"

Evangeline sighed. "I suppose that is not very good reasoning, is it?"

"Perhaps it is not for mortal man to reason out such things."

"I'm sure Sabina is praying she will be the one to marry Westley. But hopefully Westley is praying he doesn't marry someone unkind." Evangeline picked the tiny wildflowers on the ground around her. "I don't want to *fight* for him. That sounds low and common. I do want to gain back his favor, though."

"That won't be easy. He was very disappointed to find that we had lied to him."

Her stomach twisted.

"But that is also a good sign, a sign that he has some feelings for you. If he did not care, he would not have been so disappointed."

"I hate to think of him feeling disappointed in me."

She should never have deceived him, even if she did have a good reason.

-ᴕᴖᴖᴖ-

That evening Westley wandered out into the garden behind his family's home.

Would Evangeline come for their Bible reading now that her secret was discovered, now that he knew she had lied and deceived him?

He shouldn't even allow her near his family's Bible. If she came thinking he did not care that she had lied to him, he wasn't sure if he'd be able to control his temper.

He kept glancing behind him at the back of the house. Then he walked along the row of trees at the edge of the garden. He still had a clear view of the house.

He had talked to her like a friend, had helped her and been kind to her, had told her all about the worst time in his life, the Peasants' Uprising, and all along she had been pretending she couldn't speak. He even got the wax tablets just so she could communicate with him, and it had all been fake. She must have been laughing at him, at so easily making a fool of the lord's son. So why was he looking for her, half disappointed not to see her there?

The sun had just sunk behind the trees, spreading its last fingers of light through the sky. Westley trudged back to the house.

"Good evening."

Eva stood in the shadowy area near the back door. Her voice was smooth and feminine and more sophisticated than the village maidens of Glynval—and he hated himself for noticing.

"I wanted to say again that I'm sorry we deceived you about my being able to speak."

At one time he would have praised God at hearing her speak. But now . . .

"I thought you were someone who could be trusted." He tried to look her in the eye, to see if she was ashamed of her sin, but it was too dark to see her expression. "I am not accustomed to being deceived for no good reason."

"Perhaps I did have a good reason."

He snorted. "What reason?"

"I will tell you, but I beg you not to tell anyone else."

He did not answer for a few moments. "Very well. What reason could you possibly have for pretending to be mute?"

"As I told you, I was trying to get away from someone. It was the only way I could think of to disguise myself."

"Why?" The word exploded from him. "If you had told me you were in danger, I would have protected you." He never shouted, and he hadn't planned to shout at her, but the heat inside him forced its way out. "You did not have to make a fool of me, making me think you had been beaten until you lost your voice. I felt sorry for you." His insides twisted and he rubbed a hand across his eyes, unable to even look at her.

His mind flashed back to a few years before, when he was going fishing with John Underhill. A young woman had approached them and asked to go fishing with them.

"My family is hungry," the maiden said, "and needs me to catch some fish, for we have no other food and have not eaten for two days."

John had laughed and told her, "Go away. Westley is too virtuous for you."

"Why did you do that?" Westley asked. "Perhaps she really was hungry."

John laughed again. "You are never suspicious of anyone, and you believe everything anyone tells you."

Westley had inquired about the maiden later and discovered that she had not been going without food. She had admitted to his sister that she simply wanted to get close to him and John because they were the wealthiest young men in the two villages.

Another time a maiden stumbled and landed in his arms. Or at least Westley *thought* she had stumbled. John told him he was naive.

"Foolish," John had said. "To feel compassion for the villeins or servants." More than once he had said, with that contemptuous tone, "Westley, you're too trusting. Do you think every last one of your villeins wouldn't slit your throat to trade places with you? You think they care about you, but they don't."

Westley's face had grown hot as he told his friend, "You are wrong. It is not foolish to feel compassion, and I pity you that you think so cynically."

But that old humiliation that had made his face grow hot at John's words now rose up inside him again. Eva had done what those other maidens had tried to do—made him feel sorry for her by lying to him.

Eva hung her head, staring down at her hands.

"I felt sorry for you, Eva, if that is even your name. But you were lying to me. How can I believe anything you say?"

"I understand why you would be angry. But I had to leave suddenly."

"Why? Why did you make a fool of us?" *Of me?* He shouldn't care. Besides, she could be lying again.

"Someone wanted to marry me, and I did not want to marry him. So I ran away. I had nowhere to go, and we were very grateful you let us come along with you and your men."

Westley remembered the king's guards, along with Lord Shiveley's, seeking someone the day after they left Berkhamsted Castle. They had been searching for two women, one who was tall and had red hair. They must have been looking for Eva and Mildred, but why would the king send his men after two servants?

"Who was this person who wanted to marry you?"

"I . . . I would rather not say."

"Why?"

"It would be safer for me if you did not know." She seemed very uncomfortable, fidgeting with her hands, staring down at her feet, looking anywhere but at him.

"Could he still be searching for you?"

"He could be."

"And why should I not turn you over to him?"

She lifted her head, her eyes wide and her mouth open. Even in the dim light, he could see fear in her face. His stomach twisted. He did not want to trust someone who was lying to him, but neither did he want to be cold and cruel.

~ ✦ ~

Evangeline's breath caught in her throat. Would Westley turn her over to Lord Shiveley? Most men would, without hesitation. Many people believed a woman should have little say in whom she married, and she should feel honored to marry someone like Lord Shiveley. But Evangeline had believed Westley was different.

Perhaps he wasn't different after all.

Or perhaps he was only hurt that she had lied to him. Either way, his words made her heart crash against her breastbone.

"Why would you not want to marry this man?" His tone had softened a bit.

"I have reason to believe . . . he would not be kind to me." She remembered his words, *"You may not care for me, but you will submit to me,"* as well as his promise that she would marry him whether she liked it or not.

"You fear he would beat you, the way you were beaten by your masters?"

"I was not beaten by my masters." Her cheeks burned. She understood why that lie would make him angry. "It was wicked of us to falsely say I was beaten and lost my voice as a consequence. We did not think about the harm our lie would cause. We were not accusing anyone in particular. Still, it was inexcusable, and I am sorry."

"But you are afraid of this man finding you. That is why you told the lie."

"Yes. I do not wish to be found. Please. I am relying on your mercy and kindness should he come looking for me."

He did not say anything for a long moment. Finally, he said, "I shall have to hear what he has to say. Perhaps he has a very different tale to tell. Perhaps you are betrothed or are already married and have run away from your husband."

"No! No, I have no husband." When she had run away from Berkhamsted Castle, she had declared herself free, as free as any free man, belonging only to God. But the king might not see things that way.

"I would not turn over one of my servants—my father's servants—to anyone without a very good reason for doing so."

"Thank you, my lord."

"The lord is my father. You should continue to call me Westley." She nodded.

"It is still difficult for me to trust you after you deceived everyone in Glynval."

Hearing him speak the consequences of her wrongdoing pricked her heart, but she forced herself to say, "Of course. I understand."

They were both silent, standing near each other but not making eye contact in the relative darkness. But it helped calm her breathing, because if he hated her, he would leave and go in the house.

"I have a request to make of you. We will be having our harvest festival in a fortnight, and there is always a singing contest. People come from the surrounding villages to compete, and I would like you to sing for Glynval."

"Oh, I . . . I don't think I should draw attention to myself."

"You shouldn't be in any danger, and I am asking you to sing. I wish it. You have a beautiful voice."

The idea of singing in front of people who had thought she was mute and now knew she was lying was not a pleasant prospect. "Everyone will scorn me because I pretended to be mute."

"They will scorn you—or not—whether you sing or not."

That was no doubt true. She looked into his eyes and her heart skipped a beat. "As you wish. I shall sing . . . for Glynval." *For you.*

"Thank you."

"I also . . . I was wondering if your memory of what happened to you when you fell in the water had come back to you."

"No. Why?"

"Has Sabina told you that there were a couple of men nearby, men who may have pushed you into the water?"

"She said something like that. How did you know?"

"I was there, as you will remember the men saying I stayed with you while Sabina went for help. But what they didn't know is that I was there before you fell in the water. I saw what happened and jumped in to save you."

He narrowed his eyes at her. Of course he wouldn't believe her, but she had to try.

"I saw the men. One of them hit you in the head with a block of wood and then pushed you into the water."

He stood still. "Are you saying Sabina is lying?"

Did she dare tell him the whole truth? She took a deep breath. "Sabina came because I was calling for help."

He crossed his arms in front of his chest.

"I know you probably don't believe me, but it is the truth, and you need to know because they may try to hurt you again." She allowed her determination to infuse her voice. "After the men ran away, I jumped in and raised your head out of the water. I wasn't strong enough to pull you up the bank and was calling for help. That's when Sabina came and helped me drag you out. I am not telling you this for any sort of thanks or reward, but to put you on your guard. Truly, I hope you will take some precautions."

"And who were these two murderous men?"

"I have never seen them before or since."

Another twist of his lips. He did not believe her.

"I shall go now. I only wanted to ask your forgiveness and to warn you about those men so you will be careful."

She turned and hurried away as tears blurred her vision.

Chapter Thirteen

The next day Westley stood by the well talking with Reeve Folsham. Several men had come from the field to get a drink at the well.

Eva and Nicola approached with their buckets. The men respectfully stood back and let them draw water, even helping them haul it up.

Just then a familiar voice called out, "Westley!"

"John." Normally Westley would greet his friend with a jovial clap on the back. But the last time he'd seen John flooded his mind, the tension and accusations.

But today John was smiling. "Good morning, Westley. A pleasant day, is it not?"

"How are you?" Westley took a step toward him, then someone yelled.

"Stop! These are the men!" Eva pointed at John and his servant, Roger Cox.

"What?"

Everyone was staring at Eva as if she had lost her mind.

"These are the two men who tried to kill you!"

John's face paled and he took a step back. Westley's own face grew hot. "You are mistaken, Eva. These men would never—"

"I am not mistaken! I saw this man strike you and push you into the river." She pointed at John again.

"That is enough. Go back to the house." How dare she accuse his best friend of trying to kill him? Would the girl never stop lying?

She stared back at him. Her cheeks were red and she pressed her lips together, her eyes sparking with green fire. She picked up her buckets and glared at John.

"What is this about?" John chuckled nervously.

"She is addled," one of the men said.

"She's been pretending to be mute when she first came here."

"Full of stories."

The men laughed, including John and Roger Cox.

Eva lifted her chin and stalked off, carrying her buckets of water.

Westley stared after her, his stomach churning. Surely she was wrong about John.

Westley and John made small talk. "We are on our way to meet with the men of Ox Creek about . . ."

Westley's mind wandered while John talked. Soon John and Roger took their leave from him and continued on their way down the road. The reeve's eyes narrowed as he stared after John and Roger. Did he suspect Eva was telling the truth?

Westley hated that Eva's words had planted a seed of doubt in his mind. His friend had changed quite a bit in the last two years since the Peasants' Uprising, but surely John would not have tried to kill him. Surely this was just another one of Eva's deceptions.

Either way, he felt sick in his stomach as he made his way back to the house with Reeve Folsham.

⁓

Nicola caught up with Evangeline on their way back to the castle. "You can speak?"

Evangeline cringed. "I'm sorry I pretended to be mute. Westley knows. And now he thinks I'm lying, but, Nicola, I'm not lying. Those men struck Westley in the head and pushed him into the river."

"But, Eva, do you know who those men are?"

"No."

"John Underhill and one of his servants. John owns all the land on the other side of the river and the entire village of Caversdown. He is Westley's best friend."

No wonder Westley had been angry.

After a few moments of silence, Nicola expelled a breath of air. "Why did you do it? Why did you pretend to be mute?"

"I was trying to make sure the man who wanted to marry me would not find me. It actually worked, for they came after me the first day after I escaped, but they thought I was mute."

"I'm glad it worked. And I'm glad you can speak."

"Thank you, Nicola. You have been kinder to me than anyone, and I hope I can repay your kindness someday."

The next morning it was still dark as they walked toward the barn to milk the cows. Evangeline and Nicola entered the barn, found two short stools, and started milking. Or Nicola started milking.

"I'm squeezing but nothing's coming out." Evangeline spoke softly so as not to frighten the cow. She kept a wary eye on the heavy back hoof of the enormous animal.

"You have to squeeze and pull down," Nicola said from the cow beside hers, "but gently, like you're working your hands down the teat."

Evangeline tried again. A tiny squirt of milk hit the bucket below. She closed her eyes and concentrated, resting her cheek against the soft, warm coat of the cow's side, squeezing and running her hands in a downward motion again and again. More milk started to flow until she finally managed a mighty spurt of white liquid with each squeeze-pull. She was much slower than Nicola, but at least she was doing it. And the soft, fleshy teats did not hurt her open blisters the way the carding brush handles did.

Nicola milked two and a half cows before Evangeline's cow ran out of milk.

"I'm sorry I'm making you do more work since I'm so slow."

"You caught on fast, and you'll be as fast as me in a few days."

"You are very generous to say so." Evangeline picked up her full bucket and carried it to the door of the barn.

When Nicola finished the fourth cow, she took up two of the buckets and Evangeline picked up Nicola's other one, and they walked toward the kitchen. Even if she was a lot slower than Nicola, her chest filled with air at the bucket full of milk in her hand.

The sun was just brightening the sky. Halfway to the kitchen, Evangeline saw Sabina coming toward them. Just behind Sabina strode Reeve Folsham and Westley, heading toward the fields.

"Nicola and Eva! Up and working so early this morning," Sabina exclaimed, breaking the hush of the semidarkness.

"What are you doing up so early, Sabina?" Nicola asked her.

Sabina smiled, looking up at the sky. "My father sent me to borrow some eggs."

Just as Sabina reached them, she stuck out her foot and tripped Evangeline.

Evangeline stumbled and cried out, struggling to hang on to the milk and not fall on her face. She landed on her knees on the hard ground. Milk sloshed from the buckets, but she managed to keep them upright.

Reeve Folsham was suddenly at her side, Westley hurrying to her other side. Together they helped her to her feet as she kept hold of the buckets.

"Are you hurt?" Westley asked her.

"No." She hid her grimace of pain as she put her weight on her knee.

"Are you injured?" Sabina pretended to look concerned as she leaned close to Evangeline's face. "That looked like a hard fall."

Evangeline drew herself up and ignored her.

Reeve Folsham stared.

Sabina faced him. "You may have noticed that Eva screamed and spoke. It seems she can talk after all. Isn't that right, Eva? I'm sure everyone will be so pleased that you can talk."

Nicola was giving her a look of sympathy, and Evangeline felt rather than saw the others staring at her. She hurried on toward the house.

She blinked back tears—more of rage at Sabina than of pain in her knee, which was slowly fading.

Sabina was determined to have Westley for herself. Well, let her have him. Westley thought she was the lowest liar now that she had accused his best friend of trying to kill him, and Evangeline was practically betrothed to Lord Shiveley. Westley would probably turn her over to him when he found out Evangeline's true identity.

Once in the kitchen, Golda instructed her to pour one of the buckets of milk into a large pottery bowl on her worktable. Evangeline struggled to lift the bucket high enough. She bit her lip and concentrated on not spilling it. Finally, she had emptied every drop into the bowl.

"There is less than usual in these buckets," Golda said. "Did you spill it?"

"I spilled a little."

The head cook looked startled at hearing Evangeline speak.

"She fell," Nicola supplied behind her. "But it was because Sabina tripped her. Eva saved most of the milk."

Golda stared at them both for a few seconds. "Very well. Take the rest of the milk to the dairy and start churning."

Evangeline followed Nicola with the remaining buckets to a small stone building at the edge of the woods behind the castle and to the east of the kitchen. There were no windows and one lit torch to light their way down some stone steps.

"Have you ever churned butter?"

"No."

"It isn't difficult." Nicola set down her buckets in a corner of the room, which was quite cool belowground. The dungeon at Berkhamsted Castle must feel about the same.

Evangeline set her bucket beside it, then watched as Nicola picked up another bucket sitting on the opposite side of the room.

"We don't use the fresh milk. We use the milk from the previous milking, which was last night."

"Why?"

"I don't exactly know. Maybe to give the butter a slightly sour flavor." Nicola approached a large square barrel that lay on its side and had a hole in the top. "So you pour the milk into here." She poured in the milk—a bucket and a half—and closed up the hole. Then she poured the other bucket and a half in a second churn—an upright one on the floor—and Evangeline sat and used the wooden paddle to agitate the creamy milk inside while Nicola turned a handle on the side of the barrel-like churn. They occasionally switched places, as their arms grew tired of the repetitive motion.

Evangeline had to wrap her hands in some discarded cheesecloths to keep the wooden handles from chafing her blistered hands as badly.

"Don't your hands hurt?" Nicola asked when she saw the bloody mess on the palms of Evangeline's hands.

"Not as much anymore."

"You should be careful they don't become septic. You should ask for some of Lady le Wyse's salve she uses on wounds."

"I'm sure it's fine." Evangeline had something else on her mind—the fact that Westley, or someone else, could turn her over to Lord Shiveley's or King Richard's men. And if that happened and Evangeline did find herself in that man's power, she wanted to be able to defend herself against him.

"Nicola?"

"Yes?" Nicola calmly rotated the handle on the butter churn. She was quite pretty, with her pale-blue eyes and blonde hair pulled back in a single braid.

"How would I go about learning archery and sword fighting and knife throwing? Is there someone who might teach me?"

Nicola smiled. "Why would you want to learn those things? I don't know any women who know how to sword fight."

"Is it strange that I want to learn those things?"

"I suppose not. But why do you want to?"

Evangeline took a deep breath. "I might need to protect myself."

"Glynval is a safe place, mostly. I have never had to defend myself from anyone trying to harm me. Although I did see what Sabina did to you, tripping you in the yard."

"Sabina does not like me very much."

"Sabina doesn't like anyone she thinks might catch Westley le Wyse's attention."

Evangeline smiled ruefully at the accuracy of Nicola's statement, then they both laughed. She was immediately struck with the thought that she had not laughed enough in her life, and to laugh with a friend was quite lovely.

"A lot of people think Westley will marry her, but I hope he will not be that stupid. She isn't the kindest person. But you've already seen that."

"Unfortunately."

"Did someone hurt you? Is that why you want to learn how to fight?"

"No. But there is someone . . . someone I might have to defend myself against someday."

"Reeve Folsham knows knife throwing and archery. He regularly teaches some of the servants, as well as his daughters. His daughters, I am told, can defeat any man who might be foolish enough to try to harm them. As for sword fighting, Westley is the best at that."

Evangeline would have to stay alert to opportunities to learn some fighting skills.

⁂

Looking for the reeve, Evangeline stood outside the dairy and searched the men coming back from the fields that afternoon. But after several minutes she still did not see him. She also kept a wary eye out for Sabina.

It was Evangeline's turn to help serve dinner to the other servants. She was late, so she ran across the courtyard toward the kitchen behind the castle. When she reached the kitchen door, someone called, "Eva! Wait."

Sabina hurried toward her. She carried something inside her apron as she held the hem up to her chest. Behind Sabina, Evangeline spotted Reeve Folsham.

"Golda asked me to pick these mushrooms for the pottage tonight," Sabina said to Evangeline. "She will be so angry with me if I don't get them into the pot immediately. Please, won't you take them in for me? I have to go home and help my little sister. Please? I'm sorry for making you fall this morning."

Evangeline stared. Part of her wanted to turn away from Sabina without a word and ignore her request. But she also wanted to show she was not as heartless as Sabina—and if she didn't hurry, she'd miss getting to speak to the reeve before he left. So she held out her own apron and let Sabina dump the mushrooms inside.

"Thank you, Eva!" Sabina ran back the way she had come.

"Reeve Folsham," she called as he was walking past. "May I speak to you a moment?"

The large man walked toward her.

"I wonder if you might be willing to teach me how to throw a knife or how to shoot a bow and arrow."

He looked at her askance. "Can you be trusted with knives?"

Her face burned as she realized what he was thinking of. "I-I only thought . . . if you were teaching a group of-of men, you might let me watch."

"It is good for girl children, especially ones as fair as you, to learn how to defend themselves." His expression was sober. "The next time Mistress Alice gives you some time away from work, come and find me and I'll teach you."

"Oh, thank you, Reeve Folsham. Thank you."

He nodded and walked on. He did not eat with the other servants but went to his own home for his evening meals.

Evangeline's shoulders felt lighter, and she couldn't help smiling.

She looked down at the mushrooms in her apron and remembered what Sabina had asked her to do. Perhaps she was not such a bad person, and Evangeline might win Sabina's good opinion the way she had won Reeve Folsham's. Sabina had even said she was sorry for tripping her. Perhaps she was sincere.

Evangeline strode over to the large pot bubbling over the cook fire and dumped the contents of her apron inside. Golda's back was turned as she inspected the bread that was being drawn out of the oven. When she saw Evangeline, she said, "Go take those trenchers to the table."

Evangeline placed the slabs of stale bread at regular intervals on the trestle table. Then she filled all the goblets with ale. Next she helped slice the fresh bread and put it on a wooden serving platter, then took it in and set it in the middle of the table. The other servants were starting to come in and sit down.

"Eva, can you help spoon up the pottage into the bowls?" Golda pointed to the stack of wooden bowls in the corner.

Evangeline grabbed the stack of bowls while someone else spooned the pottage into them. She took two bowls at a time to set beside the trencher at each place. Meanwhile, another servant dished a portion of roast pork and gravy onto their trenchers.

The workers began arriving, sat down, and started to eat. Suddenly one of the men spit something forcibly from his mouth.

"What is it, Robert?" the servant beside him asked.

"Poison! Poison mushrooms in this pottage."

Several people cried out or stood up. Several others spit their food back into their bowls or into their hands.

"Who did this?" a large man with beefy arms demanded. "Who would put poison mushrooms into the pottage?"

Chapter Fourteen

Chaos swelled as everyone spoke at once. Then a voice rose above the others.

"Someone wants to kill us."

"It was the new maiden," a woman said. "The one who pretended she couldn't talk. I saw her put the mushrooms in the pottage when she thought no one was looking."

"No, I didn't know." Evangeline's knees trembled and her face started to tingle.

Angry eyes turned on her.

"I saw you," the maidservant Cecily said. "I saw you put them in the pottage."

Voices rose so loud Evangeline could not hope to be heard.

"Who is she? Why is she trying to kill us?"

"She's the one who claimed to be mute! She's a liar. No one even knows where she came from."

"She wants to kill us all."

"Take her out and flog her!"

Hands grabbed her by the arms and shoulders. They began pushing and pulling her toward the door.

"No! Stop!" She struggled against them, trying to pull her arms free, but they only squeezed her harder. Her heart pounded and her vision began to spin. Would she faint? What would they do to her?

Muriel was arguing with them as they dragged Evangeline through the doorway and into the waning light of late afternoon. But they were not listening. Muriel's voice was lost in the shouting.

They pulled her toward the courtyard. Evangeline's feet dragged over the ground, and she lost her shoes.

"I'm going to tell them!" Muriel leaned into Evangeline's face so she could hear her. "I will tell them who you are!"

"No! Don't! Please!"

"If I don't tell them, they will fasten you to the pillory and beat you."

Evangeline's stomach roiled at the thought of being beaten and at the sight of the pillory looming ahead. She could never fight them off.

Both men and women hurled accusations at her. Some large men, their faces red and contorted, shouted, "Devil's servant! Poisoning us with Satan's cap mushrooms! Take her to the pillory!"

God, help me! Please have mercy on me.

The man holding her left arm wrenched it nearly out of its socket as he jerked her up the pillory steps and onto the stage at the corner of the courtyard.

"Halt, I said!" A man's voice rose above all the others.

Everyone quieted as they looked behind them.

Lord le Wyse strode toward them. Westley was beside him.

Evangeline stood on the wooden stage with the man still holding on to her arm. On her other side was the wooden board that was used to clamp a person's neck and wrists and hold them long enough to serve their sentence of public humiliation, and sometimes a beating.

"What is the meaning of this?" Lord le Wyse's voice was a steely scale, weighing the men surrounding Evangeline. "Do you dare seize one of my servants? A woman under my protection?"

"My lord, she tried to kill all of us with poisonous mushrooms in our pottage."

Westley's face was like a mask in the fading light of late day, hiding his thoughts as he stood beside his father.

"Let her speak for herself, if she can speak." Lord le Wyse glared with his one good eye, holding his shriveled hand against his middle.

"I can speak." The breath returned to her lungs.

"What is your name?"

"Eva, my lord."

"Can you defend yourself against these accusations?"

"Sabina gave me the mushrooms. She said Mistress Golda told her to bring mushrooms for the pottage, and she begged me to put the mushrooms in the pot for her."

"Did you know they were poisonous?"

"No, my lord."

"Fetch Sabina."

A few men ran off in different directions. While everyone waited for Sabina's retrieval, Muriel stomped up the three steps to the pillory platform and shoved the men who were still holding Evangeline's arms.

"Get off her, you fiends!" She slapped at their arms until they loosened their painful grips on her arms and let go.

The people talked low among themselves, sending furtive glances Evangeline's way. She tried to ignore them. She tried to keep her eyes focused above the tops of the crowd's heads, but her gaze kept flitting to Westley. Did he think she was lying again, that she had deliberately tried to kill the other servants with poison mushrooms?

Reeve Folsham arrived and pulled Westley aside and spoke with him at the back of the crowd. Then Sabina arrived, walking between two men, her eyes wide and her lips closed. The men prodded her forward, toward the pillory.

"Sabina." Lord le Wyse's voice boomed, silencing the already quiet crowd. "Did you give Eva the mushrooms she put into the pottage?"

"Me? No, of course not! Is that what she said?" Sabina turned wide eyes toward Eva.

"I saw her."

Every head turned toward the back of the crowd.

Reeve Folsham strode through the crowd toward them. "I saw Sabina give Eva the mushrooms and heard her tell her to put them in the pottage."

Several people gasped.

"Sabina," Lord le Wyse said, "shall I ask you again?"

"I-I didn't know, my lord. I was trying to hurry and do as Mistress Golda bid me and gather the mushrooms, and I didn't realize they were the poisonous ones." Sabina sobbed. "You must believe me. I would never hurt anyone."

"What kind of mushrooms were they? Does anyone know?"

A woman's voice rose above the others. "They were fool's toadstools."

Someone else said, "Fool's toadstools are not deadly. They will only make you sick for a few hours."

Another person added, "They look very much like the harmless moon's caps."

"It was just a mistake," someone else called out.

Reeve Folsham reached the platform. He mounted the steps and stood beside Evangeline. "You all falsely accused this young woman. Now, Eva"—he turned toward her—"what must they do to gain your forgiveness?"

Eva rubbed her arm where she could feel a bruise, then stopped when she realized what she was doing. Everyone was staring at her while Sabina continued to sob nearby.

Eva drew herself up, straightening her shoulders. "Nothing. I forgive them."

"They will at least ask your forgiveness, every man who laid a finger on you." He glared at the men standing on the platform with her who had dragged her forcibly from the castle and across the courtyard.

The men looked sheepish, barely lifting their gazes from the ground. "Will you forgive me?" one man said, then the others followed suit, mumbling, "Forgive me."

"I forgive you," Evangeline answered.

Sabina cried more quietly now as everyone seemed to have forgotten her.

The crowd trickled away. Muriel took Evangeline by the elbow to help her down the steps of the platform. As soon as she took a step, she cringed at the pain in her ankle and limped down the steps.

"You are hurt." Westley was by her side when she reached the bottom.

Evangeline shook her head. "No." She kept her voice strong and steady and her head down as a tear dripped from her eye. She quickly willed away any more tears.

Muriel led her toward the manor house undercroft.

"You have not had your dinner," Westley said, still following alongside them. "Come to the house. Let my mother see to you. I think you are hurt."

"I am well. I can walk." Defiance rang out in her voice . . . in her heart. He had not believed her, had at least half believed the accusations that she had tried to poison them. It was on his face. Why could he not simply leave her alone and let her go to her bed and cry her tears in peace?

She limped toward the manor house undercroft, clinging to Muriel's arm.

Westley's heart sank as Eva turned away from him. But he could not let her limp away without finding out how badly she had been hurt by that mob of angry servants bent on punishing her.

"Please." Westley jumped in front of her to block her way. "I insist you allow me to take you to my mother."

Eva and Mildred stopped. Eva lifted her head but refused to look him in the eye.

"Perhaps you should," Mildred said to her. "Let Lady le Wyse make sure you have no broken bones from those evil brutes."

Eva nodded, still not speaking.

They walked toward the castle. Eva continued to cling to Mildred and look straight ahead as he led them into the house and down the corridor.

His mother stepped out of the Great Hall where they had all been dining when they heard the commotion.

"Lord le Wyse told me what happened. Oh, you poor thing." His mother, ever eager to nurse someone's wounds, reached her hands out to Eva. "I shall take good care of you. And, Mildred, you can come too." She put her arm around Eva's shoulder and led her away.

Westley followed them, in spite of not being invited.

Mother and the other two women went into Mother's sick room, where she sometimes treated the servants and other villagers. Mother's care was an option for those who could not be helped by the village barber, who would bleed the sick person or sew up the injured, or Joan the herbal healer, who prescribed plants and dried herbs for just about everything that could ail a person or animal.

Mother would be able to help her. But he had a sick feeling in the pit of his stomach that he could not have saved her the anguish of being wrongfully attacked by a mob—a horrendous thing to happen to a gentle maiden. And he felt even worse that initially he had not believed in her innocence. Thanks be to God for Reeve Folsham, who had been a witness and could vouch for the truth of Eva's words.

What else might she have been telling the truth about?

Chapter Fifteen

Evangeline followed Lady le Wyse into a room with bandages and vials and small lidded pots on shelves on the walls.

"Mildred," Evangeline said quietly, "I don't want you to miss your dinner. Why don't you go?"

Muriel hesitated.

"I will take good care of her." Lady le Wyse smiled.

"Very well." Muriel turned to leave.

Evangeline lifted her head to watch her go—and noticed Westley standing just inside the door. She jerked her gaze back to Lady le Wyse, who motioned for her to sit on a chair padded with cushions.

"Where do you hurt, my dear? The leg? Or ankle? I saw you limping."

"My ankle, but it is not badly injured."

Westley came closer as Lady le Wyse lifted Evangeline's foot and examined her ankle. She pressed her fingers all around. "Does this hurt?"

"Not very much. I'm sure it will be better in a few days."

"Nevertheless, I want you to rest it for at least tomorrow. What else did they do to you?"

"Nothing. I am not hurt." Evangeline had managed to hold back the tears that had started to fall earlier, but Lady le Wyse's kind attention and sympathetic looks were beginning to undo her efforts. She blinked several times to drive away the moisture flooding her eyes.

"I am so sorry, Eva. It isn't like Glynval's people to become so angry and violent. Let me see your arms."

Evangeline wore her work dress with the floppy sleeves that hung to just below her elbows. She pushed up one, and Lady le Wyse covered her mouth and shook her head.

"You poor dear." She pushed up her other sleeve and found more of the same little round fingerprints of purple and dark blue.

Westley leaned closer to see.

Evangeline suppressed the urge to slap his face and order him to get away from her. How dare he let those men grab her and drag her and threaten to beat her? Tears suddenly overflowed her eyes and ran down her face.

"Westley, fetch some cold water in a basin and some water in a cup for Eva."

More tears slipped down her cheeks, and she hoped Westley had not seen them as he hurried out.

Lady le Wyse dabbed Evangeline's cheeks with a cloth. "My dear, are you in pain somewhere you haven't told me about?"

She shook her head.

"Only in your heart?"

Evangeline shrugged and nodded. Lady le Wyse let her take the cloth and wipe her eyes and nose. She had to control herself before Westley returned.

"I will not let anyone hurt you again," Lady le Wyse said stoutly. "And from now on you will work only here in the house with me, where I can keep a close eye on you."

"I do not want you to go to any trouble for me, my lady. I am—"

"It is no trouble. I am outraged on your behalf, and I want to make up to you the feeling of safety you have lost over this."

She said the words so gently, warmth spread through Evangeline's middle. Was this what it was like to have a mother?

To have someone care what happened to you and concern herself about your feelings?

The warmth inside was replaced by an ache, a hollowness that hurt. Her mother had died in childbirth. Westley had a kind mother who loved him, but Evangeline would never know what that was like.

"Here is your water." Westley entered the room, balancing a basin in one hand and holding a cup in the other. He handed the cup to Evangeline.

The hands that reached for the cup shook. She bit her lip at not being able to hide the weakness. Evangeline sipped the cold water and closed her eyes, again willing the tears away, trying to push down the memory of the pitying looks on Westley's and his mother's faces.

"I will wrap this ankle and make it snug so you won't twist it or turn it walking back to the undercroft. And tomorrow, if you feel like walking, you can come back here and let me make sure it isn't too swollen. Westley told me you enjoy reading our Latin Bible." A smile graced Lady le Wyse's lips. She was indeed a beautiful woman, even at her age. Westley resembled her quite a bit, but his hair was darker, and he had his father's chin and jawline.

"Yes, I do. I did not have a Bible at . . . where I lived before."

"We are pleased to let you read it"—she continued to wrap Evangeline's ankle—"especially tomorrow since I do not wish for you to work."

"I thank you, Lady le Wyse."

Evangeline gave her back the cup, and Lady le Wyse stared as if something had caught her eye. Then she grabbed Evangeline's hand, twisted it palm up, and gasped. She grabbed her other hand and did the same. "Eva! What happened to your hands?"

"Only blisters." Evangeline's cheeks burned, and she wished she could hide as Westley bent and stared down at her hands as well.

"Those look worse than ever," he said.

"Get me my healing salve," Lady le Wyse said, still studying her hands with a troubled downturn of her brows. "And some bandages. My dear, I'm so sorry."

"It is only because my hands were too soft. I should have kept my hands wrapped after . . . after Westley put some salve on them two days ago. They will toughen up soon and be like the other servants' hands."

Lady le Wyse made a clicking sound with her tongue against her teeth. "You should have told someone. Westley should have told me. You don't have to suffer wounds like this untreated. It is dangerous, besides. Open sores like these could become septic."

Her hands were quite bloody and raw. "I am sorry. Forgive me."

"Child, it is not your fault. There is nothing to forgive." She took the pot of salve from Westley and smeared it on Evangeline's palms.

"Mother!" Cate's voice called from another part of the castle. "Mother, we need you! The little ones won't stay in bed."

Lady le Wyse wiped her hands on a cloth. "I'd better go see what is amiss with my children." She smiled apologetically. "Westley, you can finish this task. You know what to do. He is very gentle." She patted her son's cheek and then hurried out.

Westley looked hesitant as he stood over her with the little salve pot in one hand and a roll of bandages in the other. Then he sat in front of her on the stool his mother had vacated.

"I'm very sorry about tonight. This should not have happened."

Would he say it was just a misunderstanding, as the other servants had done? Did he believe Sabina was sincere in her tears and protestations of innocence, that she had not known the mushrooms were poisonous?

He looked into her eyes. "I don't want to think what might have happened to you."

"Yes, I am grateful your father and Reeve Folsham came to my aid. Those people would have fastened me in the pillory, at the very least." There was that tone of defiance in her voice again. She wasn't even sure why she was so angry at Westley. But she was. "I cannot blame them. They thought I was trying to poison them with Satan's cap mushrooms."

He was quiet as he took her hand in his, his skin warm and tingly. But she clenched her teeth, refusing to find his touch pleasant.

He smeared the thick yellow salve on her open blisters, his face tense as he concentrated on the task. The open wounds reacted to the cold salve with a slightly painful sensation that sent chills across her shoulders and down her back. But his hand was gentle and warm.

When he finished, he closed the jar, wiped his hand, and took up the bandage roll. He wrapped it around her hand.

"Can you make it tighter? I'm afraid it might fall off."

He glanced into her eyes. Then he undid the bandage and started over. "I was trying not to cause more pain."

"It does not hurt." *At least, not as much as you believing I would lie about your friend trying to kill you, or that I would try to poison people.*

"I am sorry I did not check your hands again."

"As I said before, it was my fault. I should have wrapped them. I can wrap my own hands, after all."

"Well, I should have checked since I knew you had blisters."

"It is not your place, as the lord's son, to check the servants' blistered hands."

"I am only trying to be kind." He tied the bandage snugly, then grabbed her other hand.

"Oh, you are very kind, my lord." Evangeline bit the inside of her mouth at the sarcasm in her voice. *Stop, Evangeline. Just stop.*

He glanced at her face, then down again as he wrapped the second hand. "Is this not too loose? Too tight?"

"It is perfect, my lord." Again she bit the inside of her cheek. She should not have baited him with the unwelcome address of "my lord."

The moment he tied the bandage in place, she rose from the chair. But he held on to her hand, his fingers wrapping firmly around her wrist.

"I am sorry about what happened to you, Eva. It was wrong, and I am ashamed of my people for their violence and rush to judge."

"You do not have to apologize for what they did. Their consciences are not your responsibility. Besides," she said pertly, "I have already forgiven them." She tugged her arm, trying to pull away from his hold.

"Then why will you not forgive me?" He kept hold of her wrist, drawing closer to her.

"Forgive you for what?" Her tone was still hard, but the breathiness betrayed the way he affected her when he was this near and she was staring into his blue eyes.

"For not believing immediately that you would never try to poison anyone. For not running up to that pillory and knocking those men to the ground and snatching you away from them."

"And for not believing me when I said your friend tried to kill you?"

He hesitated, then said, "I was still upset that you had deceived us by pretending to be mute. And it is hard for me to accept such a terrible thing about my childhood friend."

"Yes, I imagine it is." She should not be staring at his lips. But they were just so perfect, so appealing.

But he did not care about her. And Sabina would do anything, obviously, to make sure he married her and no one else.

If he wanted someone as despicable as Sabina, then he was not worth desiring. Or mourning over. Even if he did make heart-swelling apologies and have a deep, gentle voice and an even gentler touch.

She spun around on her heel, forcing him to let go of her hand. "I forgive you. And I thank you for the bandages." Over her shoulder she added, "Please tell your mother thank you."

She limped to the door.

"I will walk you to the undercroft." He caught up with her in two long strides. "Wait. You have not had your dinner."

"It is all right."

"No, no, we will go to the servants' dining room. They should still be there."

"I would rather not go in there."

Understanding dawned on his face. "I will go get you some food. We can go together, to the kitchen."

She sighed, deciding not to protest, and followed him out.

It was dark already as they walked across the yard to the kitchen. She waited outside while he went in. A few minutes later he came out with a large bundle.

"You must think I'm very hungry."

"In case you get hungry again during the night."

They continued on to the undercroft. At the door she took the warm bundle from his hand. "Thank you."

Perhaps it was wrong for her to be angry with him for not trusting in her. After all, she was still hiding some rather big secrets. If only she could tell him who she was. But she could not risk it.

"Be careful of that ankle."

"I will see you tomorrow, perhaps."

"You will." He gave her that smile again. She did not like the way it made her breathless, and she especially hated that Sabina was so in love with this man that she would try to get Evangeline beaten or even killed just to make sure Westley would not look favorably upon her. Surely no man was that exceptional.

Evangeline got out of bed before the break of day and hobbled toward the cow barn. She found Nicola already milking one of the cows.

"I thought you were resting today," Nicola said.

Evangeline took her place under a cow. "I am well enough to help you milk the cows. I did not want you to have to do all the work by yourself."

Nicola gave her a concerned look over her shoulder. "I heard what happened yesterday. Are you sure you are all right?"

"Yes, I only sprained my ankle." Evangeline shuddered a little as she remembered her terror and the people's determination to do her harm.

"Why did they think you were trying to poison everyone? Did you put poison mushrooms in the pottage?"

"It was Sabina." Evangeline told Nicola everything that happened.

"Sabina." Nicola was silent for a few moments before continuing. "She would do anything to make you look bad to Westley. I'm so sorry, Evangeline."

"Don't worry. She cannot fool me again."

"I suppose she cried to get out of being punished."

"How did you guess? She said she didn't know they were poisonous and sobbed until everyone seemed to feel sorry for her. Why is it that you and I are the only ones who know she was lying?"

"She doesn't show her true self to most people. She's sneaky. But you and I have seen it." Nicola stood and moved her full bucket near the door, then grabbed an empty one and moved her stool to the next cow. "The other servant girls are afraid of her, so they try to please her and do whatever she wants."

"But you don't do that."

"No. And she hates me for it. And she hates you because you're pretty and Westley has noticed you. Most men aren't very wise when it comes to women."

Evangeline knew little about such things, having never been around anyone except the Berkhamsted Castle servants, and they did not share intimate details with her about their love affairs. She had always believed love was what she sang about in the minstrels' ballads. But life seemed much different from anything in those love ballads.

"Why are men not wise about women? I mean, why would Westley not see that Sabina is not very kind?"

Nicola lifted her head off the cow's side.

"She behaves much differently around him. Besides that, men become addled by their own lusts. A man's judgment becomes clouded by a pretty face."

Muriel had told her something similar before.

"Women think with their hearts, and their judgment is clouded by compliments. A man tells her a few flattering words and she will do anything he wants and will fancy herself in love. That's what happened to my sister."

Surprised that Nicola was talking so much, Evangeline waited for her to go on.

"One of the blacksmith's sons, Hugh, lured her into the woods, telling her she was pretty. She never thought she was pretty, and I suppose she wanted to believe that he loved her. He got her with child and then ran off to join a band of outlaws. Then he got himself hanged for attacking travelers and robbing them. She cried for weeks and weeks, even though she knew he was a knave."

"That is very sad."

"But I must say that Westley seems a much more noble young

man than most others I've known. I hope he is too wise, ultimately, to marry Sabina."

"I saw him rescue a little girl from a runaway horse once. And he was very kind to me when he thought I was mute. The other men only looked askance at me. At that time I had no idea he was the son of a wealthy lord." And he had walked her back to the undercroft last night, taken care of her blistered hands twice now, and . . . She should not think about him anymore.

Evangeline finished milking her first cow and then moved on to another one before Nicola finished her second.

"You're getting faster." Nicola flashed her a smile.

After finishing the milking, Evangeline walked with Nicola to the servants' dining hall to break their fast. Her heart thumped nervously. She was about to encounter the same people who had wanted to commit violence against her only the night before.

Chapter Sixteen

Westley came around the side of the kitchen, just catching sight of Nicola and Eva as they walked—Eva was barely limping at all now—through the door to the servants' dining hall. He followed at a distance, slipping in with some other men. He stood in the corner, watching.

The atmosphere was subdued. A man brushed against Eva's arm. When he turned to see who was there, he stepped back. "Excuse me." He politely nodded to her.

Eva nodded back and moved away.

People gave her furtive glances, humble looks on their faces for the most part. Sabina was not there, of course. He didn't know what she had been doing picking mushrooms for the cook. She was always nearby, it seemed, instead of at her home at the mill on the edge of the village.

The other servants were starting to notice him standing there watching them. Eva seemed safe, as she stayed next to one of the other maidservants, but he wanted to make sure.

He waved Robert over. "All is well, but I wonder if you would keep watch over Eva."

"Of course. Piers, Aldred, and I will make sure no harm comes to her."

"Thank you, Robert." Westley slipped outside.

Westley hurried toward the back of the castle. After helping his father all morning in the planning of a new dining hall for the servants, he hoped he might sit with Eva for a bit while she was reading, but he did not see her in her usual reading alcove. Had she decided not to cease working today, even though his mother had told her to rest all day?

Just as he was about to go in through the back door, he spied her with Reeve Folsham at the other end of the garden, in the open space between the meadow and the fruit trees. They were facing the back of the oat barn, and the reeve seemed to be offering some sort of instruction.

Westley walked toward them. Eva lifted a longbow, drew back the string, and let the arrow fly toward the barn wall. It stuck fast in the wood.

"Very well done," Reeve Folsham said. "Now try again, only this time, let your cheek rest against your hand, hold only as long as you need to get your sights perfect, and then release."

The reeve and Eva turned to see him.

"Good morning to you, Westley."

"Good morning, Reeve Folsham. Eva."

She nodded, then drew back the bowstring, her face as taut as the string as she focused on the bull's-eye drawn in charcoal on the barn wall. She let loose the bowstring, and the arrow shot fast and straight, striking the middle of the target.

"You have a talent for archery, you do." The reeve looked as cheerful as Westley had ever seen him—strange, since his first interaction with Eva was when she cut a line across his side.

"How long have you been shooting?" Westley asked.

"For a couple of hours," Eva said with a smile.

"When did you learn?"

"Yesterday."

Westley nodded, pretending not to be surprised. Though she wasn't very good at servant tasks like feeding pigs, cutting wheat, and knowing which mushrooms were poisonous, she was apparently very good at archery.

"It's as if she was born to shoot an arrow," Reeve Folsham said. "Now, Eva, come over here and I will show you how to strengthen your arms. That is all you need to be a good longbowman, indeed."

They walked over to the barn, and the reeve put his hands on the wooden wall, stepped back a couple of feet, and pushed himself off the wall. "Put all your weight on your arms, and do this over and over every day. It builds the muscles in your arms that you need to shoot long distances."

Eva imitated his exercise.

"And when you get good at that, you can do it on the ground, like this." The reeve got down on his stomach, holding himself up on his hands and toes, and demonstrated lowering himself, then pushing himself up again.

"Ah yes, that should strengthen my arms very well," Eva said cheerfully. "Will you teach me knife throwing and sword fighting now?"

The reeve smiled—or at least one side of his mouth went up. "I have work I should attend to now, but I shall return later. Perhaps Westley can teach you sword fighting."

"Thank you so much for teaching me archery." She smiled so big at the reeve that Westley felt a pang in his chest, wishing he could have been the recipient of that smile, which brought out the dimple in each of her cheeks.

The reeve strode away, leaving them alone.

"You have never been a servant, have you, Eva?"

Her lips parted and she looked away, facing the orchard and fiddling with her bowstring. "Whatever makes you say that?"

"You have a way about you. It's different from the other maidens in Glynval."

"Are you saying I am special?" She gave him a coy half smile.

A warning went through his gut, like a tiny bolt of lightning. "The main reason is that you don't know how to do anything."

"That is an insulting thing to say." She drew her brows together, but the look of outrage never reached her expressive mouth.

"You don't know how to cut wheat or make bread or spin wool into thread. You haven't built up the strength in your arms to carry a full bucket of water, and your hands turned to blisters in one day. But you do know how to read Latin, something no servant I know is capable of. Who are you, Eva? Where do you come from?"

Her face had become pale by the end of his list.

"You can either tell me the truth or tell me some outrageous tale like the one about your master and mistress beating you until you were mute. But I will not be likely to believe any more lies." He would not be easily fooled, as John Underhill had taunted him.

Her jawline hardened as if she was clenching her teeth. "I told you the truth. I told you I ran away because a man wanted to marry me, and I did not wish to marry him."

Again he remembered the Earl of Shiveley's men, along with the king's men, looking for two women, one of whom had red hair.

"Was this man who wanted to marry you Lord Shiveley?"

She looked away. But surely Lord Shiveley would not marry anyone who wasn't of royal blood, or at least aristocratic. Perhaps it was the captain of Shiveley's guard or someone of his household staff who wanted to marry Eva.

Suddenly Eva grabbed Westley's arm and pulled him down. "What is it?" He squatted beside her and followed her line of vision.

John Underhill was walking across the small area between the back of the main house and the garden, heading around the side.

"There he is again—the blond one who struck you and tried to kill you!"

He and Eva squatted behind a bush as John wandered around the gardens.

"Are you sure you are not mistaken?"

She still gripped her bow. "That man is not your friend."

"But why would John try to kill me?" His stomach was sinking.

"You exchanged angry words with him, then he struck you and pushed you into the river. It is he. I saw him."

Her gaze bored into his. Could she know how hurtful it was to think of John doing such a thing?

John started walking in their direction and waved, as he must have seen the tops of their heads.

Eva stepped back, retrieved an arrow off the ground, and nocked it to her bowstring. She raised the weapon and aimed it at John.

Chapter Seventeen

Evangeline pointed her bow and arrow at Westley's friend John, the same man who had tried to kill him.

"Don't come any closer!" Evangeline had faced a throng of angry men and women, so she could surely take on just one—or two—if Westley still did not believe her. Her heart beat fast, sending the blood racing through her body.

Now she had a weapon, and she knew how to use it. She almost smiled.

The man stopped and held up his hands.

"Eva," Westley said, a growl in his voice, "what are you doing? Put that bow and arrow down."

"This man tried to kill you."

John Underhill scrunched his face at Evangeline. "What are you talking about?"

"You know very well what I'm talking about. You did not see me when you passed by on your way to attack Westley with that block of wood in your hand or you might have tried to kill me too."

"You're insane!" John barked out a laugh, but there was no humor at all in his hard, dark eyes. "Westley, tell this lunatic woman that's ridiculous."

Westley warily kept his body partially angled toward John, but he did not speak.

"I don't believe I have met this servant girl." John stepped toward her with an arrogant smile.

Evangeline did not lower her arrow even an inch but kept it trained on the man's chest. "I advise you not to come any closer."

John halted again.

"Westley, do you allow your servants to threaten your friends? I do believe this little firebrand would do me bodily harm."

"Do you know what she's talking about? Why does she say you attacked me, John?"

"How would I know that?" John's voice rose in pitch and volume as he flung his arms out. "She is addled, or drinking some kind of strong ale. I heard you fell in the river and hit your head, but I don't know what kind of satanic dreams this little servant girl has been having."

The man was obviously trying to insult her, for as tall as she was, no one had ever called her a "little" anything.

Westley glanced from her to John Underhill.

"Is anything amiss, sir?" One of the stable boys approached them.

"Go fetch Sabina, the miller's daughter," Westley said.

"Yes, sir." The young man turned and ran.

"Do you not trust me, Westley? Can this be?" John's face was a mixture of amusement and anger. "Who is this little annoyance? This . . . girl?"

"I am neither little nor a girl," Evangeline said, her voice as icy as her blood was boiling. "And you are the man I saw strike Westley le Wyse in the head and push him in the river. If I had not been there, he would have drowned."

The man studied her, his eyes so cold he surely would have frozen her heart if he could have. But the fact that he was pretending to be Westley's friend, bold enough to lie to his face after trying to kill him . . . He must have heard that Westley could not remember what happened.

Instead of feeling afraid, strength coursed through her. Nothing would keep her from at least wounding the man should he make an aggressive move toward either her or Westley.

Westley said nothing. John Underhill crossed his arms over his chest.

Finally, someone was approaching from the direction of the castle.

"Sabina," Westley said in an expressionless voice, "is this the man you saw running away when I fell into the river?"

Sabina shook her head emphatically. "No, of course not. This is John Underhill. Why would he want to harm you? The two men I saw running away from where you fell in had, um, black hair and red hair. Neither one of them could have been John Underhill." She smiled openmouthed, as if the idea were ridiculous.

Evangeline's stomach roiled, but she gripped the bow and arrow even tighter, the bow and string digging into her fingers.

"Eva was not even there when you fell in the water." Sabina made a derisive sound with her lips.

"It is Sabina who was not there. She only said she saw two men running away because I told her there were two men."

"Westley," John said, "if you are just going to stand there and let her accuse me of trying to kill you, pointing an arrow at me, then I'm leaving. I did not know our friendship meant so little to you."

John Underhill turned to leave. Westley opened his mouth to speak but ultimately said nothing.

Sabina smiled slowly as she stared at Westley, her eyes trained on him even as she started walking back the way she had come.

Evangeline lowered her bow and arrow and let the string go slack.

"I . . . I don't know what to think anymore," Westley said softly, "but John has been my friend for a very long time." He rubbed his temple, near where John had struck him, and closed his eyes. "I just don't remember what happened. I wish I did, but I don't."

"Perhaps your memory will come back to you."

"Perhaps." Westley let out a heavy sigh. "Either way, I think you should not go anywhere alone."

"Me? You are the one he wants to harm."

"Perhaps you only saw someone who looked like John. I stopped a man from beating his wife a day or two before I fell in the river. Perhaps he was the one who struck me. He had the same blond hair as John, now that I think of it. But either way, you should not tell anyone what you saw. If someone is trying to harm me, they should not hear that there was a witness to their actions."

"No one believes me, so I think I am safe." She gave her words a wry tone. "Even if I am mistaken—which I am not—and the two men I saw try to harm you were not John Underhill and his servant, if you do not agree to take precautions, I shall be forced to follow you around with my bow and arrows."

"Ha!" He cocked his head to one side and frowned. "How in the world did you get Reeve Folsham to teach you how to use a bow?"

"I asked him."

"After you cut him with the scythe, I didn't think you were his favorite person. But you seem to have won him over."

"I did him a good turn. When a barrel of ale was about to fall on his head, I pushed him out of the way."

The look of admiration in his eyes and slight smile made her heart flutter.

"I think he also wanted to help me after what happened to me two nights ago." She lifted her face to the sun, which was high overhead. "I also wanted to learn how to sword fight. I don't suppose that would be helpful, however, since I don't own a sword."

He smiled at her. "No, I don't suppose it would be."

As she stared at his perfect teeth, a glint of suspicion shone in his eye. He wasn't sure if he could trust her. She couldn't blame him, perhaps, but it felt like a challenge, to win him over the way she had won over the reeve. *Someday, Westley le Wyse, you'll be offering to teach me how to sword fight.*

"And now it is time for the midday meal, so we should go."

She took the bow and arrow and stowed them away in the inside corner of the oat barn. When she came out, Westley was standing in front of her.

"I've never had anyone defend my life before. You looked as if you would have shot John if he had gotten any closer to me."

"I would have. And you should take it more seriously. He could have been hiding a knife, just hoping to get you alone and then kill you with it."

His eyes were gentle but searching.

"I should go."

"After the meal, will you come and read a bit?"

She nodded. "I need to give my ankle a rest."

As they walked back together, he said, "And when you're rested, I want you to answer my question about Lord Shiveley."

"You asked me earlier if I was betrothed." Her heart pounded. "I am not. But it is true that Lord Shiveley's men may be looking for me."

He was silent for a moment. "Perhaps later you will explain."

And perhaps you will forgive me when I choose not to explain.

~ ♪ ~

Evangeline sat amid the pillows behind the castle, her back propped against the stone wall. She read from the Latin Bible while Westley read from the English version. The problem was that she only understood *most* of the words in Latin. She glanced over at Westley.

He looked up. "Is something wrong?"

"I don't understand some of these Latin words. Do you think I could . . . That is, do you mind . . . ?

"Do you want to read the English one?"

"I don't want to take it away from you, of course."

"We can read it together. Which book were you reading from?"

"I was about to start reading the book of Ruth, but I can read whatever you are reading."

He stood and carried the book closer, then sat beside her. "Shall we take turns reading aloud?"

"That sounds like a good idea."

He found the book of Ruth and let Evangeline read the first chapter. It felt strange to read the Holy Writ of God in the common language, but after a few verses, she lost herself in the story and ceased to think of the language she was reading it in. She handed the book back to Westley, and he started the second chapter in his even, masculine voice.

Evangeline read the third chapter. She read about Ruth going to the threshing floor where the men were sleeping, uncovering Boaz's feet, and lying down beside him. Evangeline stopped.

"What is it?"

"It seems strange that she would risk her reputation as she does. Why does she lie down with a man when he's with his workers at the threshing floor? How does she know she can trust him?"

"I think the intention was to signal to Boaz that she was willing to marry him."

"I suppose. But why do it like that? Why not just speak the words? I cannot imagine doing such a thing with a man who was practically a stranger."

"Have you always had trouble trusting men?"

Evangeline thought for a moment. "I like to think I would not trust a stranger, but the truth is, I trusted you when I knew you and your men not at all."

"Perhaps you have more in common with Ruth than you thought." His crooked smile seemed flirtatious.

"I have always had the idea that I should not trust men. I suppose . . ." She almost said, *I suppose I got that idea from my nursemaids*, but of course, a peasant did not have nursemaids. However, he already knew she was not a peasant, and certainly not a servant.

"From the very first time I saw you, there was something about you, something in your face. I trusted you. I trusted you not to molest Mildred and me, at least. Besides, when I saw you save that child from the runaway horse, I knew you had a good heart."

"You saw me . . . in Berkhamsted Castle's bailey?"

Evangeline's stomach sank. Had she said too much? When he figured out who she was, would he take her back to Berkhamsted Castle?

"Where were you? I did not see you. You must have been inside the castle."

"I . . . I was. May I please finish this book before you question me further?"

He held up his hands. "Very well. Go on."

Evangeline took a deep breath and resumed reading to the end of the chapter.

Westley took back the book, their hands brushing as she helped lift it from her lap.

He read the last chapter and looked over at Evangeline. "So you would not let a man know that you wanted to marry him by lying down at his feet?"

"Um, no. But perhaps it was the custom of the day. Would you marry a woman who came to you while you were sleeping, uncovered your feet, and lay down beside you?"

He smiled as if amused. "Possibly." Then his smile disappeared. "How did Lord Shiveley tell you he wanted to marry you?"

Evangeline stared down at the book between them. "I never said Lord Shiveley wanted to marry me." She had to be careful. She did not want to tell a lie, but she also did not feel she had to tell Westley everything. He was better off not knowing, especially if his conscience were to tell him he should take her back to Berkhamsted Castle to do the king's bidding.

"Are you betrothed to Lord Shiveley?"

"I already told you I am not."

If Westley wanted to marry her himself, she would reveal all to him. If he were committed to her, perhaps he would fight for her, would think of some way to protect her from the powerful Lord Shiveley. But she did not believe Westley wanted to marry her. After all, she was running not only from the Earl of Shiveley but also from the king of England. How could she ever escape? They were bound to find her sooner or later.

Westley did not behave like a man who was in love with her. She wished he was, but she had no idea how to make him fall in love with her. Besides, he had only known her for a short time. She could not trust him to protect her from Lord Shiveley. "May we please keep reading?"

"You are not betrothed to Lord Shiveley, but someone wanted to marry you, and you ran away to avoid marrying him. Was that man Lord Shiveley?"

"Why do you want to know so badly?"

"I want to know what manner of trouble my family will encounter in the future."

"I do not intend to cause your family any trouble." Evangeline avoided looking at him and kept her jaw tight, even as she struggled to keep a tight rein on her emotions. "I shall leave Glynval now if you wish."

"I do not wish you to leave. I also don't want you to have to marry anyone you don't wish to marry. I was only trying to discover the reason for you running away from your previous home. Come. Let us forget about it and read. It is your turn."

Evangeline chose to skip ahead to a different part of the Bible and read the gospel of the Apostle John. After several chapters, Westley put down the book and sighed. "I can't read any more. Would you like me to teach you knife throwing?"

"Reeve Folsham said he would teach me the fighting skills that he taught his own daughters." She should think of an excuse to get away from Westley before he asked more questions about her past and about Lord Shiveley. But what she should do and what she wanted to do were two completely different things.

"Come. I can teach you something." He stood and held out his hand to her.

Chapter Eighteen

Westley extended his hand to Eva to help her up. Even though he still wasn't sure he trusted her, something about her made him want *her* to trust *him*. Was it because she was so pretty, with her lovely red hair and green eyes and fair face? Or was it because he still felt bad about the way his people had treated her about the poison mushrooms? Besides, if she was telling the truth, she'd been the one who saved him from drowning.

When she placed her hand in his, he felt it all the way to his shoulder.

She let him pull her to her feet. A strand of hair had come loose from her braid and dangled by her cheek. Why could he imagine himself brushing the hair off her face and behind her ear? He never had a thought like that when he was with Sabina. And now, after what Sabina had done to Eva, lying about the mushrooms and possibly lying about who she saw running away from the river, he no longer had any interest in the miller's daughter. But Eva . . . He must be careful. After all, she was still hiding something from him.

He walked toward the barn where she had practiced archery with Reeve Folsham that morning.

He turned and said over his shoulder, "Are you coming?"

She started to follow him and pulled a knife out of her pocket.

When they reached the barn, he showed her how to hold the

knife properly for throwing. He demonstrated, throwing his own knife and driving the point straight into the side of the barn. Eva tried it. The side of her blade hit the wooden wall and bounced off.

"This is more difficult than it looks." Eva bit her lip.

"After a bit of practice, you will be as good at it as you are at archery."

She was preparing to try again when Reeve Folsham approached.

"I see your teacher has returned. I shall go. I need to speak with my father. And I'm glad your ankle is better."

"It is much better. I thank you." Her smile was captivating. He actually stumbled as he walked away.

⁓✺⁓

Evangeline hid her amusement behind her hand as Westley stumbled. He was nearly as clumsy as she was.

Reeve Folsham began his instruction by saying, "I am going to teach you how to defend yourself the way I taught my own daughters. Knife throwing is a good skill to know, but it is no good if your attacker is in your face, grabbing your hands, or if you cannot reach your knife."

Evangeline nodded.

"Now, if you don't have a knife, look around for something to use as a weapon—a rock or a block of wood or something else heavy or sharp or hard. If you find something, strike your attacker in the head or the throat or between the legs. If you don't have a weapon, use your knuckles to attack his eyes or his throat. Strike hard and fast, then run. And always scream as loud as you can to raise the hue and cry."

Evangeline nodded.

"Now, if I were to attack you from behind, like this—" He went behind her and put an arm around her neck. "You can try to elbow me"—she tried but missed, as he was standing too far back—"but that won't work, so you have to stomp on the middle of my foot."

Instead of stomping his foot, Evangeline stomped beside it. "Then what?"

"Then when your attacker loosens his hold, you can take a step back and reach his midsection with your elbow. Slam him a good one to his ribs. That should loosen his grip enough so you can get free. Then turn around and ram your knee between his legs. Or if that doesn't work, strike his throat with your knuckles."

Evangeline followed his every word and move. They practiced several moves until Evangeline almost wished someone would attack her so she could use her new skills.

"Thank you for teaching me, Reeve Folsham. Here are your bow and arrows back."

"You may keep them. I insist. Every peasant maiden should be able to defend herself against violent men or unwanted attention."

Every peasant maiden," he said. But did his rule apply to every maiden who was not a peasant, but a ward of the king, told she must marry a man she found loathsome? Yes, Evangeline needed these skills even more if she was ever found by Lord Shiveley.

Westley discovered his father sitting at his desk in his study, a small room next to the family's library.

"Father, I need to speak to you."

He turned his attention from his task to Westley. "What is it, son?"

"Eva, the new servant girl—"

"The one who claimed to be mute and was accused of trying to poison everyone?"

"Yes, she said she saw John strike me and push me into the river."

"And you still do not remember what happened?"

"I remember walking to the river to fish but nothing after that until I woke up in bed with Mother hovering over me."

"Perhaps this girl is lying. What do we know of her?" The brow over Father's one good eye lowered.

"She and her friend Mildred joined the men and me when we left Berkhamsted Castle on our way back here. Mildred claimed Eva was mute after being beaten by her former mistress. But Eva has admitted that was a lie. She said she was trying to get away from a man who wanted to marry her, and it was her way of disguising herself." He decided not to tell Father that he suspected the man she did not want to marry was the Earl of Shiveley or one of his men.

"I thought it was Sabina who found you after you fell in the river. Did she say anything about seeing John push you in?"

"At first Sabina said nothing about anyone pushing me in. Eva said nothing because she was still pretending to be mute. But then Sabina said she saw two men running away after I fell in."

"What else?"

"Eva said Sabina was lying, that she wasn't there when I fell in. She said she was the only one around when John and his man, Roger Cox, approached me at the river. She said John and I exchanged angry words, then he struck me with a block of wood and pushed me in."

"This is a grave matter. Why did she did not tell us this right away?"

"She said she asked Sabina to tell me that she saw two men running away after I fell in so I would be on my guard. But she did not know who the man was who struck me until she saw John and Roger Cox at the well two days ago. And then he showed up again this morning."

"What did John want?"

"I don't know." Westley rubbed his temple, trying to bring back the memory that had flashed through his mind when he saw John scowling at Eva and her raised bow and arrow. "But it is strange that I have hardly seen John these past three years and now he is showing up so often. And John behaved strangely when she accused him."

"She accused him to his face?"

"While aiming a bow and arrow at him."

Father raised his brows.

"Reeve Folsham was teaching her to shoot."

"Reeve Folsham? Did she not throw a scythe at him her first day here?"

"The scythe slipped out of her hand and gave the reeve a small cut. But that seems to be forgotten now."

Father was still staring at him in disbelief.

"I believe she won him over when she saved him from a rolling barrel of ale that fell off a cart and nearly onto his head. And then when the other servants falsely accused her of trying to poison them, he defended her. I think he agreed to teach her because he wanted her to be able to defend herself."

Father cleared his throat—something he sometimes did when he wasn't sure what to say.

"I don't like to think that John Underhill would try to kill me, but I had a strange little flash of a memory . . . a memory of his enraged face and his arm raised. I don't know if it was a memory or just my mind playing with me. And then his answers to Eva did not ring true. And yet . . . it seems ridiculous to believe this girl over John, especially when she deceived us all."

They were both silent for a few moments.

"When was the last time you had talked to John, before you fell in the river?"

"He met me one day a few days ago on the path through the woods near the oat field on the north side. He looked angry and he argued with me, saying his father was a good man and that it was our fault the villeins rose up and killed him." Westley hated to tell his father that.

"You know that isn't true, don't you?"

"I tried to get him to remember what a hard man his father was, how he had beaten those two men in the weeks before the uprising before they killed him."

"John is still angry about his father's murder. He has found someone to blame in you and me. I am still not convinced John tried to kill you, but if he did, he will probably try again. I don't want you going anywhere alone, and the same for this servant girl. From now on I want her to work and sleep here at the castle. You will probably regain your memory, and when you do, if Eva was telling the truth, we will need to send for the hundred bailiff."

His father's words lowered a heavy weight onto his chest. Thinking that his old friend could kill anyone, especially him, brought home the very unpleasant truth of how much John had become like his father—irrationally angry, suspicious, and violent.

Westley fingered the petals of a red rose as he stood in the flower garden. He should stop standing around, stop waiting to see if Eva would come and read with him.

"Westley!" his mother called to him as she walked out to meet him. When she was still several yards away, she said, "Your father just told me that someone may have been trying to kill you when you fell in the river. Why did you not tell me?"

"I did not know until two days ago, Mother."

The pained look on her face only made his heart sink a little lower than it already was.

"Do you think Eva is telling the truth about John being the one who struck you?"

"I don't know." He sighed, then pulled off a loose rose petal and made indentations with his fingernail in the easily bruised flower's flesh. "At first I was angry that she would even accuse him. But I don't want to falsely accuse her of lying either. It's just so hard to believe that John would try to kill me. Why? He has no reason to hate me."

"You have not seen much of him the last three years, have you?"

He shook his head, still watching the rose petal grow more limp and wilted in his hand.

"What did she tell you about why she lied about being mute?"

"She said she was trying to avoid marrying someone. I suspect she may have meant the Earl of Shiveley."

"Oh." His mother's mouth opened and her expression changed. "Did you tell your father that?"

"I don't think I did."

"Don't you remember that your father's cousin was Lord Shiveley's first wife?"

"I had forgotten that. What was her name?"

"Margaret. It was nearly fifteen years ago. She married him, and for the next few months, every time her mother and father saw her, she had bruises on her face and arms. And then she was dead. We all suspected that he murdered her."

"Was nothing ever done about it?"

"Nothing. It is difficult to cast suspicion on an earl, especially one as wealthy as he is."

"I don't remember you telling me anything about that." He felt a burning in his stomach.

"Well, you were only a child at the time. We didn't want to tell you something so sordid and terrible. And you did not know poor

Margaret." Mother's face was sad as she stared out into the distant trees.

Just the thought of Eva marrying someone so despicable . . . No wonder she was so desperate to leave him, to disguise herself however she could to get away. But again, he did not know if she was fleeing Lord Shiveley. Even so, it was his men who had come after her.

"But don't you realize? If she was to marry Lord Shiveley, and if she was living at Berkhamsted Castle, she must be . . . the king's cousin, the one who supposedly sings so beautifully she can enchant the birds out of the trees."

Westley's mind raced. Could it be? After all, she knew nothing about the work of a servant, and her hands had blistered so badly she obviously had never done any hard work. But she knew how to read Latin and owned a Psalter—and she had a beautiful voice. He had heard her sing in the clearing near the river. Had he been so distracted by the fact that she had lied about being mute that he hadn't realized hers was the same voice he'd heard from the upper window of Berkhamsted Castle?

"We must protect her!" Mother's eyes widened and her expression was intense. "We must keep her hidden until we can tell the king what we know about Lord Shiveley's first marriage. Surely he will not force his cousin to marry someone who murdered his first wife."

"But the king might not believe that." *Perhaps we can keep her here forever, and the king need never know.*

Mother bit her lip. "I cannot bear to think of her being mistreated the way Margaret was. I shall speak to your father about this."

Westley watched her go.

Eva is the cousin of the king of England.

Westley and Aldred walked around the North Meadow where the Harvest Festival would take place. Sellers would come from miles around with their booths and wares, and they would need plenty of room.

Horses' hooves sounded on the road just beyond a stand of trees. When they came into view, the horsemen spotted Westley and Aldred and proceeded toward them.

They wore the colors of the Earl of Shiveley.

Westley stepped forward.

"What village is this?" the horseman in the lead asked.

"Glynval. Ranulf le Wyse is the lord here, and I am his son. Is there some way I might help you?"

"We are searching for a maiden with red hair, seventeen years old, very tall. She is thought to have left Berkhamsted Castle on foot almost two weeks ago. Have you seen her?"

Westley squinted and cocked his head to one side. *God, please let Aldred stay quiet.* He didn't dare glance Aldred's way.

Westley shook his head. "May I ask who is looking for her? Berkhamsted Castle is one of King Richard's royal residences, is it not?"

"King Richard himself is searching for her, as is the Earl of Shiveley." Raising himself up in his saddle as if trying to look imperious, he said, "Lord Shiveley is concerned for her safety. It is very important that she be found safe and well, so if you were to find her, Lord Shiveley would reward you well for escorting her back to Berkhamsted Castle. King Richard has also promised to add his own reward for her safe return."

"It would be enough for me to see a maiden of the realm safely home," Westley said with a bow.

"What did you say your name was?"

"Westley le Wyse of Glynval."

"Are you certain this maiden is not taking refuge in your village? She was probably traveling with another woman, fifteen years older than the red-haired maiden."

"It is a small village. My father and I would notice if someone new came here."

"Very well."

"Is she Lord Shiveley's betrothed?"

The guard placed his hand on his sword hilt, shifting in his saddle. Finally, he said slowly and deliberately, "Yes. She is."

Westley's gut twisted. "I shall not detain you any longer." He stepped away from them.

The guard nodded and turned his horse around. The men rode away.

"Why did you not tell them?" Aldred asked. "They must have meant Eva and Mildred."

Westley looked him in the eye. "I believe Eva may be in danger from these men, and I don't want you repeating any of this to anyone, Aldred. May I depend upon you?"

"Of course. You are our lord, even if you do not allow us to call you that. And you can depend on the rest of Glynval."

"Perhaps not all of Glynval." Westley rubbed his jaw. "I don't want you to say anything to anyone else. Let these men move on to the next village. With God's good favor, perhaps they won't come back through here."

It was a shaky hope at best, but it was the only hope Eva had.

The man said she was Lord Shiveley's betrothed. Had she lied to him again?

Chapter Nineteen

Evangeline was always in the castle now. She even slept in the same small room with Lady le Wyse's closest maidservant above Lord and Lady le Wyse's own bedchamber.

As she was sweeping the hearth in the library, a voice behind her said, "Eva?"

She stopped sweeping and turned to face Westley.

"You have not come to read with me the last two days."

"Oh." She stared down at her broom. "I have been busy cleaning. And Reeve Folsham keeps thinking of new things to teach me. He taught me how to throw a grown man over my shoulder and onto the ground on his back." She put down the short straw broom, propping it against the wall. She smiled into Westley's bright-blue eyes as she remembered it. "Could you ever imagine me doing that? I never knew it could be so thrilling to exert my own strength. You men must often feel that."

"Oh yes, I am so strong, I entertain myself with seeing how far I can toss men of various sizes."

"You are laughing, but it is something new for me. I've never been allowed to—" She stopped abruptly as she realized what she had been about to say. As smoothly as she could, she went on. "—learn how to use a weapon or defend myself. Reeve Folsham is the first man I've ever met who thought defending oneself from attack was important for a woman to learn."

"Did he tell you he has taught my sisters?"

"Lord le Wyse allowed him to teach his daughters?"

"My father asked him to teach them so if they ever needed to, they could fight off someone trying to hurt them. My mother was once attacked when she was still a young maiden and got away by fighting back."

"Oh." She covered her mouth with her hand at the thought of someone attacking Lady le Wyse. How wonderful that men like Reeve Folsham and Lord le Wyse would provide ways for women to defend themselves.

"One reason I was hoping you would come to read with me is because I have something particular to tell you."

"Yes?" Already the buoyant feeling was fading.

"Eva, some men rode into Glynval two days ago and asked me if I'd seen a young woman with red hair, seventeen years old, who had run away from Berkhamsted Castle two weeks ago."

Eva felt the warmth drain from her face. Her vision began to spin.

Westley grabbed her by her arms. "Are you going to faint?"

"No," she whispered, even though the room was still spinning.

He still held her upper arms and stared into her eyes, his face only inches from hers. "Why is Lord Shiveley, and even King Richard, searching for you? Are you betrothed to the Earl of Shiveley?"

"Please." Tears pricked her eyelids. "You did not tell them I was here, did you?"

"I pretended I didn't know who they were speaking of and told them you were not here. But you need to tell me the truth. Shiveley's men said you were his betrothed. Did you lie to me, Eva? Did you deceive me again?"

Her stomach twisted at the pain in his eyes. "Please, Westley. Please understand. I can't marry Shiveley. It would kill me. Please

forgive me." It was impossible to look away from his eyes. If only . . .
But she would not ask for his love. Only his mercy.

"I want to understand, but you won't tell me the truth. You haven't
even answered my question."

"I am not betrothed to him. That is, it is not official or sanctioned
by the Church. But King Richard came to Berkhamsted Castle—you
were there—and immediately called me into his presence and told
me I must marry Lord Shiveley." Westley was still holding her arms.
She grabbed his shirtfront. "I begged the king not to force me to
marry that man." Tears burned their way down her cheeks.

"Eva, who are you?" he asked quietly. His breath brushed her
forehead as he leaned even closer.

"Evangeline, the illegitimate daughter of the king's uncle, Lionel
of Antwerp."

"I suppose I should have guessed," he said, his voice even softer.
"You are the king's ward, as well as his cousin. It is your duty . . ." His
voice trailed off.

"It is my duty to marry whomever the king wishes me to marry.
I know it is, but I cannot . . . cannot bear it." Tears streamed down
her cheeks now, but she didn't even attempt to wipe them away.
Something drove her to keep speaking, to make him understand.

"If I were to marry that man, it would mean—" Tears choked off
her voice, but she swallowed and pushed on. "It would mean that I
am not worthy of being loved, that I am just a pawn, that my feelings
do not matter. Don't you see? My father didn't even love me enough
to marry my mother. I grew up with only servants to take care of me.
Some of them treated me well, others did not, but never, never did I
feel like any of them actually loved me. I thought if only I could be
free, if I could live like a servant, I could find someone—"

The pain, like broken knives inside her, wrenched the breath
from her chest, forcing her to stop. She forced in another breath. "If

I could find someone who would love me and marry me, then maybe I am not unworthy after all. Perhaps I am not just a pawn in someone's game. I want to be a human person with feelings, someone who can inspire love in another."

"Perhaps the king believes Lord Shiveley loves you."

She shook her head. "The king . . . He is deceived in Lord Shiveley's character. Believe me when I say the earl doesn't love me. You didn't hear what he said to me, how he . . . he just wants to control me, and to be able to boast that he is married to royalty—one king's granddaughter and another king's cousin."

Did Westley think, as Muriel did, that she should do her duty and obey the king? "I will not go back. You cannot force me. I will not marry that man. I'll run away again where you'll never find me." A sob escaped her throat, and she struggled to control herself and not weep aloud.

The violent feelings suddenly drained out of her. She should not be this close to Westley, should not be clutching his shirt. He would think she was like Sabina, trying to trap him into marrying her. Her hands went limp.

"Let me go," she said softly, uncurling her fingers and pushing gently away. Unable to lift her eyes to meet his, she stared at his chest and wiped her cheeks with her hands.

But instead of letting her go, Westley pulled her closer, his hands slipping from her arms to embrace her.

Her cheek was pressed against his chest, against his soft linen shirt, as his hand caressed the back of her head.

"Do not cry anymore." His deep voice was warm in her ear. "Lord Shiveley will not harm you. I will not allow it."

Could this be happening? His embrace felt so good, so safe and warm and lovely. If only Westley loved her. How brave she could feel with his arms, and his love, to surround her. If only he loved her as much as she loved him. She would imagine that he did, just for a moment, as she closed her eyes and breathed in his freshly laundered shirt and masculine scent.

Her heart ached, but it was a lovely ache. She would remember this moment for the rest of her life, just like the moment after she saved him from drowning, the moment she realized he was alive and she had saved him.

She stood very still, afraid if she moved he would break the closeness. But he continued to hold her until they heard footsteps in the corridor outside.

Evangeline pushed away, breaking free from his arms, keeping her face turned away from him.

She walked over to where she had left her broom. "I should get back to work." She reached for the broom, rubbing away the tears from her cheeks with her other hand, but Westley touched her shoulder.

"Don't look at me." She lifted her apron to wipe her nose. "I must look like a red, blotchy mess after all that crying."

"I just want you to know," he said, his hand still warm on her shoulder, "that I think you are very brave and that I understand. I will speak with my father, and we shall find a way out for you, out of this unwanted marriage."

"You won't tell the king I am here, will you?" She gazed up at him before remembering her tear-streaked face.

He caught her hand in his. A strand of hair fell over her eye. Just as she was about to push it out of the way, Westley brushed it back, his hand grazing her forehead. The breath stilled in her throat.

"I think you are lovely, even after all that crying." A tiny smile raised the corners of his lips.

Her heart flipped inside her.

"I will do everything I can to keep you safe." He hurried out of the room, leaving her staring after him.

⁓◦◦∘⁓

Westley rushed out of the library, his heart pounding, before he completely lost his mind.

Eva—Evangeline—had finally broken down the wall he had always felt with her, had opened her heart and told him the truth. She had looked so vulnerable, so desperate and determined . . . and so beautiful. Her lips were plump and red and her eyes sparkling and bright green from the tears swimming in them. Holding her made him feel completely alive. He'd never wanted anything so much in his life as to kiss her.

He could not be thinking this way. His mind was churning even faster than his heart was beating.

He practically ran through the house. His father was walking down the staircase.

"Father, I need to speak to you."

"Let's go into the library."

Eva—Evangeline—was in there. "No, let's go . . . in here." Westley led his father into a small empty bedroom.

"What is it, son? Did you see John Underhill again?"

"No, Father, but I did see the Earl of Shiveley's men. They came here looking for a red-haired maiden who ran away from Berkhamsted Castle two weeks ago."

He rubbed his cheek beneath his black eye patch. "Your mother told me you suspect Eva is Evangeline, the king's cousin and ward."

"I just spoke to Eva and she confessed it, without me even asking her."

"She is the girl they were seeking."

"Yes. It seems the king wants her to marry Lord Shiveley."

"And she does not wish to?"

"Exactly."

Father took a deep breath and sighed. "What did you promise her, Westley?"

His face grew warm. "I said what anyone with any kindness and mercy would have said. I told her I would do whatever I could to keep her safe. I don't think she even knows that Shiveley probably murdered his first wife."

Father was already shaking his head.

"Do not make me out to be a child who does not know anything of the world, Father." Westley's ire rose. "The Church says a woman cannot be forced to marry someone she does not wish to."

"But you know as well as I do that women are often coerced to agree, especially in situations such as this. She is the king's ward. She is obligated to do whatever the king asks of her. People of her birth do not have a choice whom they marry. They agree because they know it is their duty."

"Are you saying that it is right? That she should do her *duty* and marry a man who will beat and mistreat her?"

"No, but—"

"Evangeline will never agree to marry Lord Shiveley. You should have seen her, Father. She was crying and saying she would run away again if I tried to send her back to Berkhamsted."

"We do not want it on our consciences that we forced a maiden, no matter who she is, to marry someone she is determined not to." Father sighed again. "If nothing else, we can help her find refuge at Rosings Abbey."

"Perhaps she could hide here until the king and Shiveley forget about her."

"I suppose it is possible, but sooner or later it's likely the king's men, or Shiveley's, will find her. After all, if those men had asked almost any other person in Glynval besides you, they would have known the men were looking for Eva, and they would have said so. But let us hope they do not return."

"If the king believes we are knowingly hiding his ward from him and from the man he wants her to marry, we could lose everything, could we not?"

"Yes." Father looked thoughtful but not afraid. "Losing everything is sometimes the price one must pay for doing the right thing. I could not save my cousin, but perhaps . . . perhaps we can save the king's. And if it comes down to it, we will seek an audience with King Richard and tell him what we know about Shiveley. He isn't likely to believe us over one of his advisors, but we can try."

Westley imagined the king taking away their home, their lands, everything. They might be forced to move back to Father's place of birth in Lincolnshire. But they would lose even those holdings if the king had a political friend he wanted to reward. People out of favor with the king often found themselves destitute—or exiled from the country.

"How can I ask you and Mother to risk your home?"

"I don't see it as you asking us to risk it. I am willing to risk it for the sake of mercy and righteousness."

"Thank you, Father."

"But, son, I can also see that you are in danger of letting your heart become attached to this woman. Don't be guided by your emotions, Westley. Be wise and guard your heart. You hardly know anything of this woman's character, and she has deceived us once already."

"She says she saved my life when John pushed me in the river."

"But are you certain she is telling the truth? It has not been proven."

Westley said quietly, "I shall be careful, Father."

Would he and his family have to face the king's wrath for Evangeline to be free from marrying Shiveley? Only time would reveal her destiny. And his. But for now, it seemed wise to rein himself in where the king's ward was concerned. He was too eager to forget that he had only known her for a short time.

As his father and mother had quoted to him on numerous occasions, "The heart is deceitful above all things."

Chapter Twenty

Evangeline was sitting on a cushion on the ground in the little reading alcove when Westley came and held out a wooden bowl to her.

"What is it?"

"Apples and cream." Westley sat beside her with a second bowl.

She held the bowl up to her face and breathed in the aroma of cooked apples, cinnamon, and cloves. "Mmm." Her mouth watered.

Westley handed her a spoon. The adorable smile on his face made her forget the apples, but when he started eating from his own bowl, she dipped her spoon in.

"Did you eat apples and cream at Berkhamsted Castle?" he asked between bites.

"Yes. But our cook was not very generous with her cloves and sugar. It didn't taste as good as this." When she glanced up at him, he was grinning.

"I'm glad you like it. A king's ward should have good things to eat."

Evangeline lowered the bowl even as her stomach sank.

"I'm sorry," he said. "I should not have brought up . . . that. I won't speak of it again, if you wish me not to."

"I suppose I cannot change it. I'm glad you know the truth. It was a relief to finally tell you."

He was quiet for several moments. "What is it like being a king's ward?"

"It is very lonely. I used to dream of being a peasant. You must think that was foolish."

"No, but I think any peasant would be astonished."

"And would think me foolish?"

"Yes. But they don't know what you have experienced."

"People probably think my life has been blessed and favored." Evangeline stared down into her bowl, unable to look him in the eye. "It is true that I have never had to worry about food or clothing or shelter. But one of my earliest memories is of my nursemaid pinching my leg so hard it left a red-and-purple mark. I had done something she didn't like, I suppose. I don't remember much else about that time. When I was seven, Mildred—her real name is Muriel—became my personal servant. She has been taking care of me ever since, but she is more of a companion now than a servant. I came to Berkhamsted Castle ten years ago when King Edward, Richard's father, was still king. He ordered that I had to stay in the castle and could only go outside when at least three guards were with me. He was afraid one of his enemies might kidnap me and hold me for ransom, or force me into marriage."

She finally got up enough courage to look across at Westley. He had set his bowl aside and was leaning toward her. His eyes peered directly into hers.

"And now we are forcing you to stay in our castle."

"But it is not the same. You must not think it is. I am around people such as you and your mother. Your mother speaks kindly to me, and she did so when she thought I was only a peasant. Your father is kind, too, in a different way. And you." Her stomach turned a somersault as she looked into his eyes. "I saw you save that little girl while I was standing at my window, and I knew you were a good person." She put her bowl aside as he had done.

He shifted so his body was facing her. "I remember seeing you. I heard you singing."

"I liked to sing every morning, standing at my window." Her cheeks warmed. "I started doing that when I was a little girl. I tried to stop a few years ago, but the servants complained, so I kept singing, at least one song every morning."

"You have a beautiful voice. My men and I talked about the voice from the castle for days. I . . . I even dreamed about meeting the person behind the voice."

"Were they pleasant dreams?"

"Very pleasant dreams."

She cleared her throat. "You were so courteous to me on our way here. You have always been . . . very courteous."

"Not so very courteous. I forgot to check your hands again." He reached out and took her hands from her lap and turned them over. She cringed, knowing they were still far from healed. In fact, they still looked a mess.

"Eva." His voice was soft and deep. "You must keep these hands wrapped." He raised one of her hands so close to his face, her insides trembled. Would he kiss her hand?

He closed his eyes, a pained expression on his face. His breath fanned her wrist, making her skin tingle.

She shouldn't long for his kiss. She did not know what the future held for her. But she did long for it. Her heart ached with longing.

He lowered her hands and stared at them. Neither of them spoke for several moments. Finally, he said, "What would your guardian say if he could see these hands?" He seemed to try to make his voice lighthearted, but he was failing.

"I'm sure the king is quite angry with me right now. He thinks I deserve this and worse." Her stomach twisted at the truth of that. "Even Muriel thought I was foolish. She thought I would go back to Berkhamsted and agree to marry Lord Shiveley after spending a few days as a servant."

"She underestimated your will." Westley looked at her, still holding her hands in his.

"I do have a strong will, I suppose, although I am usually quiet about it." She smiled at a memory. "Maudie, one of my nursemaids—not the one who pinched me—once said, 'She will smile like a cherub and say, "Yes, Maudie," but then she will run away when your back is turned.'"

"That sounds like a normal, healthy child's will to me." Westley was smiling now. He finally let go of her hands.

"For my place in life Muriel would say I have an unnatural will. I do not acquiesce to the king's requests as a king's ward ought to do."

"And I am very grateful that you do not."

Her heart took a tumble at his words. Did he mean that he was grateful she had not obediently married Lord Shiveley because he . . . wished to marry her? *Oh please, God, let him mean that.*

"If you had not run away, I would have drowned."

The breath rushed out of her. Of course he had not meant he wanted to marry her. "Oh. Yes. I thought you were dead for a moment." She averted her eyes while she recovered from her foolish disappointment.

⁂

He must keep his head.

Westley forced himself to remember that he had only known

her for two short weeks. He let go of her hands so he would not be as tempted to kiss her soft skin.

She was telling him about when he almost drowned.

"Did I open my eyes at all?"

"No, you looked very much dead. Your skin was pale, blood was trickling from your head, and you did not seem as if you were breathing. I was glad when I turned you onto your side and you vomited. Sabina screamed and ran."

"How very romantic. The minstrels will no doubt be singing of this story for years to come."

She actually laughed, a lovely sound. She covered her mouth.

"It is very well. You may laugh. If I had died, though, you would be sorry for laughing."

"But you did not die."

How could he not sacrifice everything for a woman who saved his life? Had quite possibly saved his life twice, since she warned him about John Underhill?

"You have been a blessing from God to me. And I have not treated you nearly so well."

"I think you have treated me well. You bandaged my hands. You told Lord Shiveley's men that I was not here. You allowed me to travel with you and your men. You brought me apples and cream."

"Speaking of your hands, stay here." He got up and went into the house, grabbed the jar of his mother's healing salve and some bandages, and hurried back outside. He sat in front of her.

She trustingly gave him her hand. She had such an innocence about her. She had lived in a sheltered world all her life, which had given her the childlike wonder he had seen when she had gasped over every butterfly and flower on the road to Glynval. She had chased pigs and fallen in the mud like she had no care for her appearance.

She had pulled him from the river and had not run away screaming when he threw up, half drowned and bleeding.

He needed to talk about something to distract himself from how soft her hand felt.

"You are still planning to sing for us at the Harvest Festival, are you not?"

"I don't think it would be a good idea."

"King Richard is unlikely to attend the Glynval Harvest Festival." He gave the words a wry tone. "And I will look out for you."

She gazed up at him. "Perhaps I do not sing as well as you think."

"You can practice on me and my family tonight."

She frowned. "You are very persistent."

"Yes, I am." He smeared the salve over her open blisters. "Besides, I know you sing beautifully. I've heard you sing twice now."

"Ah yes, you did. What is in this salve? It smells like honey and herbs."

"That is what it is, mostly. Honey and comfrey. My mother has used it on many people. She even gives it to people to eat if they have stomach problems." Better to talk of disgusting things so he could keep his thoughts in line.

"I have not seen Sabina around here lately."

"She says she has been sick since she gave you those poison mushrooms. Perhaps she is ashamed to show her face here, or afraid the other servants are angry with her."

"Most people seem to believe it was an accident, that she did not intend to pick the poison ones."

"Do you believe that?"

"No. Although I would hate to falsely accuse her, especially since she helped me save you from the river. I suppose it is possible she did not intend to poison everyone or to have me accused of the deed. It is possible."

He rubbed over a particularly raw-looking spot on her palm and she sucked in a quick breath between her teeth.

"Forgive me." He dipped his finger in the sticky salve, applied it to both hands, then finished bandaging them.

"You seem to be good at everything, even bandaging servants' hands."

He studied her face. Now that he knew she was the granddaughter of a king, he couldn't help seeing her a bit differently. "I hope the king does not put me in a dungeon for making you work as a servant."

"I only mean that you seem so good at making everyone like you. All the servants think highly of you. They are not intimidated, but they respect you nevertheless."

"It is important to me that I earn my people's trust and loyalty, especially after the Peasants' Uprising. I don't want them to see me as a cruel master. And I don't want to be a cruel master. As Christians, we are all brothers and sisters."

She looked confused.

"There is a passage in the Bible that says, 'Masters, provide your slaves with what is right and fair, because you know that you also have a Master in heaven.' I imagine it works the same with villeins as it does with slaves."

She was so beautiful when she was thinking and staring at nothing. She creased her forehead in that thoughtful way of hers. "No wonder you are so loved by the people. And so disliked by the other lords."

Westley rubbed the back of his neck. "I always wanted to be like my father, but the truth is, I'm not like him. He often says wise things, and he is very intense and seems to know when mischief is afoot. If something is amiss, he knows what, why, and how to fix it." He stopped. Did he truly want Evangeline to know how incompetent he felt?

"Is that why you were so angry when I said John Underhill had tried to kill you?"

"What do you mean?"

"Well, if he tried to kill you and you thought he was still your friend . . ." Evangeline shrugged.

She understood better than she pretended. "You are reminding me of my father at this moment." He shook his head. "If I could not even see that my oldest friend hated me so much he wanted to kill me, well, how could I even be worthy of inheriting my father's lands and responsibilities?"

The confession left him hollow inside, but at the same time, it felt good to admit it.

"I am angry with myself for not seeing how much he has changed, how he hates me enough to murder me."

"How could you have known? It is nothing to blame yourself for."

"But how could I be so mistaken?"

"Perhaps it is because you are so kind, you could not imagine your own friend being so evil. You are a good man, Westley."

She looked intently at his face with those enchanting green eyes.

"Forgive me for not trusting you more. It seems I was mistaken again."

She smiled and squeezed his hand. "The fact that you admit your mistakes makes you even more admirable."

Her words seemed to fill an empty place inside him. How pretty she was—fragile and yet strong. His arms ached to hold her.

His father's cautionary words came to him. *"Be wise and guard your heart. You hardly know anything of this woman."*

But he did feel as if he knew her. Was his heart being deceptive? How could he know? He turned away from her before he acted on his impulse.

"I suppose we should read a little while before we have to get back to our duties."

Evangeline let go of his hand as she realized he wasn't going to put his arms around her. If Westley loved her enough to marry her, she might be safe. King Richard might not be willing to break their marriage vows and force her to marry Shiveley.

Foolish hope. And yet, the more she knew of him, the more she wanted to be close to him, to spend time with him, and the harder it was to imagine herself married to anyone else.

Truly, she was setting herself up for pain.

They read together from the book of Romans until the sun started to set and spread the clouds and sky with bright pink and orange.

Evangeline handed the book back to Westley. "I need to get back inside to help the other servants."

He was looking up at her with a worried crease in his forehead. "What is it?"

"It does not seem right for you to work as a servant."

"You know it is my disguise in case Lord Shiveley's or the king's men come around. They would not expect me to be working as a servant. Besides, if I lived in Glynval and did nothing, it would seem suspicious."

"I know. But it feels wrong."

She smiled. "Better to work as a servant than to marry someone I do not love."

"Do not forget you promised to practice your singing with my family tonight. Come to the Great Hall immediately after dinner."

"It will be my pleasure to sing for your family." But the thought of singing at the festival gave her an uneasy feeling in the pit of her stomach. Westley had said that only the people of the four nearby villages attended. She was being overly cautious, no doubt.

Chapter Twenty-One

Evangeline ate quickly. At every meal, she remained quiet around the other servants, ever since they thought she was trying to poison them and dragged her to the pillory. Though now she ate in a smaller room, with the few house servants who worked only in the castle.

As soon as Evangeline had finished, she left the table and went to see if Westley and his family were ready for her. But when she peeked through the doorway to their family table in the Great Hall, her stomach fluttered. She pressed her back against the wall and closed her eyes to pray.

"Eva?"

Westley stood staring at her. "What are you doing? Are you coming in to sing?" He touched her elbow and tugged gently.

"But I don't know what to sing."

"Sing that song you were singing to Mildred."

She nodded and let him lead her inside.

As she walked across the room with Westley, the others turned their heads.

Several children were seated at the table—six, since Westley had six brothers and sisters—and Lord and Lady le Wyse.

Lady le Wyse bestowed her with a welcoming smile. "We are so pleased you are willing to sing at the festival, my dear."

"Thank you." After feeling so incompetent at everything since she'd arrived in Glynval, she felt rather pleased at the thought of singing for the people who had welcomed her and allowed her to feel free for the first time in her life.

The children sat quietly watching her, as did Lord le Wyse. Westley sat on the bench, too, facing toward her.

"Do you need a stool? Would you like to sit?" Lady le Wyse asked.

"No, I thank you." Evangeline closed her eyes and took a deep breath. Preparing to sing, she let herself dwell on joyful and pleasant thoughts. The moment she realized Westley was still alive after drawing him out of the river . . . the moment she first hit the target with her arrow . . . being held in Westley's arms . . .

As Evangeline began to sing, pleasant memories of Glynval mingled with the pictures conjured up by the words of the song, a story about a shepherd boy and a goose girl falling in love and getting married in the springtime. Halfway through the song, she opened her eyes. The family was completely focused on Evangeline's face, including Westley, his mouth slack.

As soon as she finished, they all began to exclaim and talk at once. Westley smiled broadly and clapped his hands together. Lady le Wyse embraced her. The children were calling out, "Sing another! Sing another!"

When they all quieted, Lady le Wyse said, "I don't think I've ever heard more beautiful singing."

"I've never heard better," Lord le Wyse said. "If you do not win the contest at the festival, it will be an injustice."

"Thank you," Evangeline said, unable to stop smiling. It felt good to hear their praise, but seeing Westley's genuine smile was the best of all.

"Will you sing one more for us?" Lady le Wyse prompted.

Evangeline nodded, then closed her eyes to choose another song.

She finally thought of one, a lullaby she and Muriel sometimes sang together.

As she sang, even the youngest two, who could not have been more than eight or nine, gave her their rapt attention.

When she finished, they all reacted as before. Singing in front of an audience of Glynval's people would be much more rewarding than singing for a wealthy, privileged king and his equally wealthy, privileged retinue.

Evangeline was gradually getting to know the other house servants, but she missed Muriel and Nicola, whom she rarely saw now, as they did most of their work at the dairy and the kitchen.

When Sunday came again, Evangeline searched through the crowd of servants walking toward the Glynval Church until she spotted Muriel. She hurried toward her and the two women embraced, then continued on behind the others.

"Evangeline." Muriel's eyes were swimming in tears.

"What is it? Did something happen?"

Muriel's chin trembled. "You will have to forgive me, Evangeline, but I cannot stay here any longer. I am traveling back to Berkhamsted Castle with a group of men who are taking a load of cheeses to the castle."

Evangeline stared, trying not to let Muriel know how panicked her words made her.

"I'm not a servant, not the kind I have to be here. I want to go home." Tears streamed down Muriel's cheeks. "And I want you to come with me. Evangeline, think what you are giving up, what you sacrifice every day. Look at your hands. Are you not in pain? Why are you putting yourself through that? You could go home with me and live in luxury and at ease as Lord Shiveley's wife."

Tears formed in Evangeline's eyes at her friend's distress. "I cannot." They were both crying now.

"Are you so in love with Westley? Do you think you might be able to get him to marry you?"

"I . . . I don't know."

"If you think he will marry you, I could tell the king and Lord Shiveley that you died, and they would stop searching for you."

"Are you that miserable, Muriel? Is it truly so bad? I will ask Lady le Wyse to let you work with me in the castle. I think she would agree."

She shook her head, staring down at the road instead of at Evangeline. "I'm leaving. I have made up my mind."

"What if they don't believe you when you say I am dead? What if they force you to tell them the truth? Or ask you where my grave is so they can make sure?"

"I don't think they would."

"But what will you do when you go back to Berkhamsted? What if there is no place for you there?" Since Evangeline would be gone, she would have no one for whom to be a companion.

"I shall ask the king to take me into his household and give me a place there."

Evangeline could think of no other objections. "Are you sure you are willing to lie to the king?" Her insides trembled at the thought that Muriel might decide *not* to lie. After all, she thought Evangeline should return to Berkhamsted Castle and marry Lord Shiveley. Perhaps she'd tell them where Evangeline was, to ensure she had no real choice in the matter.

They were nearing the church. Evangeline caught hold of Muriel's arm. "Please don't leave."

"You only want me to stay so you will not be found out. But I hate it here."

"Why? Is someone mistreating you? I will do something to stop them."

"No, it isn't that. I just . . . I am homesick. I . . . I miss someone."

"Who?" Who could she mean?

"Frederick, the stable master."

Evangeline stopped and stared. "The one whose wife died a year ago?"

Muriel nodded.

"Why did you never tell me?"

"You are young. And I suppose . . . I was a bit ashamed of myself."

Evangeline waited for her to continue.

"He is below my station. And I . . . I knew you would not approve."

"Why would I not approve? Look at me. I am working as a servant, cleaning hearths, making food, and emptying slop buckets in the pigsty."

Muriel wiped the tears with the backs of her hands. "You know how I always said falling in love before marriage was something only peasants did, that falling in love was low and common. It was prideful of me. My foolish pride . . . Perhaps that's why he hasn't asked me to marry him. But when I go back, I vow I will not care. I will ask his forgiveness for thinking he was not good enough to marry, and I will marry him—if he will have me."

Evangeline had never thought about Muriel getting married, or even imagined her falling in love before. But she loved Muriel and wanted her to enjoy her life, not to be miserable. Evangeline threw her arms around her. "I am so pleased for you, Muriel."

"But I am afraid. What if King Richard disapproves? Is it selfish for me to get married?"

"No, not at all. After your service to King Richard all these years, you deserve to marry whomever you want." Evangeline squeezed her arm. "Come, let us go into church before someone comes looking for us."

They went inside and stood near the back of the nave, listening to the plainsong hymn. Evangeline's mind wandered. What was to happen to her? Could Muriel persuade Lord Shiveley and King Richard that she was dead and to call off their search for her? Surely the earl did not want to marry her that much. He could find someone else, another relative of the king's, though perhaps more distantly related, to marry.

Muriel had asked her if she thought Westley would marry her. She was afraid to even hope for such a thing. Westley was free and wealthy. He could marry anyone he wanted, or no one at all. Why would he marry her? He'd caught her in a blatant lie, pretending she couldn't speak. She'd also accused his best friend of trying to kill him. Why would he ever want to marry her?

She *had* saved his life. But she could offer no proof that she was telling the truth.

She tried to force her mind to concentrate on the priest's words, but her thoughts were scattered. Muriel was to leave her.

Perhaps it would be better for everyone if Evangeline left Glynval. If she moved on to another village, then Muriel could have a clear conscience by telling the king the truth about where she was. Evangeline would simply have to leave when no one else was watching so no one would know where she had gone. That would involve leaving at night, with no escort to protect her.

But she knew how to protect herself now. She could use a longbow, she was learning how to throw a knife, and she knew how to fight back if someone attacked her. Still, Reeve Folsham had warned her that she might prove to be no match for a man who was determined to harm her. And if there was more than one man, it would be even more difficult. She had to rely on surprising them, hitting them quickly, then running away and screaming for help. Unless she was able to use a weapon, of course.

She was only half listening to the priest's homily when his words caught her attention. "Jesus carried your sins to the cross. Why, O man, do you insult the Lord God by continuing to carry the burden of your sin? Lay your burden down."

When the church service was over and everyone began filing out, Evangeline whispered to Muriel, "I want to be alone for a few moments to pray."

Muriel nodded and left with the others.

Evangeline moved into the corner of the nave, into the shadows. When everyone was gone, including the priest, Evangeline went to the place where she had carved into the stone wall at the back of the church. She traced the words *Absolve me* with her fingers, then traced the three crosses underneath. "I can't bear this awful feeling of guilt," she whispered. It was as if she carried a tree trunk on her shoulders.

But Jesus took that guilt away when He sacrificed Himself. Wouldn't He feel hurt to know she was refusing to lay it down? That she was still carrying it?

"I believe You took my sin, and I am forgiven."

Air filled her lungs, and she felt so light she might have lifted up to the ceiling. "Thank You, God."

She waited until the feeling passed, then she whispered, "What will happen to me, God?" She placed her finger on the middle cross. "I'm afraid to ask." She closed her eyes and Westley's face loomed before her mind's eye. "Is it a sin, God? To ask for Westley's love?"

A tear slid down her cheek. "I won't ask You to make him love me. He should have the freedom to choose whom he wants. But I'm all alone, God. I need . . ." What did she need? A friend? A husband?

Disquiet filled her heart at the thought of asking for either. It didn't seem right to *need* a person.

"I need an all-powerful God who cares for me. I need You." Her spirit quieted within her. "You'll never leave me or forsake me, and I'll always trust You. I know I'll be safe with You in my heart. I'll not fear the terror of night, nor the arrow that flies by day."

Her tears dried on her cheeks. She would miss Muriel, and she did not know what would be her fate, but somehow the fear and guilt and pain were so weak and faint, they no longer oppressed her spirit. She was at peace.

Eight days later, Evangeline awakened to Muriel standing over her, shaking her shoulder.

She held a burning candle, which spread just enough light to illuminate Muriel's face in the darkness of the predawn. "I wanted to bid you farewell," she whispered.

Evangeline sat up and hugged her friend. "I will pray for you."

"And I you."

After a few more whispered words, Muriel disappeared, leaving with three of Glynval's men carting a load of cheeses to Berkhamsted Castle.

Evangeline lay awake until it was time to get up, thinking about Muriel, praying for her, and praying Shiveley would give up and stop searching for her.

Later in the day, Evangeline was taking all the linen sheets off the beds and bringing them down to be washed. When she walked out the back door, Sabina sat beside the washtub talking with the servants who were doing the wash.

Evangeline's stomach clenched and heat boiled up inside her.

She pretended not to see her. The last time she'd seen Sabina was the night when she gave her the poison mushrooms to put in the pottage. All the emotions from that night rushed over her, sending her heartbeat into a strange rhythm.

"Good morning, Evangeline," Sabina said, smirking.

"Good . . ." Evangeline let her voice trail off. She could not in good conscience tell Sabina she wished her a good morning.

"What's the matter? You aren't mute again, are you?"

Several of the other maidens giggled.

Evangeline dumped the sheets on the ground and turned to leave.

"Oh, don't go away like that," Sabina called after her. "You are not still angry with me about the mushrooms, surely." She ended her words with a laugh.

Evangeline turned back and said, "Next time you pick mushrooms, I hope you eat them." She walked away to the snickers of the other servants, hurrying before Sabina could say anything else.

When Evangeline was on her way back outside to take the last of the linens, Westley stepped out of one of the rooms along the corridor.

"Sabina is back today, I see. I can send her away if you wish."

"No, no. I will not allow her to bother me. I did not do anything wrong. She is the one who should be uncomfortable." Evangeline brushed past him.

"Wait." Westley touched her arm. "Let me see your hands. Come into the light." He pulled her toward a window. She placed her hands in his, palms up.

"You aren't covering them."

"I can get more work done with them uncovered. They are nearly healed now."

"I don't want you letting them get worse again."

"They need to toughen up, don't you think? If I am to be a servant for the rest of my life, I need tough hands."

He was still holding her hands in his as he stared into her eyes. There was a serious, sad expression on his face. He said softly, "You were never meant to be a servant."

"But I can work. I can be free and . . . do what I like." Only if she could manage to stay free from the king and Lord Shiveley.

And only if Muriel would not tell them where she was.

"Besides, we are all meant to be servants of the Most High God. Even you."

Westley smiled. "Yes. Even me." He suddenly let go of her hands. "Tomorrow is the first day of the festival, when you are to sing."

Evangeline sucked in a deep breath. "I am ready."

Even if the worst happened, she was at peace.

Chapter Twenty-Two

Evangeline sat on a stool at the back of the castle and closed her eyes as Nicola prepared her long, wavy hair by adding tiny braids and weaving wildflowers into the plaits. Lastly, she pinned a crown of white flowers on top of her head.

Nicola handed her the small looking glass. Evangeline gasped. "How did you get it to curl so perfectly?" Normally her hair was wild and unruly. Somehow Nicola had calmed her hair into perfect ringlets, with tiny braids interspersed. "It's beautiful. You have a special talent for hair dressing."

"Thank you very much." Nicola curtsied, smiling. "And now I can hardly wait to hear you sing."

Evangeline placed a hand over her stomach. "I don't know why I'm nervous. I have been singing every night with Lord and Lady le Wyse and their family."

"And have you been singing privately to Westley?" Nicola winked at her.

"No, I have not."

"I have heard that the two of you can be seen sitting alone together every day just before the evening meal."

"We are reading."

"Reading? Has he kissed you?"

"No."

"Why don't you kiss him?"

"I cannot do that." Evangeline gave Nicola her best horrified look. The thought, in truth, did not horrify her much at all.

Evangeline straightened the belt around her hips. "Westley is an honorable young man. He does not go around kissing girls."

"Perhaps if you kissed him, it might help him make up his mind."

"Make up his mind about what?"

"About whether he should kiss you, whether he should marry you."

"Why would he want to marry me?" Evangeline turned away from Nicola and bent to put on her shoes, then reached for her overdress.

"Because you are beautiful. You know how to read. You apparently come from a wealthy family."

"A wealthy family?"

"It is obvious, Eva. You don't know how to perform the ordinary tasks that any other girl would have been doing since she was six years old. But you know how to read." She gave Evangeline a pointed look.

Evangeline's heart suddenly ached to tell Nicola her whole story, ached for a deeper friendship with another girl her age. But wouldn't that put Nicola in danger?

"I did have an unusual upbringing," Evangeline finally said. "I was an orphan and my guardian kept me a prisoner, you might say. He wanted me to marry someone I didn't want to marry, and I ran away."

"Why didn't you want to marry him? Was he rich?"

"Yes."

"But he was old and ugly?"

"Yes."

Nicola shook her head and sighed. "I would have done the same." She stepped toward Evangeline and helped her on with her overdress. Then she made some adjustments to her hair. "And now, if you can get Westley to marry you, you will not have to marry that other person." She smiled.

Even if she were married to Westley, Lord Shiveley could have her marriage annulled, could steal her away and have the king "make amends" to Westley and his family. But now that she had her newly learned skills of defending herself, he would not find her an easy conquest. She would literally fight him at every turn if she had to.

"You look beautiful in this dress." Nicola stepped back to look at her. "The green brings out your eyes, and when you are singing at the festival, Westley will forgive you for when you pretended to be mute. Perhaps he will even kiss you at the festival."

"Let us not speak about me anymore." Evangeline's cheeks burned. "Westley can kiss whomever he wishes. What about you, Nicola? Do you have a sweetheart?"

"My sweetheart died last winter."

Evangeline covered her mouth with her hand. "Oh, Nicola. What happened?"

"He was a poor villein, only seventeen—we both were. He caught a cold that went into his chest. He lived for two weeks, barely able to breathe, and then he died." Tears puddled under her eyes. "I almost never talk about it."

"I am so sorry. I did not mean to cause you more pain."

"No, no." She shook her head as she wiped her face with her apron. "It is good for me to speak of it sometimes, I think. No one ever wants to speak of it. Probably they don't want to see me cry again. But the pain . . . It doesn't seem to get any better. My mother tells me I shall love again, but . . . I can't imagine it."

Evangeline suddenly felt selfish and thoughtless. She was so absorbed with her own problems, she had not thought to even ask Nicola about her life.

"But I don't want you to think about me today." Nicola sniffed and seemed to force a smile. "Today you can make me very happy if I can hear you sing, see you win the contest, and then hear tomorrow that Westley has kissed you and declared his love for you."

Evangeline shook her head. "You are teasing me."

"Not a bit. Now, let us go or you will be late, and then I shall have to tell Westley that it was my fault, and I don't want his wrath falling on me."

Evangeline hugged Nicola. "I am sorry for what you have suffered, Nicola."

"It is the way of this world, as the priest told me. Life is fleeting."

"But it was a cruel thing to have happen." Evangeline looked down into her friend's eyes. "I wish it had not happened to you."

"Thank you, Eva." She hugged her back. "Now, let us be going."

They hurried out and found Reeve Folsham waiting for them. "Ready?"

They nodded and walked with him to the far meadow. People crowded the road as they were all walking that way. Colorful booths were set up all around the outside edge of the open space. People were pressing in on every side. Evangeline had never seen so many people in one place. Nicola greeted three young maidens who smiled and hugged her, while Reeve Folsham pushed his way through toward the stage that had been built at one end.

Evangeline stayed near him, losing Nicola in the crowd. The reeve inquired of some people who were standing nearby, then turned to her. "They will not begin the singing contest for several more hours." His brow creased as he put his hand on her shoulder, as if to make sure she didn't go anywhere while he looked all around the big meadow area, now teeming with people. "I think you'll be safe if you stay in the crowd and don't leave this area."

Evangeline nodded. But she swallowed, even as she noticed all the strangers—men, women, and children—jostling each other and her. Her stomach clenched as she remembered being dragged outside among all the servants who thought she'd tried to poison them.

But nothing was going to happen. Reeve Folsham would be nearby. Westley should be somewhere not too far. Evangeline stood for a moment, looking for an opening so she could see what the people were selling. She'd never been to a festival, or even a market fair, except when she went with Muriel on the second day of their trip to Glynval.

Evangeline moved toward the closest booth where a woman was selling buns. "Get them while they're still hot," she called. Evangeline had some coins in her purse, which was attached to her belt. She drew one out and gave it to the woman, who smiled and handed her a bun. "Enjoy it."

She checked over her shoulder to make sure the reeve was still where she had left him. He was, so she moved to the next booth. A man was selling leather purses with a burn etching of flowering vines, and some had decorative stitching in the shape of animals. Hanging from his booth were also large saddlebags, as well as some thick leather vests and mantles—protective gear for hunters.

"My wife makes the designs." The man pointed to the swirling vines burned into some of the bags.

Evangeline smiled and nodded. They were beautiful, but she had no need of a bag or leather armor. She moved on to the next booth. She continued looking around, occasionally seeing some other servant she recognized, but no one talked to her. She moved about without attracting much attention, and she soon felt at ease.

The next booth she came to was at the edge of a stand of trees. It was full of candles, some of them with bits of aromatic herbs or flowers—little stalks of lilac, lavender, and rosemary—pressed into the wax. Evangeline picked up the lavender one and sniffed—it smelled just like Westley's shirts. Her eyes fluttered closed.

Suddenly someone stepped around her, pushing her aside with his body. Immediately hands came in front of her face, covering her mouth and nose, and her feet left the ground.

She tried to fight back, but her wrists were pinned behind her back and a rough hemp sack was yanked over her head. She was carried like a flour sack, her head lower than her body.

She tried to draw in a breath, but the dusty bag clung to her mouth, and the stale air inside it choked her. She could not draw in enough air to scream. Instead, she concentrated on just breathing in enough air so she would not faint.

Several people had hold of her. Was no one looking when these people grabbed her? Were these Lord Shiveley's men? Was she being taken back to Berkhamsted Castle?

She kicked and writhed and fought, but it availed her nothing. They only walked faster, holding her waist so tight it hurt. Someone else must have had hold of her feet inside a narrow bag, preventing her from kicking out very far.

"What you got there?" A muffled voice came to her from somewhere nearby.

"A sow and her piglets," said the gruff voice without slowing down.

Evangeline's arms were burning and she could barely breathe. She felt herself fading, losing consciousness. She was being carried down some stone steps, then lowered to the ground. Someone snatched the bag off her head, ran up the steps, and slammed a heavy door shut.

Evangeline gulped in air, pushing herself up off the cold stone floor. It was quite dark, but there was just enough light for her to see buckets, two stools, and a few butter churns in the small open room. She was in the dairy, where they stored the milk and where she and Nicola had churned butter.

She rubbed her wrists, finding they were not tied together as she had assumed. Someone must have been holding them while they carried her.

She sat up and wriggled out of the rough hemp bag, pushing it off her legs and feet. She wiped her face with her hands, trying to get off the dust from the bag that still clung to her skin.

Why had Shiveley's men thrown her in here? Why had they not slung her over a horse and rode her out of Glynval as quickly as possible?

She got to her feet. Her knees wobbled, but she ran up the stone steps, stumbling a bit as she reached the top. She grabbed the door handle, but it would not budge. She jerked and tugged, but it still would not open.

Evangeline stood on the tips of her toes to reach the tiny open space at the top of the heavy wooden door, the only source of light in the room. With her unusual height, she was just tall enough to see out. Some men were walking away, and one of them was John Underhill.

Was he planning to hurt Westley? Why had he attacked her? Perhaps because he knew she was a witness to what he had done to Westley, but it was strange that he had not hurt her. Would he come back and kill her? And was he now on his way to kill Westley?

Westley! She had to get to him, had to warn him.

"Hey, Eva, can you hear me?" Sabina's taunting voice came from outside.

"Sabina, let me out of here."

"How did you find yourself in there?" Sabina giggled.

"Some men threw me in here. Can you please let me out?"

"Oh, I don't think I will."

Evangeline's stomach sank and her face burned. Her mind raced as Sabina continued to speak.

"I thought I wanted to marry Westley le Wyse. Everyone knew I wanted to marry him."

Sabina must have been standing off to the side because Evangeline could not see her through the tiny window.

"And I always get what I want. But when you came and Westley looked at you the way I wanted him to look at me, I could not let him make a fool of me."

Evangeline leaned against the door. What was it Reeve Folsham had taught her? She stared hard at the bottom of the steps, looking for something she could use as a weapon. Sabina continued talking, but Evangeline hardly heard her as she ran down the steps and found a heavy pottery churn. She took out the paddle and the lid and threw them on the floor, then carried the heavy churn up the steps.

"Westley is not so saintly as everyone thinks. John Underhill told me how he always speaks ill of his father, Hugh Underhill. He blames Westley's father for his father's death. But either way, John is the one who has what I want—the will to gain the most wealth, the most land, and the most power."

Evangeline raised the heavy churn over her head, then brought it down as hard as she could on the handle of the door. The churn fell to the stone step and broke into several pieces, but the handle also broke off and lay among the broken pottery pieces.

She pushed the door open, still holding on to the largest piece of the broken churn, and thrust it into Sabina's face.

Sabina's eyes widened and she screamed. Evangeline charged at her with the giant piece of broken pottery and used it to shove her to the ground, the broken edge near her throat. Sabina screamed again.

Evangeline fell to the ground beside Sabina and used her knee to press down on the pottery and Sabina's chest. She grabbed Sabina's hands and pinned them down on either side of her head. The pressure on Sabina's throat halted her screaming.

"Where are they? Where were they taking Westley?"

Sabina's face was turning red and her mouth and eyes were wide open. Evangeline eased up on the pressure to her chest. Sabina sucked in a gulp of air.

"Tell me now or I'll—"

"They were taking him to the woods"—she gasped for air again—"behind the meadow."

"If you're lying to me . . ."

Sabina shook her head, her face a cloudy white now instead of red.

Evangeline left the broken pottery on top of Sabina as she stood. She ran as fast as she could to the oat barn, then she barreled out of the barn with her bow and arrows.

The reeve rushed toward her. "Where did you—?"

"Westley is in trouble! John Underhill is here. I think he intends to kill him."

Reeve Folsham turned, and they both raced toward the meadow.

Chapter Twenty-Three

Westley and his father spoke with some of the traveling minstrels they had hired. When they had arranged for them to stay through the evening to entertain the crowd and had decided on a fair wage, he headed to the meadow where Evangeline and the others were supposed to sing. He wanted to make sure the stage his men had just built was holding up well.

Westley plunged into the crowd but could see neither Evangeline nor Reeve Folsham, who was supposed to keep watch over her. Nicola was nearby, talking to another servant at a booth selling silk scarves. He took a step toward her, and a tall burly man stepped in front of him. Something sharp stuck into his back and a voice behind him said, "We have Eva. If you don't come with us, we will kill her."

Westley clenched his teeth as a hand clamped down on his arm and turned him away from the crowd. The two men pressed in close on either side of him, as if trying to hide him from view, as they guided him toward the trees.

"Who are you?" Westley ground out.

"Just keep walking."

The knife point pressed harder into his side. If it was only the one man and his knife, Westley would risk grabbing the knife handle and wrenching it from him. But since there were two men and Westley had no weapon of his own, he would wait for a better opportunity.

First he needed to find out where they were keeping Evangeline.

John Underhill and a few of his men stood in the middle of the trees. John's face and eyes bore a dark look that was never there when they were children. Even his lips looked thinner, giving him a harder, colder expression.

"John. Why are you doing this?"

"Don't pretend you don't know." The sneer on his face transformed him even more into someone Westley had never seen before.

"What have you done with Eva?"

"My father was right and you were wrong all those years ago." John stomped closer, sticking his finger in Westley's face. "He knew we were too soft on the villeins and servants, and they would turn against us. But you said that was not true. You said the better we treated them, the better off we would all be. And then it was not half a year later that they slaughtered my father.

"Then when my father was not even cold yet, your father was giving out extra food to the peasants, paying them wages for work they had always done for us as an obligation." John lowered his finger but snarled, lifting his top lip like an animal. "My father always said, 'If you don't take control of the villeins, if you don't weigh them down with more work than they can do, then they will take control.' And he was right."

"I'm sorry your father was killed, John. No one, least of all me or my father, would ever have wanted that to happen. We would have done anything to prevent it."

"You didn't care about my father. He always said you were too soft. He didn't even want me to play with you as a child, but I believed my father was wrong. I would sneak away and go fishing with you. I listened to you, but my father was right and you were wrong."

Westley tried to remember those conversations. "Your father loved you, John, and you loved him. That is a good thing. God would not—"

"Shut your mouth! Don't talk about my father, and don't talk to me about God!" John stabbed his finger at Westley's face and spittle flew out of his mouth as he yelled, "You were wrong, and now I want you to admit it. Admit you were wrong!"

Madness seemed to shine out of his bloodshot eyes. A dark vein in his neck bulged as if ready to explode; another swollen purple vein at his temple throbbed.

"You and Lord le Wyse killed my father. With all your softness and talk of all men being equal in God's eyes. You filled the villeins with these notions, and they rose up and killed my father. And I blame you."

"Then why are you trying to hurt Eva? What did she do?"

"I was only using her to lure you here. But if she doesn't do as I say . . ." He curled his lip again. "She must have seen me when I pushed you in the river. I wasn't planning to kill you. You just made me so angry. But now . . . You will admit you were wrong about the villeins, that your father was wrong, and that my father was right."

"Sabina must have been lying."

"I didn't know Sabina then." He actually smiled. "But when I explained to her that you are not the perfect man everyone thinks you are, she told me she was sorry she ever helped that other girl save you. Now she wants to be my wife." His smile grew wider.

"When did you become so full of hatred?"

"What I am full of is justice and truth. I want justice for my murdered father, and I want you to say that he was right, about everything."

"So, will you hit me in the head and push me in the river again?" The knife was still pressing in between his ribs, but he was trying to buy some time.

"I should kill you the same way they killed my father—with a knife through the chest and beaten with sticks until his face was unrecognizable."

Westley glanced around. He had to make a move soon. But the oaf beside him tightened his grip on his arm. John pulled out his own knife and held it up to Westley's nose.

His stomach twisted. How would he get out of this?

Suddenly a high-pitched yell split the air. They all turned around to see Evangeline holding a bow and arrow aimed at the man behind John. She let the arrow fly.

The man screamed. "She shot me!"

Just as suddenly, the man on his left grunted and fell face-forward into the ground, his knife still clutched in his hand.

The man to Westley's right, with a block of wood in his hand, suddenly disappeared behind Westley's back. Scuffling, like two people fighting, ensued behind him.

Seeing the shock on John's face, Westley tried to snatch his knife away. But John did not let go, and they both struggled for control of the weapon.

Westley was slightly taller, and he used his height to push down on the knife handle, pushing it toward John's forehead and forcing him backward so far he fell to the ground on his back. Westley pinned his left hand to the ground while he pounded and squeezed John's right hand until he knocked the knife loose.

_____

Evangeline aimed her next arrow at the man's left shoulder and let it fly. The arrow struck him just where she aimed it.

The man screamed and grabbed at the arrow shaft. "I'm killed!" He stared at her, then roared like a bear. He started toward her, and she tried to snatch another arrow from the leather pouch at her hip. Her fingers fumbled and nearly dropped it. Finally, fitting it to the string, she pulled it taut and aimed at the man's chest.

His eyes bulging, he stared at the arrow.

"You should go get that shoulder bandaged." Her voice was surprisingly even.

The man backed away, his left arm hanging limply at his side.

Evangeline kept her arrow nocked. The man Reeve Folsham had attacked first was lying on the ground, still not moving. The reeve had been struggling with the other man, but he suddenly slammed his fist into the man's temple and he sunk to his knees, then fell forward.

Westley seemed to have overcome John Underhill as well. They were on the ground with Westley holding his wrists.

Evangeline ran over, aiming her arrow at John's chest.

Westley let go of John's wrists, snatched up the knife lying on the ground, and stood. "Very impressive, Evangeline."

"You did well too."

He looked back at Reeve Folsham. "Thank you, old friend. The two of you saved my life."

"Eva found out from Sabina where they were taking you. You should thank her."

He turned his sky-blue eyes on her. One corner of his mouth quirked up. "I will."

A few people burst through the bushes and trees toward them. Reeve Folsham sent a couple of men to find some of Lord le Wyse's strongest men to help secure John and his henchmen and escort, drag, or carry them, as the case warranted, back to the castle where they would be locked in one of the outbuildings.

Westley, Reeve Folsham, and Evangeline kept watch over their foes—Westley with John's knife, the reeve with his block of wood, and Evangeline with her bow and arrow aimed and ready. When help returned, more people came with them, asking what happened.

Westley tried to answer their questions as briefly as possible.

Some of them left to follow and heckle the prisoners. In the chaos Westley took Evangeline's bow and arrow from her, gave them to Reeve Folsham, and clasped her hand.

She followed him away from the crowd while the reeve tried to get everyone to go back to the festival and enjoy themselves.

Westley led her to the clearing where he'd first heard her sing, the place where he'd discovered she'd been deceiving him about being mute.

He faced her, holding on to her arms and standing quite close. "Thank you for saving me, both today and when you saved me from drowning. John confirmed that it wasn't Sabina." He took both her hands in his. "I'm sorry I didn't believe you. Will you forgive me?"

"Of course I forgive you. I cannot blame you for not believing me."

He was beautiful. After she had heard that John Underhill was going to kill him, her whole body exploded with strength. She assaulted Sabina and held her on the ground. She shot an arrow that could have killed a man and did wound him in the shoulder. She had not even been afraid, because she was too furious that anyone would try to hurt Westley.

"Did John's men hurt you?" he asked. "Or was he lying about capturing you?"

"I am not hurt, but they grabbed me and put something over my head and carried me to the dairy." Her heart pounded and her knees went weak as she recalled it. "They left me at the bottom of the stairs, and I . . . I broke the door handle with a churn. I'm sorry, but you will have to repair the door."

His arms enfolded her, pulling her close. She pressed her cheek against his, her height a perfect match for his. He only had to lean down a bit.

He squeezed her shoulder. "I'm so sorry they did that to you. But . . . you amaze me," he said softly, stroking her shoulder.

"Did they hurt you?" Evangeline closed her eyes, memorizing the way it felt to embrace him, his arms around her . . . warm and solid and comfortable . . . the way he smelled . . . like lavender and fresh air and Westley.

"No, I am well," he said, his breath warm on her neck, "now that I know you are well. And later I shall think more about how much I want to punish those men for laying hands on you."

Do not think about that now. Just think about what I'm thinking about, which is how much I want you to kiss me.

"Evangeline?" His deep voice rumbled next to her ear.

"Yes?"

"I don't want you to work as a servant anymore."

"Why not? What shall I do?"

"You are the king's cousin."

"Perhaps your mother would allow me to do some mending. I embroider very well, and I imagine mending would not be so different from embroidery."

He leaned back and gazed intently into her eyes, an unhurried searching, before saying, "Are you sure you aren't hurt?"

"I am sure." Why didn't he kiss her? She might just kiss him. Nicola would applaud her, but what would Westley think? Kissing him was no different from Ruth uncovering Boaz's feet. But would he react to her the way Boaz reacted to Ruth? The uncertainty kept her lips six inches from his.

"Westley?"

Evangeline pulled away and turned around. Westley's sister Cate approached them.

"There you are. Mother is very worried and wants you to come to the castle right away. Both of you." Cate raised her brows at them, a half smile on her lips.

Evangeline started after his younger sister, but Westley stayed her with a hand to her shoulder. He bent and brushed his lips against her temple. After squeezing her hand, he started walking behind Cate.

Her heart fluttered and she squeezed back.

"What were you two doing out here by yourselves?" Cate asked with a backward glance.

"Talking," Westley said.

As they emerged onto the road, people stared at them, but Westley seemed to purposely avoid making eye contact as he hurried toward the castle. One called out a question about whether someone was trying to kill Westley. He simply shook his head, smiled, and waved as he kept up his fast pace. Evangeline followed beside him.

People were staring at their joined hands. Westley would have a lot of questions to answer—when he slowed down long enough to hear them.

Lady le Wyse was waiting for them in front of the castle. "I am so relieved to see you both! Your father is questioning John and his men. I hope they did not harm either of you."

"We are well." Westley let go of Evangeline's hand to embrace his mother. "Neither of us are hurt."

Lady le Wyse reached for his side near his waist. "Then what is this blood on your shirt?"

Chapter Twenty-Four

Evangeline gasped at the circular red stain about the size of a fist that had soaked through Westley's white linen tunic. His mother pulled his shirt up to show a small wound in his side.

"Mother, please. It is nothing." Westley pulled his shirt out of her grasp and back down over his stomach.

"Come inside then. I must put something on that."

As they followed her inside, he gave Evangeline an apologetic look.

"Your mother is right. Let her take care of it."

"What happened?" Lady le Wyse led the way into her small room where she kept the bandages and her homemade remedies.

"John's man stuck me with his knife."

Evangeline and his mother gasped at the same moment.

"Nothing more than a scratch. A prick of the knife point while he was forcing me to walk with him into the woods. It is not as if he stabbed me through my liver."

Westley laughed, but neither Evangeline nor Lady le Wyse even smiled.

His mother ordered him to sit on the stool in the middle of the room, and Evangeline hovered close where she could see. Lady le Wyse lifted his tunic, exposing his side and a swath of his lean stomach as she peered down at the wound. "Hold this," she said, and Westley took the hem of his tunic from her, holding it up so she could see.

"It is not very deep," his mother said.

"I told you," Westley muttered.

"Evangeline, get me that jar there, will you?" Lady le Wyse pointed to a shelf behind her.

Evangeline fetched the container. Lady le Wyse finished wiping the blood from the wound, which seemed to have almost stopped bleeding.

As his mother smeared the healing salve on the small puncture wound in his side, Evangeline said softly, "I'm so sorry I didn't even notice you were bleeding."

"It is nothing." Westley gave her a jaunty half smile. Evangeline's stomach flipped.

Lady le Wyse took up a roll of cloth and wrapped it twice around his middle. "It should heal without much more bleeding, but it is difficult to tell with puncture wounds, since I don't know how deep it is."

"Thank you, Mother. I'm sure it will be fine. Evangeline will think this is too much fuss over a little knife prick. She is so tough herself—working all day every day with bleeding hands."

"My hands are not bleeding anymore." She smiled back at him as his mother took the shears from her and cut off the bandage, then handed them back to Evangeline and tied the bandage in place.

"There." Lady le Wyse stared at him, then blinked rapidly.

"Mother, please, do not cry. I am very well, as you can see."

"But you were nearly killed." She placed her hand over her mouth.

"There, now." Westley looked a bit awkward as he stood and embraced his mother, patting her shoulder. "I don't think John would have actually killed me."

"He would have left you in the river to drown."

"Yes, but Evangeline will not allow anyone to kill me, you see." He pulled away from his mother and gave Evangeline another jaunty smile and a wink. "We are both safe as long as we have each other."

"And Reeve Folsham," she added.

Lady le Wyse turned to Evangeline and threw her arms around her. "Yes, thank you, my dear. You are our guardian angel. I could not bear it if anything happened to Westley."

Nor could I. "I am only grateful I was able to help. God guided me, no doubt."

"Of course." Lady le Wyse sniffed, drew out a handkerchief, and dabbed at her eyes. "God is merciful and has kept us all safe once again. Forgive me, my dear. I am just a bit overcome at the thought of someone trying to harm my son."

"Of course. There is nothing to forgive."

"Come, come," Westley said, his voice loud as he laid one arm around each woman's shoulder. "This is a strange way to spend the Harvest Festival. Let us go and enjoy ourselves."

Lady le Wyse clasped Evangeline's hand and looked into her eyes, her gaze at once penetrating and kind. "Thank you," she whispered.

"Mother . . ."

"Very well. Go on." She took a few steps away from them. "I must check on my youngest son and daughter upstairs, and all three of us will be there soon."

Westley was already holding Evangeline's hand again, heading toward the door.

"See you at the singing contest," Westley said as they left the room.

"I nearly forgot." Evangeline put a hand over her mouth.

"Forgot you will be singing this evening?"

"Yes."

"I should get some food in you so you don't faint on the stage."

Evangeline laughed. "I won't faint. I have sung for—" She stopped herself.

They seemed to be alone as they walked through the castle

toward the front door, but she still did not think it wise to make any indiscreet announcements.

As they reached the door, Westley stopped and whispered near her ear, "You sang for the king. Is that what you were about to say?"

"Yes."

"Evangeline." He moved to stand in front of her, the smile gone from his face. "I know you are far above me in social status. You are the granddaughter of a king and King Richard's cousin, but do you think you could—?"

"Westley! There you are." Lord le Wyse started toward them from the other end of the corridor.

Westley seemed reluctant to tear his gaze from hers and glance at his father. Evangeline turned to face him as well.

"We must discuss what to do with John Underhill. He is making all sorts of threats. And when the men from Caversdown hear we have their lord locked away . . ."

"They might come and demand we set him free."

"At the very least," Lord le Wyse answered.

They stood talking over the possibilities while Evangeline listened. It was Lord le Wyse's responsibility as the local lord to deal with lawbreakers, but John was also a lord, making it a more complicated situation. When they mentioned taking him to Berkhamsted Castle in the hopes that King Richard would still be there to hear the accusations against him, Evangeline felt her stomach dive like a swallow after an insect. The king would surely find out that she was in Glynval.

Lord le Wyse seemed to notice her. He bowed. "Forgive me, Evangeline. I will let you and Westley enjoy the festival for now, but he and I need to make a decision by tonight." He turned to his son. "After the singing contest I want you back here."

"Yes, Father."

They hurried away, Westley's hand on her elbow as he ushered her away from the house.

"As I was saying." Westley cleared his throat. They were walking across the grassy area in front of the castle, headed back to the road that would take them to the meadow and the festival.

"Yes?"

"Would you ever consider marrying me, a man without a title, if it meant defying the king?"

"Yes. I would consider it."

Did he say what she thought he said? It was not exactly a proposal of marriage, but very nearly. Her insides seemed to go numb at the thought of being so close to her greatest wish coming true. They stared into each other's eyes.

"Westley! Eva!" A group of people, including his brothers and sisters and several townspeople and servants, approached them on the road.

"Where have you been?"

"We heard someone tried to kill you."

"Was it John Underhill?"

"Are you injured? What happened? What did he do?"

Westley said in her ear, "We will talk more of this later."

She squeezed his hand.

He smiled at the people surrounding them.

"Leave the poor young man alone," someone said. "Cannot you see he wants to spend time with the pretty maiden?"

Westley raised his voice to be heard over the crowd. "I am very well, thank you. The people who attacked me are being dealt with by my father. Now, please go back to enjoying the festival."

Someone else shouted, "The man is obviously not injured. Stand back and let him through."

Westley managed to work his way out of the crowd, and he and

Evangeline made their way toward the festival. Soon they were entering the area where the vendors were selling their wares, and jongleurs and minstrels were performing.

Westley bought some buns and some freshly roasted meat, and Evangeline walked beside him to the rear of the newly built stage. He pushed back the curtain that was strung over some rope between two trees, and they sat in between the two curtains, one at the back of the stage and the other at the front. They were alone.

"I thought I was dreaming when I saw you shoot that man with your arrow." He swallowed a gulp of ale from a flask he was sharing with Eva.

"Did you see Reeve Folsham knock that man out with a block of wood?"

"He's as big as a bear. The man's lucky the reeve did not break his neck."

"And the look on John's face?"

"When you held your arrow pointed at him—for the second time?"

They both laughed softly. Westley's hand brushed hers as she reached for the ale flask. She took a drink, letting her shoulder press against his as they sat side by side at the edge of the stage. She put down the flask, and Westley was staring at her.

"Will you miss Berkhamsted Castle? If you stay here with us?"

She shook her head.

"We cannot let anyone know who you really are. You can never see the king again. You will have to hide for the rest of your life."

"I do not mind."

He deliberately brushed her little finger with his.

"I like Glynval Castle better."

He leaned his head until it was touching hers. "Why?"

"I like the people who live there."

"All the people?"

"Yes."

"Is there any one in particular you like better?" He took one of her tiny braids that was lying on her shoulder and rolled it between his fingers.

"Yes."

"Who?"

"Lady le Wyse."

He dropped her braid and leaned away.

She laughed at his insulted expression. She reached out and took his hand. Then she looped her arm through his and laid her head on his shoulder. She sighed, her heart dancing inside her chest.

They sat together, holding hands and not saying anything. Evangeline did not want the moment to end, the feeling that Westley enjoyed being with her, that he liked her, that he was even thinking of marrying her.

He finally pulled away enough to gaze into her eyes. "Are you ready?"

"Ready?"

"To sing?"

Westley brushed her hair back from her eyes, then let his fingers trail down her cheek—and she was no longer thinking about singing. Her breathing shallowed. They were alone. No one was watching as his blue eyes focused on her lips.

He bent lower, his eyes nearly closing.

She lifted her hand and touched his face. Her stomach did a flip. He touched his lips to hers, and she pressed in closer, bringing her lips flush against his.

His hand on her cheek, he kissed her firmly and boldly, stealing every thought from her mind except how it felt to kiss Westley le Wyse.

Chapter Twenty-Five

*Evangeline's eyes fluttered open to see Westley's hand-*some face only inches from hers.

"You are the most beautiful archer in England. Thank you for saving my life. Again."

Pure, delicious joy welled up inside her as he pulled her into a tight embrace.

Westley thought she was beautiful! Westley *kissed her*. The only thing keeping her from floating up to the clouds was her arms around him.

"Where is Eva of Glynval?" a woman asked just before someone pulled the curtain aside.

"Yes?"

"It is almost time for the contest. The other singers are waiting in front of the stage. You shall be the second one to sing." The woman, whose eyes were as wide as her smile, turned and opened the front curtain the rest of the way.

Evangeline and Westley stood as the woman motioned with her hand to a young woman. They both climbed the three steps to the stage. Then the woman faced the crowd and announced, "Maud Waldgrave of Caversdown shall be our first singer. Our four judges here in front of the stage shall decide which of our singers shall be crowned the winner of the Harvest Festival singing contest."

The older woman left the stage and the young woman began to sing.

Westley and Evangeline stood in front of the stage. He kept hold of her hand, and she found herself completely unable to listen to the singer on the stage representing Caversdown village. All she could think about was Westley's kiss . . .

Suddenly the woman was motioning to Evangeline. Westley let go of her hand and nudged her forward. She hurried toward the woman and climbed the steps with her.

"And now we have Eva . . ." She paused, waiting for her to supply her surname. When she did not, the woman continued. "Eva of Glynval."

Evangeline turned to face the meadow full of people, some of them looking up at her, some talking or otherwise not paying attention to her. But a small group of people in front of the stage seemed to be attentively waiting for her to sing.

The woman left her all alone on the stage.

Evangeline was surprised not to feel nervous. Instead, her mind and senses were still filled with Westley's kiss. She closed her eyes for a moment.

She opened her eyes and started to sing the song she had planned, a song she had sung several times already to Westley and his family. She concentrated on the words and the sound coming out of her mouth as the buoyancy lingered. She even smiled as she sang.

When she finished the song, most of the people near the stage were smiling and clapping, while others all over the meadow had stopped to look at her. Some older people at the other end of the stage—perhaps they were the judges—put their heads together and were talking, nodding, and gesturing with their hands.

Westley smiled broadly. She caught sight of Lady le Wyse standing farther out in the crowd, smiling much like her handsome son. Lord le Wyse was probably dealing with his new prisoners.

Evangeline walked off the stage, practically skipping down the steps. Westley met her at the bottom. "You were wonderful." He took her hand. "You sing more beautifully than a songbird."

"You are flattering me."

He drew her hand through the crook of his arm and walked her into the crowd.

"My dear Eva!" Lady le Wyse was holding on to the hands of her two youngest children. "Your singing was the most beautiful! I cannot imagine anyone's voice as lovely as yours."

Evangeline impulsively hugged Lady le Wyse. The woman embraced her in return as if it were the most natural thing.

Later, after Lady le Wyse was occupied with talking to one of the other ladies who pulled Westley into the conversation, Evangeline suddenly had a thought. She turned to Westley. "Where is Sabina?"

"Sabina?"

"Yes. She was helping John Underhill. She taunted me after John's men locked me in the dairy and told me that John Underhill had taken you."

Westley's brow creased. "I don't know where she is. We did not see her when we captured John and his men. But I will tell Father and our men to look out for her."

"She boasted about marrying John. And she told me that John blamed you and your father for his father's death."

"His thinking is so warped. He isn't remembering his father the way he actually was." He stared past her shoulder, a dazed look in his eyes. "I suppose his father influenced him much more than I did, in the end."

Evangeline nodded. Who had influenced her? Muriel? The other servants and her early nursemaids? The priest at the castle, whom she had been inexplicably afraid of until a couple of years ago? She had no parents, and one of her nursemaids had abused her. What had that done to her thinking?

But she had also read her Psalter until she memorized it. Surely God was guiding her through those psalms. Her thinking could not be all bad with those scriptures in her head.

"I am sorry you lost a good friend, Westley."

"And I am sorry you were treated roughly by those vile men. I assure you, they shall be punished and will never hurt you again."

"I am safe now." She drew closer to him, and he put his arms around her. "And you are safe, and that's all that matters."

He kissed her temple.

Suddenly everything quieted around them. The woman who had led her onto the stage to sing now stood on the stage again.

"After hearing the five singers from each of the five villages who are participating in this festival, the judges have come to a decision. The winner of the singing contest is . . . Eva of Glynval."

The woman locked eyes with Evangeline and motioned for her to come up on the stage. The crowd parted for her as she made her way through. She kept hold of Westley's hand. He helped her up the steps but left her to go onstage without him.

Lady le Wyse presented her with a basket full of wares from the sellers at the festival, which included a scarf, candles, flowers, and several other items. Evangeline hugged her, and Lady le Wyse kissed her cheek.

Sabina stood on the ground below her, scowling up at her with a contemptuous curl of her lip, hate glaring out from under her lowered brows.

Evangeline smiled anyway, pretending not to see her as Lady le Wyse said, "You were wonderful. I'm very proud of you."

As Evangeline made her way back down the steps, Reeve Folsham approached Westley from behind with a grave look on his face. He leaned down and whispered near Westley's ear. Westley's smile disappeared, and she decided not to tell him just now that she had seen Sabina in the crowd.

Evangeline hurried toward them. Had John Underhill escaped? "What is it? What has happened?"

Reeve Folsham bowed to her. "Come and you will see."

Westley's blue eyes seemed serious. He asked someone to take her basket to the house for her, and they both followed the reeve out of the crowd.

They walked across the courtyard at the manor house to where a man stood watering his horse from a bucket. It was Frederick, the stable master, the man Muriel had said she was in love with.

He looked up and saw Evangeline. He immediately bowed his head and sank to one knee.

"Frederick." Evangeline prayed no one else saw him do this.

The steward and Lord le Wyse strode toward them, the lord's expression harsh and angry. Evangeline's heart sank. What would Lord le Wyse say when he learned that the king wanted her to marry the Earl of Shiveley? Or did he already know? Would he send her back with the stable master to prevent trouble from assailing his village?

"Lord le Wyse," Reeve Folsham said when they were all assembled. "This is Frederick, the stable master of Berkhamsted Castle. He has a message for us."

"Greetings, Lord le Wyse. Forgive me for interrupting your festival, but I came here to ask for your help, and also to warn you. Over a fortnight ago, the Earl of Shiveley accompanied King Richard on a visit to Berkhamsted. He planned to marry the king's ward, Evangeline." He glanced uncomfortably at her. "When she ran away with her companion, Muriel, whom you know as Mildred, the king and Lord Shiveley searched for them. Then a few days ago Muriel returned to the castle. Lord Shiveley tried to force her to tell where Evangeline was hiding. She told him Evangeline was dead but he did not believe her—and he threw her in the dungeon. He's been torturing her ever since."

"What?" Evangeline's hands clenched into fists. "Does the king know of this?"

"No. I tried to get word to the king, but the earl intercepted the message. I left before he could capture me and came here."

Evangeline's vision flitted and her face tingled as if she was about to faint. She held on to Westley's arm.

Frederick went on. "I believe the Earl of Shiveley planned to marry Evangeline, the granddaughter of King Edward, hoping he might someday claim the throne. And I have more bad news." He paused a moment. "I saw two of Shiveley's men. I'm afraid they may have followed me here. They were at the back of the crowd watching Evangeline sing."

Westley tightened his arm around her.

"Where are these men now?" Lord le Wyse asked.

"They left as soon as Evangeline finished singing."

"Reeve Folsham. Take some men and see if you can overtake them and capture them. But if you don't see them within five minutes, come back. We're going to need you."

"Yes, my lord." Reeve Folsham left quickly.

"Is Muriel all right?" Evangeline asked. "What has he done to her?"

"She was not seriously injured when I left." Pain filled Frederick's eyes. "But they are increasing their abuse of her. Lord Shiveley would do anything to find out where you are."

"We must do something." Evangeline looked desperately to Lord le Wyse as she squeezed Westley's arm.

Lord le Wyse gave her a quick nod, then turned back to

Frederick. "Why do you believe he wishes to take the throne from King Richard?" He fixed the man with a hard gaze from his one eye.

"He has been talking to the king's knights, offering them more money and lands if they will promise loyalty to him. He has a lot of men out searching for Evangeline. Lord le Wyse, England and your king need your help."

O God, don't let him hurt Muriel. Fury ignited into a full burn inside her. Energy surged through her limbs. Evangeline's gaze moved to Lord le Wyse, then to Westley and the steward.

"Father." Westley's jaw was rigid. "We must save Muriel, and we must warn the king. And we cannot allow Shiveley's men to take Evangeline."

Lord le Wyse's jaw twitched, his one eye fixed on his son with a fierce look. Finally, he said, "We will send word to my family and allies in the north."

"But it will take days to get word to them, then several more days for them to reach us."

"Then we must round up as many men as we can and go ourselves to rescue the king and Muriel." Evangeline had not planned to speak, but the words flew out of her mouth anyway.

They all stared at her.

Frederick spoke first. "I would be terribly grateful if you did, Lord le Wyse."

"How many of Lord Shiveley's men are at Berkhamsted Castle?" Lord le Wyse asked.

"Only about twenty when I left."

"Twenty armed men trained to fight against however many of my men—mostly farmers—I can convince to go with me."

Evangeline seemed to lose all the breath from her lungs.

"We can do it, Father." Westley looked around the small circle. "We all know how to use a longbow." He even glanced at Evangeline.

Lord le Wyse was silent as they looked to him to speak next. Finally, he said, "Perhaps we could use stealth to sneak into the castle. I could go and speak to the king while the rest of you free Muriel."

"Yes," Evangeline said as her breath returned to her. The other men nodded and mumbled their agreement as well.

"But we must be as discreet as possible," Lord le Wyse said. "Anyone you speak to about coming with us must agree to keep our plans quiet. No braggarts or loudmouths are to be told anything. I prefer you get young men without families. Once we have fifteen to twenty men, we will set out."

Lord le Wyse and Frederick moved away, talking and making plans. Evangeline turned to Westley. "I will come too."

"No, you will not." His brows drew together. "You will stay here and keep out of sight. I'll set some men to guard you, Mother, and the children at the castle."

"But I know how to fight."

"You have been through a few hours of learning how to defend yourself. You cannot fight soldiers and knights with weapons, men who have trained all their lives."

"I can use a longbow. I can help."

"No. You will stay here. Shiveley's men are looking for you. If they were to capture you, all would be lost."

She slammed her fists on her hips and stomped her foot. "I am going. I can help save Muriel. It is my fault she is . . . is being tortured." Her voice hitched at the thought.

"Evangeline, this is madness."

"Perhaps it is best if she goes," Frederick said. "The earl is after Evangeline. Perhaps we could offer her as a trade."

Her blood went cold.

"Begging your pardon, Evangeline." Frederick's eyes were round and desperate. "We could rescue you after we've spoken to the king."

Westley gave Frederick a tight-lipped scowl. "Excuse us for a moment." He grabbed Evangeline's arm and pulled her a few feet away. "You see? It is too dangerous," he said in a harsh whisper. "You heard what the man said."

"But you would protect me, and I can shoot a longbow and give you and the other men cover if you have to storm the castle."

"This is ridiculous." Westley stared out over the courtyard, still keeping hold of her arm. "I know you are brave and very capable, but I cannot let you risk your life." He expelled a harsh breath. "I have to go help round up men for this trip. But you are to stay here. Do you understand? Stay. Here."

She would never win this argument. Better to let him think she would be obedient. "Yes, Lord Westley."

He narrowed his eyes at her.

"You should go help your father."

He sighed. "You know I only want you safe. That man over there would throw you into a pack of wolves to save Muriel and the king."

"He cares about Muriel."

"And I care about you." He pursed his lips and looked away. "All the more reason—"

"But I cannot bear to do nothing when Muriel is being tortured."

He reached out and brushed his fingers over her cheek. "I have to go." But he didn't leave. He kept staring at her face.

Her thoughts were churning. She would not be left behind, not when it was her fault Muriel was in danger of being killed.

Westley waved at someone over Evangeline's shoulder. Nicola advanced toward them.

"Take Eva to the castle and make sure she is safe," he said to her. "Will you do that?"

Nicola looked confused. "Of course."

He placed his hands on Evangeline's shoulders. "You will understand later." He stared into her eyes for a moment longer, kissed her quickly on the forehead, and ran off in the direction his father had gone.

"Did he just kiss you? And why did he say you would understand later? Eva?"

Evangeline took Nicola's arm and turned her toward the castle. "Come. He's watching us. Make him think we are obeying." They started walking.

Evangeline quickly told her the whole story. They entered the castle, which seemed empty except for one manservant who appeared to be guarding the front door, and were walking toward the back of the house when Evangeline whispered, "Can you help me find some men's clothing? And I'll need a longbow and arrows—and a horse."

"Oh, I just happen to have all those things stuffed under my bed."

"Nicola, this is serious."

"I realize that. But it won't be easy to take those kinds of things without being caught."

"But you will help me, won't you?"

She stopped and looked at Evangeline. "You love Westley, don't you?"

"Yes."

"Then perhaps you should stay here. He will be very angry with you when he sees you ignored his wishes. It might be wiser to do as he asked."

Was she right? Would it be wiser? She thought for a moment, her mind going over every possible scenario. She tried to think of herself staying hidden in the castle while they went to save Richard and Muriel.

"He shouldn't be angry. He knows I am no coward, and he would not wish me to be. Besides, he hasn't exactly asked me to marry him. I don't have to obey him."

"That is true." Nicola actually smiled. "Men are attracted to women with some courage and spirit."

"I truly know *nothing* about men. And I so want Westley to love me." The admission made tears come to her eyes. "And yet I cannot stay here. Even if it means death to me, I must go and do what I can to save Muriel and Richard. But I don't want Westley to hate me."

"Evangeline, you are the king's ward, the daughter of the Duke of Clarence, and the granddaughter of King Edward. You can do anything you wish, and Westley would be a fool not to marry you at the first possible moment."

Her words made Evangeline's heart flutter, not with joy or anticipation, but with fear. Would Westley want to marry her only because she was of royal blood?

She did not have time to waste worrying about such things. She and Nicola hurried to find what Evangeline would need.

Chapter Twenty-Six

Westley rode at a brisk walk on his favorite horse, Gallagher. They'd been riding most of the day and only had an hour or two of daylight left, so they pressed on before they would be forced to stop.

It had only taken them about three hours to round up twenty men, gather supplies and weapons, and start out. The road was hard packed and dusty, as they had had little rainfall for a few weeks. Trees lined most of the way, but occasionally they passed close enough to a village to see some fields, mostly empty, as the grain had already been harvested.

Westley still was not sure who all the men with him were. He had been mostly riding and talking with his father and his friends, Robert, Piers, Aldred, and a few others. Finally, when the sun had set and it was completely dark, they halted.

None of them had ridden so far in a long time, and some of them had never sat a horse for so many hours. Westley could see the suppressed groans on everyone's faces as they dismounted, took out their blankets, and got ready to lie down to sleep.

One of the men raised his voice. "Who are you?"

Westley turned in time to see one of the larger men push the shoulder of a thinner one. "What is amiss there?"

"This one says you asked him to come"—the man pulled the skinny one forward by his upper arm—"but none of us know who he is."

Westley stepped forward to meet them. The skinny one's face was mostly covered by an oversize hood. He wore loose leggings and a tunic that was cinched by a leather belt.

Westley took hold of the hood and flung it back, revealing a head of wavy red hair.

Evangeline's defiant eyes looked back at him.

His heart sank to his toes and his breath rushed out of him. Did his expressed wishes mean nothing to her? She was dearer to him than his own life, and yet here she was, a glaring target for the man who wanted to harm her. She was deliberately putting herself in danger. Did she not understand that he could not bear the thought of Lord Shiveley harming her?

"What are you doing here?" His voice sounded raspy.

"I have come to help free my friend." She spoke loudly so everyone would hear her.

How would all these men react to having a woman among them? They'd be angry, horrified, or even downhearted. "I asked you to stay in Glynval. What have you done?"

"I can help, but you are too stubborn and proud to admit it." She lifted her chin, her green eyes sparking.

Heat rose into his face. "You're being foolish. You know Shiveley wants nothing more than to have you back at Berkhamsted. You will only make trouble by being here." He clenched his fist around his sword hilt. He should stop talking before he said anything else to hurt her. "What do you plan to do? Give yourself up to Shiveley in exchange for Muriel? Do you want to marry him now?"

Her cheeks turned bright red. "How dare you?"

"How dare I?" No one had ever said that to him before. Now he was seeing for the first time how the spoiled ward of a king behaved.

Her eyes were narrowed, and her chest rose and fell rapidly. She pointed her finger at his nose. "If you think I am some pathetic girl child willing to hide wherever you tell me to and do nothing when my friend is being abused in a dungeon, then you do not know me at all."

Had she not listened to him? Did she not know that he would do anything to keep her safe?

His father stepped toward them. Westley walked away from her, his head and heart both pounding like thunder to keep from saying something else that he shouldn't. Perhaps Father could speak sense to her. But even if his father could make her understand, it was too late to send her back to Glynval now. The obstinate girl would have to come with them.

~∂∂∂~

Evangeline forced herself to push away Westley's words and ignore the way he stalked away from her, as if he could no longer stand the sight of her. She could not let herself cry or she would appear weak.

Lord le Wyse came to stand before her, the other men hanging back but staring intently. "You'll have to come along with us, in any case. We cannot spare a man to escort you back. Try not to get in anyone's way." Then he started barking orders to the men to get busy tending to their horses.

Her chest felt hollow. Westley would hate her now. She had defied him. She had made him both angry and sad. But he had called her foolish and asked her if she wanted to marry Shiveley. How could he say such things? Did he not know how much they hurt her?

Everyone was getting ready to sleep for the night.

She turned to retrieve her bedding from her horse, aware that the men kept glancing her way or outright watching her. Did they think she was as foolish as Westley did? Well, she didn't care what they thought. Or Westley either, for that matter. If he could get so angry and think so little of her abilities, then perhaps he wasn't the man she thought he was.

Tears pricked her eyes at that thought, but she had no time for tears. Now that the men knew she was a woman, she had to be on her guard. She had thought to sleep near Westley, but she was too angry to want to be anywhere near him. Besides, she could take care of herself. She refused to be afraid.

Westley placed his bedroll on the ground next to a large oak tree. She placed hers about ten feet away from him and the other men. While they sat in a circle talking and eating with each other, Evangeline went into the woods to relieve herself. When she returned, Westley watched her walk back to her blanket.

She pretended to look straight ahead. She sat by herself and ate the bread and cheese Nicola had retrieved from the kitchen for her.

Would Westley get over being angry with her? Would she only get in everyone's way? If so, the men would utterly scorn her.

She would focus on saving Muriel and warning Richard about Lord Shiveley.

She put away her food, lay down, and closed her eyes. What would happen when they arrived at the castle? Would they be able to rescue Muriel? What would an actual battle look like?

Westley watched where Evangeline placed her blanket. She did not join the men as they ate. Did she have enough food? He supposed it would not be proper to invite her to sit and talk with the men. They might say something bawdy, although with his father on the trip, they were not likely to say anything very uncouth. Besides, she might not want to sit and eat with him. She was already lying down. And she was angry with him.

He had been rather harsh to her. But why couldn't she have stayed in Glynval as he asked her to? How did she not understand that she was in danger? Perhaps when he wasn't so angry, he might admire her for having the courage to come and want to fight with them. But courage would not protect her from Shiveley and his trained soldiers.

Westley left the group of men and their inane conversation. He went to his own blanket and lay down facing Evangeline. Her back was to him, and he couldn't see her very well, as dark as it was, but she seemed to be using her hands to rub her face. A moment later he heard a slight sniff coming from her direction. Surely she was not crying. He heard another sniff, barely audible, as if she was purposely trying to be quiet.

He listened for several more moments. Loud laughter from the men drowned out any sounds from Evangeline.

This was ridiculous. He got up and squatted next to her. "Can I get you anything? Do you need food or water?"

"No. I thank you." After a pause, she said, "I have food and water."

Perhaps he had imagined that she was crying. She seemed fine. "I shall see you in the morning, then. Don't go anywhere without telling me first."

His only answer was silence.

~ↀↇ~

The next morning Evangeline was up with everyone else, taking care of her horse—even though she didn't actually know how to care for a horse. She kept looking over at what the men were doing and imitating them. Then she refilled her water flask as the other men were doing. Westley seemed to be keeping an eye on her but did not speak to her.

The other men either eyed her askance or nodded politely when she came near. *See, Westley? You overreacted. No one here was so thrown off balance by me as you are.*

A few men had already mounted their horses. Evangeline took hold of her horse's reins and was about to hoist herself into the saddle when someone shouted. One of the men drew a dagger from his belt and cursed.

Evangeline spun around as a group of men rode toward them on horseback, at least a dozen, surrounding them on all sides. Their arrows were nocked and pointed at them when another group appeared with swords drawn. And riding in the forefront was Lord Shiveley.

Chapter Twenty-Seven

Westley placed his hand on his sword hilt, his muscles aching to draw his weapon. But with so many arrows and swords aimed at him, his men, and his father, he could do little.

Shiveley had caught them off guard.

Heat flowed through his limbs as a well-dressed man wearing leather body armor—Lord Shiveley, no doubt—moved forward. He seemed to be searching faces until he saw Father.

"Lord le Wyse. I haven't seen you since my wedding ceremony. My first wife was your relative, was she not?"

"How kind of you to remember." Father's wry tone and steely stare belied his indifferent manner.

Where was Evangeline? If Shiveley saw her he would surely recognize her. Westley subtly scanned the faces of their group. Where was she?

There, to Westley's left, not far from Lord Shiveley. Her hood covered her hair and most of her face. Two Glynval men stood close to her as if to hide her.

"Were you and your men out on a pleasure trip, Lord le Wyse?"

"We were on our way to Berkhamsted Castle, hoping to have an audience with the king over an attempted murder in Glynval."

"Oh, I see. Then why did you bring so many men? Did you bring the prisoner with you?"

"No, we left him in Glynval. These men are for my protection."

"For *your* protection? No, I think you were going to speak to the king about Evangeline, to convince Richard that she should not have to marry me."

"I'm sure I don't know what you mean. Who is Evangeline?"

"She is the king's ward, and Richard has ordered her to marry me, but she has run away. Are you telling me you do not know where she is?"

"I am not accustomed to having my word questioned, Lord Shiveley."

"I am sure you are not. But I finally persuaded Muriel, Evangeline's nursemaid, to tell me what she knew. She revealed that Evangeline was living in Hertfordshire. Glynval, to be precise."

Father did not reply, and Shiveley continued. "If the wench was lying, I shall have to return immediately to the castle and resume my tactics of persuasion."

Frederick made a deep sound like a growl, and Evangeline clenched her fist by her side.

"What does King Richard think of you using these tactics of persuasion on the daughter of an archbishop?"

"Oh, he doesn't know. And because I cannot risk you telling him, unless you have a better plan, I may have to ask my men to shoot you."

"So it's to be a massacre?" Father asked. "The king will hear of it."

"I might be persuaded to change my mind, if you give me Evangeline."

"And if I don't know where she is?"

"Then I shall begin by killing that one." Shiveley pointed to Westley. Two of Shiveley's guards seized him from behind, dragged him to the middle of the circle of people, and forced him to his knees. They pushed his head forward and down until his forehead nearly touched the ground.

"No! Don't hurt him!" Evangeline's voice rang out, high and clear.

Westley's heart slammed against his chest as Evangeline hurried forward and yanked off her hood. "I am here. Do not hurt this man."

"Evangeline." Lord Shiveley's eyes lit as he smiled down at her.

"This is indeed a surprise," Lord Shiveley said. "But what peasant did you rob for those clothes?"

Evangeline hastened toward Westley and shoved the shoulder of the first guard holding him down. "Let this man go. I will do what you want, just vow to me that you will not hurt this man."

"Why would you be so concerned about him, Evangeline? Could it be that you have come to care for someone else in Glynval? Let him up," he ordered his guards. "I want to see his face."

They let go of Westley's hair and shoulders, and he stood and stared defiantly back at Shiveley.

"He is rather young, and I suppose you think he is handsome."

Evangeline said nothing, her breath shallow at the thought of Shiveley harming Westley.

"Lord le Wyse? Who is this young man? Could he be your son?"

"He is my son, and if you harm him, you will regret it."

Evangeline's heart seemed to tremble at the intensity of Lord le Wyse's expression. But what could he do? They were outnumbered, and Lord Shiveley's men all had weapons trained on them.

O God, do not allow them to harm Westley or Lord le Wyse. I could never bear to lose Westley or to be the cause of it.

"You are not in a position to threaten me, le Wyse."

Evangeline's vision tilted as she waited for what would happen next.

"I have no wish to incite the king's wrath by killing you and your men. But neither can I have you attacking me on the way." Lord Shiveley flashed his serpentine smile. "I shall simply have to take you and your son with me as my prisoners. I shall inform Richard that you have been deliberately keeping his cousin from me all this time, in defiance of the king's will."

At least he wouldn't kill them.

"And that man." Shiveley pointed at Frederick. "I recognize you as one of Berkhamsted's stable servants. Did you truly ride all the way to Glynval to warn le Wyse? You shall come with us as well."

Shiveley's men forced Westley to hand over his sword while other soldiers rounded up the rest of the Glynval men and escorted them down the road toward their home village.

The men helped Evangeline mount her horse. She was surprised they let Lord le Wyse and Westley mount their own horses and did not tie their hands. But they were so outnumbered and without weapons, they had no chance to escape.

Evangeline's heart sank as they started down the road toward Berkhamsted Castle. Westley kept glancing at her, but Shiveley made sure they were separated by several guards. Somehow she had to speak to King Richard and tell him what Shiveley had been doing.

But what had he been doing? Trying to find her? Capturing the men who had essentially been hiding her? Richard wouldn't care. But he might care that Shiveley had tortured Muriel.

He would threaten Frederick's life to keep Muriel quiet. Did Shiveley know of her love for Frederick and his for her? If he did, they might never be able to convince the king of Shiveley's nefariousness.

After riding all day, Evangeline was not only desperate to get out of the saddle, her shoulders also ached from the tension of being constantly watched.

No matter how she tried, she had not been able to speak a word to Westley, Lord le Wyse, or Frederick, nor could she see that they had been able to speak to each other. How would they escape if they couldn't devise a plan?

They were close to the castle now. In fact, the lane that led to the castle gate was just ahead. But instead of taking that path, Shiveley and his men led them around to the north side as they skirted the outer moat. Where were they going?

Soon they reached the smaller Derne Gate. No doubt the king's men were guarding the main gate while Shiveley's men were guarding this one.

As they drew near to the wooden bridge that led over the first moat, Shiveley suddenly ordered them all to halt. "Tie up these men. They are our prisoners until they've earned their freedom."

They began tying Lord le Wyse's hands, but Frederick fought back. Westley suddenly leapt from his horse and snatched a sword from one of Shiveley's men.

Shiveley drew his own sword and spurred his horse toward Westley. "This one is mine!"

Westley struck Shiveley's blade with his own, but then the earl struck a blow from his much greater height on horseback. Shiveley struck over and over, forcing Westley to take a step back with every blow as Shiveley advanced.

Finally, they were so close to the edge of the moat, Evangeline cried out, "Watch out behind you!"

Just then, Westley's foot slipped, and he tumbled backward into the murky waters of the outer moat.

"Westley!" Evangeline jumped from her horse, but one of

Shiveley's guards grabbed her. She struggled against him, but he was too strong. She strained her eyes in the half-light of evening but could see nothing in the water, not even a bubble breaking the surface.

This was even worse than when he'd been struck and pushed into the river. At least she could see him and was free to jump in and save him. But now . . . He had disappeared under the water.

She recalled the tricks Reeve Folsham had taught her. She stomped on her captor's foot, then elbowed him in the ribs. He made an *oomph* sound but only tightened his hold on her. He pulled her arms behind her back, so hard it made her shoulders burn. She screamed, but he still did not loosen his hold.

"Someone save him! Lord Shiveley, I demand that you send someone in to save him."

No one moved and Lord Shiveley said nothing.

"If you save him, I will marry you! Willingly!"

"You will marry me anyway." Shiveley chortled.

She glanced around to see if there was anyone who could save Westley, but Shiveley's guards were tying cloths around Frederick's and Lord le Wyse's mouths.

O God, please! Westley was drowning!

Shiveley shook his head. "It is a pity. He looked to be a strong, healthy young man. But perhaps you will forget him when you are wed to me."

She refused to even acknowledge Shiveley's words. Except for the sickening twist in her stomach, she couldn't feel anything.

~*~

Westley hit the water, his body sinking in the cold moat.

He swam under the surface, hopefully in the direction of the bridge. He'd drawn in as much air as he could before he went under. He even managed to keep hold of the sword in his hand as he swam.

His lungs were near bursting by the time he reached the darker water that he believed was shaded by the bridge. He took the risk of raising his head and bumped it against something hard.

Wooden planks. It must be the bridge.

He lay on his back. His mouth and nose were only three or four inches from the underside of the wooden bridge, but it was enough room for him to breathe.

Soon he heard horses' hooves clomping on the wooden planks above him. Evangeline screamed, then the sound was suddenly muffled.

"Shut her up," Lord Shiveley said. "Tie something around her mouth."

"Who goes there?" A voice came from the other end of the bridge.

"The Earl of Shiveley," another voice answered him.

Several horses crossed the bridge into the castle bailey. Was anyone looking for him? They didn't seem to be. He waited until no more hooves sounded on the bridge. When he was sure no one was looking for him in the murky waters of the moat, he took a deep breath and dove beneath the surface.

⁂

Evangeline used her hands, tied together in front of her, to check to see that she still had the extra knife strapped to her thigh underneath her tunic. It was growing quite dark as they moved across the bailey toward the castle. Strangely, no one was around to see her, Lord le Wyse, and Frederick with their hands bound and gags in their mouths.

Lord Shiveley quietly ordered his prisoners to dismount. They did so, and he whispered to Evangeline, so near her face that she couldn't help but smell his breath, "If you tell King Richard anything, I shall immediately kill Lord le Wyse and your beloved Muriel before the king can intervene. Then I will tell him you are delusional and will force you to marry me anyway. So I suggest you cooperate."

He kept hold of her arm as they entered the castle and skirted around the rooms used by guests. They started up the stairs only used by the servants. Shiveley stopped her. "Remember, not a word, not a sound from you, or Muriel and Lord le Wyse will die." He untied the gag from her mouth.

"God will punish you for this."

He slapped her cheek. Hard. The sharp sound resounded through the narrow stone stairway. The stinging in her cheek brought tears to her eyes as she covered her burning face with her hand.

"That is only a small taste of what you will get if you do not obey me."

She refused to look at him, and he started up the stairs, pulling her after him. No one had ever slapped her before. She burned with the humiliation of being struck in the face.

"If you will be a good girl, I shall bring Muriel to you. But if you try to escape or talk to King Richard, I shall have my men snap her neck like a twig."

Her stomach boiled. She could possibly break free from his grasp by punching him in the throat or kneeing him in the groin, but three of Shiveley's men followed closely behind them. She could never get away from so many.

God, save Westley from the moat and from Shiveley's men. She could not bear the thought that he had drowned. Perhaps he had been able to get out of the moat under cover of darkness. After all, he was not unconscious this time when he fell into the water. *Please don't let him die. And rain down Your fire and brimstone on the head of Shiveley and all his evil men. Repay him evil for evil.*

When she reached her room, Shiveley left her inside, closed the door, and locked it. She tried to open it, just in case, but she was well and truly locked in.

She went and found her handheld looking glass. Her left cheek showed the bright-red outline of four fingers, and her lip was swollen and bleeding from a cut at the corner. "God, please keep Westley and Lord le Wyse safe from these evil men."

She wiped away her tears and dabbed at the spot of blood on her lip.

The door opened again and Muriel stumbled in. Her skin was pale, she seemed thinner, and her lip was swollen. Her dress was also dirty. And Muriel's dress was never dirty.

Afraid her embrace would not be welcome, Evangeline approached her slowly. "Muriel, are you well?"

"I'm so sorry they found you, Evangeline. I prayed Westley and Lord le Wyse would keep you safe in Glynval. I tried not to tell them, I tried to be strong . . ." Her eyes were large and strangely vacant.

"It is all right. It is my fault they found me so quickly, actually." If she had stayed in Glynval like Westley had asked her to . . . they still would have found her eventually.

Evangeline noted a bruise on Muriel's cheekbone. "I'm only sorry they hurt you. Because of me."

"Truly, it could have been much worse." Tears welled in her eyes and her bottom lip trembled.

"Oh, Muriel, I'm so sorry. It's all my fault." Her horror reduced her voice to a hoarse whisper. "I would never wish any pain on you, please believe me. I should have come back to Berkhamsted with you." An ache stabbed her heart as if it truly were breaking in two.

"No, Evangeline." Muriel shook her head. "You always think everything is your fault, but it's not. This was Lord Shiveley's doing, not yours. Besides, I knew this might happen, but I risked it because I . . . wanted to be with Frederick."

"Frederick came to tell us you were in the dungeon and he was afraid of what Shiveley would do to you. He is the reason we came, to save you and to save the king. He thinks Shiveley eventually hopes to usurp the throne."

"Yes, poor Frederick. And now he is in the dungeon. I just saw them taking him there, along with Lord le Wyse."

Someone pounded on the door, making them both jump.

"Hurry up in there! Get dressed, or I'll come in there and dress you myself."

"That's Shackelford." Muriel dashed over to Evangeline's trunk to pull out her best dress. Her hands were shaking as she held it up.

"Muriel, I'm so sorry for what they did to you."

"Never mind that. Let us make haste."

"But I learned some things while I was in Glynval, how to defend myself. Perhaps I could help us both escape."

"Shiveley has too many men. They would only capture us again. He is determined to have you, Evangeline." A haunted look shone out of Muriel's eyes, something completely unfamiliar. "We cannot escape."

She did not want to be the cause of further punishment for Muriel, so she hurried to get out of her men's clothing. "Do not worry. We'll get out somehow."

Muriel nodded but did not look at her. They both worked to get Evangeline's clothing off her and the dress on. As soon as it was in place and laced up, Shackelford pounded on the door again.

"She's ready," Muriel called.

The door opened, and Shackelford stepped forward and took

hold of Evangeline's arm, then addressed Muriel. "You go down ahead of us."

Muriel went out the door and they started down the stairs.

As Evangeline entered the Great Hall, Lord Shiveley looked up at her and smiled. "Here she is, my king. I told you my men would find her."

Richard's face was like a mask as he stared at her. "Evangeline, you made us very sad when you ran away."

She stared back at him. *Richard, please realize that this man is not your friend. He is evil!* She wanted to scream it out. But if she did, good people would get hurt, or even killed. Muriel. Frederick. And Lord le Wyse. It felt like a bad dream, seeing the king but not being able to ask for his help.

"Come, my dear." Lord Shiveley motioned to her. "Sit by me."

She moved cautiously forward and sat opposite Lord Shiveley and at King Richard's left hand.

"Evangeline," the king said, "are you sorry now that you ran away? The world is a harsh place, after all."

He wanted her to thank Lord Shiveley for bringing her back. Well, she could play along, to keep her friends safe.

"The world is a harsh place, King Richard. A place where women are used as pawns."

The king's face grew hard, so she changed her tone. "But being a peasant and trying to keep body and soul together is not an easy life."

"Lord Shiveley tells me you were on your way back to Berkhamsted Castle when he and his men found you this morning."

"That is true."

"Lord Shiveley also tells me you have agreed to say your marriage vows before the priest this very evening."

"Oh? I don't remember agreeing to that." Evangeline's heart beat hard against her ribs.

Shiveley gave her a dark look.

"It is late." Evangeline tried to smile. "And the priest will not have time to prepare . . . for the ceremony."

The king's jaw hardened again. "It's time to put away your childishness, Evangeline. We wish the marriage to take place tonight."

"If neither of you are too tired, I suppose I cannot object—after we have all eaten, of course." Evangeline wanted to scream. Instead, she clenched her fists under the table.

A servant hurried to bring her a trencher, and they all were served a large square of meat jelly. Evangeline did her best to eat a few bites of the heavily spiced jelly before a large pheasant was placed on the table in front of them. Lord Shiveley placed a portion on her trencher. She merely stared at it.

She would have to get away tonight, even though she had no weapon and no plan, and Shiveley's guards were everywhere. And she dare not think about Westley except to believe that God had rescued him from the moat.

Chapter Twenty-Eight

Westley made his way slowly and carefully to the palace building, pausing in the shadows to look around. It was quite dark now. He did see one guard—one of Shiveley's men—at the door where he had seen the earl, Evangeline, Father, and Frederick enter.

When he was nearly to the door, he took the rock he had picked up by the bank of the moat and threw it so it hit the side of the stone wall. The guard turned his whole body to face the sound. He put his hand on his sword hilt and took a few steps in that direction.

Westley ran forward and struck the guard on the back of the head. He fell facedown on the ground.

Westley stripped the man of his sleeveless surcoat, which bore Shiveley's colors. He pulled it on over his head. Then he took the man's dagger from his belt even as the guard began to moan and awaken.

Westley hurried into the palace through the door and hid himself in the shadows. He heard voices in the distance, growing fainter. Hearing nothing from above, he took the steps two at a time, soon reaching the upper floor. But which room belonged to the king? Thankfully, no guards were in sight. If the king was at dinner in the Great Hall, the guards would be with him, or at least near him. Westley went to the door that looked the most like where the king might sleep, opened it, and snuck inside.

Evangeline kept alert for any way she might speak to Richard without Shiveley hearing her, but he was just as alert, speaking only to the king and to Evangeline during the meal. She could think of no way to tell the king that Shiveley was evil that would convince him and still keep the earl from sending someone to the dungeon to kill Muriel and Lord le Wyse.

As the feast was beginning to come to a close, Evangeline's hands shook. She stared desperately at Richard, but he didn't seem to notice anything was wrong. Finally, Shiveley spoke.

"I would like to take Evangeline and have our wedding blessed by the priest. Will you be the witness to our marriage vows, my king?"

"Of course. I shall go up to my room for a few moments and rejoin you in the chapel."

Evangeline watched him go. Shiveley already had hold of her arm and was pulling her toward the stairs. "If I remember correctly, the chapel is this way."

She glanced around. Two guards were watching them as they departed through the doorway. Two more were behind them, meeting her stare. Even if she could get away from Lord Shiveley, she could not get away from so many guards.

Westley, where are you? Was he alive? Had he been able to get out of the moat before he drowned? Her heart twisted painfully. *God, I pray he is safe, and I pray You will help me escape.*

There was nowhere to run to as they climbed the stone steps to the chapel, surrounded by Shiveley's men.

⁓

Westley crouched against the wall. When no guard came at him, he waited for his eyes to adjust to the darkness. He was alone in a large bedchamber. He walked over to a trunk against the wall. Did this room and this trunk belong to King Richard? How could he know for sure?

Perhaps he should check the other rooms to see which was the largest and most sumptuously furnished. But that would take time, and he might get caught. The guard whose clothing he had stolen could be awake now and spreading the news that an intruder was in the castle.

A long garment lying across the bed caught his eye. It was purple and had ermine trim. Surely not even the arrogant Lord Shiveley would wear purple and ermine in the presence of the king.

Westley looked around the room again, taking in every wall, corner, and piece of furniture. Where did he want to be when the king of England came through the door? Would a guard precede him? Should Westley hide or immediately make his presence known? He decided to stand in full view and state his business as quickly as possible.

Just then, footsteps sounded in the corridor. Westley faced the door. It swung open and a guard walked in. He saw Westley and froze. "Who are you?" He drew his sword.

Westley lifted his hands. "I come in peace. I need to speak with His Majesty King—"

Two guards rushed at him and grabbed his arms.

"Your Majesty," he yelled as the men tried to push him down on the floor. "Evangeline is in danger."

The men managed to shove him to his knees as they ground their fists into the back of his shoulders and pulled his arms behind him.

"Stop. Let him up." A third man walked into the room. He was thin, with dark-blond hair and a matching beard.

They loosened their hold on Westley, and he stood and jerked his arms out of their grasp.

"Who are you?"

This man must be King Richard, as he held his head high and ordered them around with such a regal tone.

"I am Westley le Wyse from Glynval. Evangeline is afraid for her life if she marries Lord Shiveley. And Lord Shiveley has captured my father, Lord Ranulf le Wyse, and thrown him in the dungeon. He has also been torturing Muriel."

"How do you know all this?" The king's face was scrunched in a tight scowl. "Shiveley may have threatened Muriel and yelled at her to try to convince her to tell him where Evangeline was, but he would not strike her."

"Have you seen her, Your Majesty?"

"No, but why did Evangeline not tell me these things? I have been with her for the last hour."

"Shiveley threatened to kill my father and Muriel if she spoke a word of it."

"And you? Where did you come from? How did you get in here?"

"I escaped Lord Shiveley and his men by diving into the moat and swimming to the underside of the bridge."

King Richard had been studying Westley's face while he stroked his beard. "And why do you think Evangeline is in any danger from Shiveley? He is one of my most trusted advisors."

"My father believes he murdered his first wife. She was my father's cousin, and her family said she often had bruises on her face and arms. After she died, her mother prepared her body for burial, and she said she looked as if someone had beaten her . . . in the head. Shiveley said she fell down the steps, but her head had more than one injury, and they were all on one side."

"These are all very grave accusations. Is there anything else you have to say?"

"The castle stable master, Frederick, told us he believes Lord Shiveley has a more sinister intention for marrying your cousin. He believes the earl hopes to someday be king."

"Does he have any proof of this?"

"I believe it was based on something Lord Shiveley had said to Muriel."

"Come, then." The king looked grim as he motioned to his guards. "Let us go down to the dungeon and see whom we might find there."

Evangeline stood beside Lord Shiveley in the chapel before the priest.

"Where is the king?" Shiveley growled. He turned to two of his guards. "Go find him." He spoke from behind clenched teeth. "Ask him if he realizes we are waiting for him and how much longer he will be."

She closed her eyes and tried to block out Lord Shiveley's face. He would surely kill Muriel, Lord le Wyse, and Frederick—and Westley, too, if he found him. The only thing she could hope for was to buy their safety . . . with her compliance. At least until she was able to free them. Somehow.

Westley accompanied the king and his two guards down one flight of stairs, then headed down the dank stone steps to the dungeon. "Pardon me, my king, but is Evangeline safe?"

"She and Shiveley are waiting for me now in the chapel to say their wedding vows."

Westley's heart hitched. "You must not allow him to get her alone, if you will forgive my boldness, Your Majesty. He will do harm to her, I have no doubt."

"Did she have a red mark on her face before you left her? Or a cut on her lip?"

"You see? He has already struck her." Heat rose into Westley's face and sent a surge of energy through his limbs. If only he could get his hands around that man's neck . . .

The king reached the bottom of the steps and approached two guards there. "Open the doors of the cells where Lord le Wyse and Frederick are being kept."

"We can open those doors for no man except Lord Shiveley." The first guard stood staring back at the king, his hand on his sword.

"How dare you? I am King Richard, and this dungeon, as well as every inch of Berkhamsted Castle, belongs to me."

The man's countenance fell but still he hesitated. Then he bolted past them and up the stairs.

"What is the meaning of this?" The king glared at the other dungeon guard.

He stared, openmouthed. "Your Majesty, forgive me. Shiveley told us that if we disobeyed him, even if it were the king himself, he would have us beheaded. But if you make me one of your guards, I hereby renounce any ties to Lord Shiveley. I vow to be loyal to you forever, my king."

"Do you dare propose to bargain with your king?" He motioned to one of his guards standing just behind him. "Give me your sword."

"Forgive me, Your Majesty." The man quickly took the keys and unlocked the doors.

"Open these doors, every last one of them, for I know of no prisoners of mine down here. Treachery is afoot here."

Out came Westley's father, Frederick, and Muriel, who fell into Frederick's arms.

"Muriel?" the king asked in a shocked whisper. "What has Shiveley done to you?"

She lifted her head from Frederick's shoulder and faced the king.

"Lord Shiveley is mad. He planned to force Evangeline to marry him by threatening to kill me if she did not comply. I believe he thought if he was married to the granddaughter of a king, the people would be more likely to accept him as their king. It was his ultimate goal . . . to be king in your place."

"And I suppose he has sent away my guards?"

Frederick spoke up. "Most of them, Your Majesty, on the pretense of searching for Evangeline, and the others he imprisoned in the dungeon."

"Come. I shall confront Shiveley and we shall fight, if necessary. Who's with me?"

"We're willing to die for you," they said.

Westley and the others surged up the steps toward the chapel. *God, keep Evangeline safe, and make us victorious.*

Evangeline studied the one doorway leading out of the small chapel, the position of Shiveley and his guards, and the priest, who stood two feet in front of her with his eyelids so low over his eyes he almost looked as if he was asleep standing up.

Lord Shiveley kept glancing about the room, mostly at the entrance to the chapel behind them. He fidgeted, shuffling his feet, and avoided looking at Evangeline.

Why was the king taking so long? If only he would never come. What was happening with Westley? Was he safe somewhere?

But instead of feeling anxious, fidgety, or searching the back of the chapel as Lord Shiveley was doing, Evangeline stood calmly, almost numb. *God, You will do something. I believe in You. I believe in Your lovingkindness.* After all, God had allowed her to escape long enough to learn how to defend herself and fight off an attacker. Surely God would allow her to use that knowledge to save herself from Lord Shiveley.

He suddenly faced the priest and grabbed Evangeline's arm, his fingers biting into her flesh. "Start the vows," he growled. "We can't stand here all night. My guards can be witnesses."

The priest nodded. He opened the book in his hand and seemed about to speak when a rustling sound came from the back of the room. Evangeline turned. King Richard was walking toward them.

Would her cousin stop the wedding? She stared at him, her heart in her throat.

Richard reached them. But he only looked at the priest and nodded.

The priest read the vows, his voice droning on. Her feeling of numbness and calm left her, and she cast about in her mind for an excuse to stop the ceremony. It was going so swiftly. The priest said, "If there be anyone present who knows of any impediment or any reason this marriage would not be lawful, let him speak now."

"I have a question." Richard's voice was even, betraying no emotion.

Shiveley glared at him, his face turning red.

"I would like to know what happened to your first wife, Lord Shiveley."

"She died."

"Indeed. And how did you say she died?"

Evangeline's heart beat fast. What was the king doing? Would he save her?

Shiveley's jaw hardened and twitched. "She fell down some stairs at our home."

"I see. And how did my fair cousin get that swollen, bloody lip and the red mark on her face? Did she fall down some steps too?"

Air rushed into her lungs.

"I do not know what she did before she came to Berkhamsted."
Shiveley licked his thick lips. "She says she was in Glynval. She
may have—"

"Evangeline?" The king cut him off. "What happened to
your face?"

Shiveley pinched her arm.

"Ow! This man struck me." Evangeline stomped on Shiveley's foot.

He grunted and loosened his hold on her arm just enough that
she was able to snatch her arm away and run. Shiveley's guard
began to scramble to block the doorway leading out, but before she
had gotten very far, one of the guards sidestepped in front of her
and she ran into his broad chest. He seized her arms and held them
behind her with one hand while holding her firmly to his side with
the other.

The earl's guards snatched their swords from their scabbards,
the blades ringing in the small room.

"What is this?" Richard said, ice in his voice. "Will your guards
draw their swords on the king's ward?"

Shiveley stood straight and tall, but his pointy beard trembled.
"Have you decided not to allow your ward to marry me? I have been
loyal to you."

"Why do you want to marry Evangeline so badly?"

"Why? Because . . . she is beautiful." Shiveley seemed to be
waiting for the king to say something, but when he didn't, the earl
continued. "She-she is . . . your ward. I want to care for her. Any man
would want to marry her."

"And I thought you fell in love with her sweetness and spirit and
beautiful singing."

"Yes, of course. All of those things as well."

"Then why are your guards still holding their swords?"

"My men have been instructed to do whatever it takes to ensure that your ward stays in this chapel until the priest has finished speaking the vows," Lord Shiveley said from behind clenched teeth.

"You are prepared to defy your king, then? For I forbid your marriage to Evangeline."

Her breath caught in her throat, and she wanted to laugh in Shiveley's face. If the king intervened, she would not have to hurt this guard, for she was already planning how to inflict pain on him to get away.

She glanced over her shoulder. The guard was wearing a hood and she couldn't see his face.

"Why do you forbid it?" Lord Shiveley leaned forward menacingly.

"I do not wish it. I am the king. I do not need a reason."

"And I say, she will be mine—and so shall the throne! Men, seize the king." But before he could finish his command, shouts rang out behind them, near the entrance to the chapel.

The guard who was holding her suddenly grabbed her by the waist, threw her over his shoulder, and ran for the door.

Chapter Twenty-Nine

Evangeline screamed. Men, including Lord le Wyse and guards wearing the colors of King Richard, surged into the room and fought with Lord Shiveley's guards. But the one holding her passed right through the middle of them and out the doorway and into the corridor.

She screamed over and over, beating at his back with her fists. He set her feet on the floor and pulled off his hood.

"Westley!" Her heart nearly leapt out of her chest. She threw her arms around him as a sob escaped her throat. "You're alive. Thank You, God."

"I have to go help." He kissed her forehead and then drew his sword. He plunged back into the chapel and into the fight.

Evangeline followed and watched as he leapt into the fray. He attacked one of Shiveley's guards and immediately divested him of his sword, but the fight ended soon after. Shiveley's men surrendered. Richard held his sword point to Shiveley's throat. Lord le Wyse was standing over a man lying on the floor, as the king's men had subdued several others.

Westley stepped toward her and put his arm protectively around her waist.

The king relinquished his prisoner to one of his guards. "Take these traitors down to the dungeon and lock them up."

Westley pulled her out of the way, still holding her, until everyone had departed from the chapel except Lord le Wyse, the king, Westley, and Evangeline. Even the priest had disappeared around the chancel. They all seemed to be waiting for the king to speak.

"Lord le Wyse, I presume." He nodded at the older man.

"Your Majesty." Lord le Wyse bowed to the king.

"That was fine sword fighting."

"My son Westley taught me everything I know."

Westley responded with a slight smile, standing very straight.

"The truth is, I owe you three my life." The look on the king's face was quite somber. "I shall make certain that Shiveley and his men are no longer a threat, but I wish to speak with the three of you later in the Great Hall."

"Yes, Your Majesty." Westley and his father bowed and Evangeline curtsied as the king left the room.

Westley tightened his arm around her waist, as if afraid she might try to get away, and asked his father, "Are you well?"

Westley pointed to a thin line of blood on Lord le Wyse's chin. His father touched his chin with the back of his hand. "Only a scratch. But be sure and tell your mother and brothers and sisters that the king complimented me on my sword-fighting skills."

"I shall." Westley grinned, showing all his teeth.

"I'll go wash this off." Lord le Wyse gave a smile and nod to Evangeline and left the chapel.

Westley gazed down at her, now that they were alone. "Are you all right? I wish I could have gotten here sooner." His tone was hushed, and his thumb gently stroked beside the cut on her lip.

Her heart filled and overflowed into her eyes. She pressed her face against his chest.

"Wait. I don't know how clean this thing is." Westley pulled away and stripped off the surcoat that bore Shiveley's colors. He threw it on the floor and then pulled her to him. She didn't even mind that the clothes underneath were still damp from his swim in the moat.

They walked over to a bench against the wall near the chapel entrance and sat down, their arms around each other. She touched his hair.

"Still wet."

"I don't suppose I smell very good after being in the stinky moat."

"I don't care what you smell like. I was so afraid you'd drowned." She held him tight, pressing her cheek to his shoulder.

"Nah. I've been swimming since I was a wee child."

She suddenly wished she could have seen him swimming through the moat. "But what happened after that?"

He explained to her how he sneaked in and hid in King Richard's bedchamber and everything that ensued.

"Thank you for saving me."

He squeezed her tighter to his side and kissed her head. "Not still angry with me, then?"

"No. You were right. I should have stayed in Glynval since I turned out to be useless to you."

"That's not true. If you hadn't been here, we probably could not have proven to the king that Shiveley was a traitor."

"Do you think so?"

"I do."

It felt so good to be in Westley's arms again. But a sharp pain inside forced her to say, "You hurt me with what you said on the way here, that I was foolish and I would only make trouble."

"I shouldn't have said that." He stared intently into her eyes. "I never wanted to hurt you. I was angry with you for placing yourself in danger, and I was afraid something bad would happen to you. Please forgive me for saying those things. They weren't true."

"I do forgive you. I said some unkind things about you too."

"That I was stubborn and proud?"

"You're not stubborn or proud. Will you forgive me?"

"Of course." He placed a kiss on her temple. "Is there anything you need?" Westley said softly.

She'd never realized how warm and pleasant his voice sounded—sweet but masculine at the same time. But there was something else getting in the way of her joy, something else she needed to say.

"No, but, Westley . . . I'm sorry if I've always seemed selfish. I promise I will try not to be so selfish in the future."

"Why would you say that?"

"I was so afraid you would think I was too selfish to . . ." She was about to say, "too selfish to love," but he hadn't said anything about loving her.

"Why would you think you were selfish? You've risked your life more than once for me."

"I've always feared that if people knew how selfish I was, they couldn't possibly love me."

"But why?"

"I . . . I had a very unkind nurse as a young child, before Muriel came to me. She would yell, 'You're so selfish.' And her face would scrunch up, as if being selfish was the most disgusting thing imaginable. I would feel so hated every time she said that. I learned to hide my feelings. I didn't even tell Muriel how I felt about most things. I was afraid I was unlovable, afraid she would hate me the way that nurse seemed to hate me. I just don't want you to hate me." Had she said too much? What would he think?

Westley kissed her forehead as she kept her head down.

"Evangeline." His voice was gentle. "I could never hate you. That nurse was cruel and unreasonable to treat a child that way. All of us are selfish sometimes. We're weak men and women. But you are kind, you feel remorse when you hurt someone, and you jump into rivers to save people who are about to die."

His words made her smile and drove away the pain in her heart.

"You also point arrows at people you think might murder me, and you disguise yourself in men's clothing to try to help. You're not selfish, Evangeline. I love you."

"I love you too." Her heart ached with the truth of it as she closed her eyes. "I love you so very much."

They sat shoulder to shoulder in warm silence. Finally, she said, "I told myself I would run away from Berkhamsted Castle. For a long time I thought I just wanted to avoid marrying one of Richard's friends. But a year or two ago I began to realize . . . I longed for things."

It felt good to tell Westley this, especially since he was listening so intently. "I longed to be held, to feel safe. I longed for someone who would comfort me when I was sad. I longed for someone who would never think I was selfish, who would never hate me. I decided I wanted to be like the peasants—free to marry for love. But . . . it's not possible."

"Of course it's possible. I am holding you and comforting you right now." He pulled away, and with his fingers under her chin, he lifted her face. Very gingerly, he kissed the corner of her mouth, pressing his lips oh so softly to her cut. The tender gesture sent a thrill all the way to her toes. She closed her eyes. His warm lips caressed her cheek as well.

He whispered, "I could kill that man for striking you. Tell me what he did."

Her eyelids fluttered open, and Westley brushed a strand of hair off her cheek, letting his hand linger on her skin. It was difficult to concentrate on speaking when he was so close.

"He took me to my room and locked me in to get dressed—I don't think he liked my men's clothing. But on the way up the stairs, I told him God would punish him, and he slapped me. Oh dear." She suddenly remembered. "Where is Muriel? Is she all right?"

"Yes, she is well. She's with Frederick."

"Did you see her?"

"She looks like she's had a hard two weeks, but I think she will be well." He caressed her cheek again. "You know, you said you wanted to be held. And to be free to be married to someone you loved."

"Yes."

"Do you know what I want?"

"Tell me."

"I want to fall in love with a beautiful young woman, to marry her, and to have beautiful red-haired children." He stared into her eyes, his body turned toward her on the narrow bench. "I've already fallen in love with her. Do you think her guardian will give me permission to marry her?"

"You can ask him." Would he say no? If he did, she would run away from Berkhamsted Castle again. Perhaps there would be a place for them in France. Or the Holy Roman Empire.

Westley leaned down and pressed his lips to hers.

"What is this?"

Evangeline pulled away. The priest was giving them a horrified look. She hadn't known his eyes could open that wide.

"Are you kissing in the Lord God's chapel? There is no kissing in the chapel! Unless it is to seal a marriage vow."

Westley stood and kept hold of her hand. He did not apologize. He only nodded at the priest as they left, and he led her down the steps. "I've never been asked to leave the chapel for kissing before," he said.

"Are you sure? Because you don't seem very embarrassed about it."

"Why should I be embarrassed for kissing the woman I plan to marry?"

Evangeline bit her lip. The king had not given them permission yet. And he might not. After all, Westley had no title, and the king did not believe in marrying for love. She was Richard's political pawn, and Lord Shiveley had revealed to her just how valuable a pawn she was. Would her cousin give her up to Westley?

As they reached the main floor, Lord le Wyse and King Richard were walking into the Great Hall, talking as if they were old friends.

Westley stopped her short and turned to face her in a dark corner near the stairs. "I haven't thanked you for being willing to give yourself to Shiveley to save me."

His handsome face was so close to hers, she could almost count his eyelashes, even in the dim torchlight. His gaze was focused on her lips, but he leaned down and touched his lips to her cheek.

"I . . . I don't know what you mean."

"When you told Shiveley you would willingly marry him if he would save me from the moat. I thought you were still angry with me."

"I was very angry with you. You also accused me of wanting to marry Shiveley. But I knew you didn't mean it, and I still loved you."

His lips brushed her cheek again, but this time an inch closer to her lips.

She should probably ask him what he meant by kissing her, since the king had not given him permission to marry her, or mention that he did not smell very good after his swim in the moat. But if she spoke, he would know by her voice how much his simple kisses affected her.

"I'm sorry I doubted that you could be helpful." He kissed her other cheek, pulling her even closer.

Why didn't he kiss her lips? Didn't he know she wanted him to?

He kissed her chin.

"I already forgave you," she whispered.

"Will you marry me?" He kissed her forehead. "If your cousin the king will give us permission?" He looked into her eyes and brought his hands up, his palms cradling her face.

"I will marry you even if he doesn't give us permission." She sounded breathless.

He brought his mouth down to kiss her lips. She did her best to kiss him back. Was she doing it well? Were there rules to kissing? If there were, she didn't know them, but Westley didn't seem inclined to complain.

He ended the kiss and caressed her jawline with his thumb. "I'm so in love with you, Evangeline." His breath was warm on her temple. "And seeing you stomp Shiveley's foot to get away from him . . . I wanted to carry you off right then and there, all the way back to Glynval."

She closed her eyes and savored his words. "I felt the same way when you were sword fighting with Lord Shiveley. You looked so powerful."

His expression showed her praise affected him.

Someone cleared his throat about thirty feet away. Evangeline turned to see Richard and Westley's father standing there. Her cheeks burned.

The king said, "The servants are preparing a small feast for us in honor of our defeat of Lord Shiveley."

"Thank you, Your Highness," Westley said.

The king smiled as though amused, and Lord le Wyse raised his brows as they turned and went back toward the Great Hall.

Westley's blue eyes were staring into hers again. "I suppose we should not anger the king, not when I have something so important to ask of him. Shall we go?"

She wanted to say something daring like, "If you promise to kiss me again soon," but she only whispered, "As you wish."

⁓◦℗℗◦⁓

Westley held Evangeline's hand under the table while his father and the king discussed various political situations the king was dealing with. He waited for a chance to speak.

"Westley," Evangeline said softly, gazing at him with those beautiful green eyes of hers, "will you ask that servant over there where Muriel is?"

He waved to the servant girl, and she hurried over. Evangeline leaned away from the table and asked her, "Where is Muriel?"

"She is with Frederick, my lady."

"So she is safe?"

"I should say so. They went to the priest to ask him to bless their marriage."

Evangeline's eyes widened, but she smiled and thanked the servant. She squeezed Westley's hand under the table.

Just then, the king finally looked his way and addressed him. "Westley, Evangeline has very good instincts about men, do you not think?"

"Uh, of course, Your Highness."

"She told me she did not wish to marry Lord Shiveley and was quite emphatic that she did not think he was the kind of person I thought he was. Unfortunately, I did not listen to her and she ran away. Would you not say that showed good insight—even foresight?"

"There is no doubt she is a remarkable and extraordinary woman. And I would like to ask you, if I may—"

"I know what you are about to say." The king lowered his voice and leaned in close. "It is quite plain that you wish to ask me for

Evangeline. But the truth is, I cannot have my cousin marry a commoner with no title."

Westley's heart sank. Evangeline had said she would marry him even if the king did not give his consent. Would they have to run away to the Continent?

"I have an announcement I want to make," the king said.

Did he intend to marry Evangeline off to someone else? Westley's blood rose into his face. He would defy the king and spirit her away this very night and have their marriage blessed by the bishop near Glynval. They could hide out somewhere in the German regions of the Holy Roman Empire.

Around them sat a few of the king's knights who had spent the last several days in the dungeon as a consequence of their loyalty to the king and running afoul of Lord Shiveley's guards. And across the table from Westley sat Father. But in spite of the fact that there weren't many dignitaries to hear his announcement, the king stood until he had the attention of the entire room. Even the servants who were bringing platters of food stopped and looked on.

"Friends and loyal subjects"—King Richard looked oddly humble—"it appears my fair cousin, Evangeline, daughter of my uncle Lionel, Duke of Clarence, possesses supernatural discernment of character. If she had not rejected the traitorous Earl of Shiveley, he might have succeeded in his plot to overthrow me and usurp my crown. Cheers for my favorite cousin, Evangeline of Berkhamsted Castle!"

The room roared with cheers and foot stomping so loud it was nearly deafening. Evangeline blushed and smiled, acknowledging the crowd with a nod and a wave of her hand. When the noise finally died down, the king resumed speaking.

"I am forever grateful for the bravery of this woman, and also to the men of Glynval, who were willing to sacrifice themselves for the good of England."

More whoops and shouts went up.

"Lord Ranulf le Wyse and his son Westley risked much to come here and fight for me, and so . . . for his bravery, I shall create a new earldom to replace the Earldom of Shiveley, which upon his execution shall cease to exist, and Westley le Wyse shall henceforth be . . . the Earl of Glynval."

Loud cheers erupted. Westley's heart leapt inside him at the thought of being the Earl of Glynval. But was that all the king intended to give him? A title?

Westley stood and bowed to the king. "Thank you, Your Majesty. That is very generous."

"And because you, along with your father, not only successfully thwarted the evil intentions of my closest advisor and since you obviously have found favor with my fair cousin, I grant you the right . . . to marry the brave and insightful Evangeline."

Westley could not stop the smile from stretching across his face. "I thank you, my king. I most gladly will marry Evangeline, if she is willing." He turned to her and held out his hand, then knelt. "Do you accept me?"

"Of course. Yes!" Evangeline's red hair formed a halo around her face. She gave him her hand.

He got up, bent, and kissed her briefly on the lips. The entire room cheered and roared.

The king lifted his goblet. "I wish you joy, long life, and many children."

Everyone drank to them and shouted out their goodwill wishes, and Evangeline's cheeks shone a pretty pink.

Evangeline stood beside Westley as they were wed quietly in the Berkhamsted Castle chapel. Muriel and Frederick, whom King Richard had promoted to the position of steward of Berkhamsted Castle, stood nearby as the priest blessed Evangeline and Westley's union.

After a few days in Berkhamsted, they traveled back to Glynval. At the next Glynval hallmote, held in the manor courtyard, a jury of twelve sworn men were appointed to collect and present evidence relating to the incident at the Harvest Festival. They found John Underhill and his men guilty of seizing Evangeline and carrying her away and locking her in the dairy, as several witnesses swore an oath corroborating Evangeline's story, having seen John Underhill's men carrying a sack just the size and shape to be the maiden. They also found John and his men guilty of seizing and assailing Westley le Wyse, of inflicting a small stab wound in his side, and of threatening to kill him in very specific terms.

The jury fined John forty shillings, and his men six shillings each because they were poor, and they all were ordered to stay in their own village of Caversdown and never to set foot in Glynval again.

"I don't think John will object to such a light punishment," Evangeline said when the hallmote was over and they were having dinner with Westley's family.

"You should have seen his face," Westley said, "when he found out you were the king's ward and I had been made an earl."

Evangeline laughed.

"And Sabina has accepted an offer of marriage from someone in another village and she has already left her father's house."

"Oh?"

"Yes," Lady le Wyse said. "Sabina's mother came and told me herself, and apologized if her daughter had done anything to upset Evangeline." Lady le Wyse raised her brows in a knowing way.

Evangeline nearly said something ungracious, but she squeezed Westley's hand under the table instead. She was too full of joy to wish anyone ill, even Sabina.

"Mother, tell her," Cate said suddenly with a wide smile.

"Tell me what?" Evangeline asked.

Lady le Wyse wiped her lips with her cloth napkin and laid it in her lap. "We insist on you two having a wedding at the Glynval Church, where the villagers can be present for their young lord and lady's wedding."

Evangeline's heart leapt at the thought. "Can it be just like a peasant's wedding?"

"A peasant's wedding?" Cate said.

"The same sort of festivities, with flowers and food for everyone?"

"Of course," Lady le Wyse said, chuckling. "Just as you wish."

The day dawned bright and clear, and the cool smell of autumn was in the air. The people all followed them in eager procession to the church door, where the priest had them repeat their vows.

When the priest's blessing was done, the people followed them back to the courtyard, waving brightly colored ribbons and small boughs covered with flowers. They also brought cakes they had baked as gifts to add to the great feast the servants had prepared.

The festivities included music and dancing. In between songs, the people all insisted on hearing more stories about how their lord and his men had saved the king of England from the evil Earl of Shiveley, liberating Evangeline, the king's ward, from his tyranny, and then how King Richard had bestowed upon Westley the title of Earl of Glynval.

Westley kissed his bride as everyone around them was smiling, singing, eating, and drinking.

"I am so glad you came to Glynval, Evangeline of Berkhamsted Castle."

"I am also glad I came to Glynval, Westley le Wyse."

"Don't you mean, my lord, Earl of Glynval?"

She laughed and kissed him, aware that Lord and Lady le Wyse were looking on, as well as many others. Evangeline only hoped that the rest of them could be as full of joy as she was, could escape whatever evil fate the devil had planned for them, and could feel as grateful to God as she did for lifting her out of loneliness and pain and bringing her into the lovely life He had planned for her all along.

Acknowledgments

Many thanks to my editor, Becky Monds, who is amazing in her insights into my stories and the ways to improve them, along with all the other things she does to bless my publishing experience. You're the best!

Also many thanks to Julee Schwarzburg, a wonderful line editor who goes above and beyond her duties. I feel so blessed to have you and Becky on my side!

My agent, Natasha Kern, is a powerhouse of knowledge, tact, and friendship. She is an award-winning agent with an award-winning attitude and capabilities. Thanks for all you do, Natasha! God is blessing you.

I want to thank Jenny Sherwood, chairman of the Berkhamsted Local History and Museum Society, for helping me with my research on Berkhamsted Castle. It is one of the oldest motte-and-bailey castles in England, which disappeared, for the most part, from the landscape but will never be forgotten thanks to historians like Mrs. Sherwood. Thank you for your helpfulness and for sharing your knowledge with me.

I want to thank Kathy Bone, Mary Freeman, and Terry Bell for their brainstorming help, as well as Joe, Grace, and Faith Dickerson for listening and helping when I'm in the throes of plotting a story.

ACKNOWLEDGMENTS

I am extremely grateful to God for giving me this wonderful task to do, which I love so much, and for you wonderful readers out there. Thanks for supporting and encouraging me! You are very much loved. I hope you enjoyed my *Little Mermaid*—inspired story.

Discussion Questions

1. Why did Evangeline wish she was a peasant instead of the ward of a king? Would you have felt the same way? Why or why not?

2. When Evangeline wanted to disguise herself and hide from Lord Shiveley, she pretended to be mute, since her voice was a big part of her identity. What kind of disguise would you use if you were trying to hide your identity?

3. When Evangeline encountered the poor woman at the market who was begging for food, she gave her money and some of her bread rolls. Muriel scolded Evangeline and said the woman would probably lose the money. Do you think Evangeline did the right thing? Why or why not?

4. When Evangeline tried to work as a servant, she found she wasn't very good at some of her duties, but she still managed to make friends. What things did she do well? What things did she do badly?

5. Evangeline struggled with understanding the story of Ruth. Are there passages in the Bible that puzzle you? What do you do when you don't understand something? How do you express or deal with confusion or doubt? Is it possible to understand everything in the Bible? Why or why not?

6. Evangeline feared that no one could love her if they thought she was selfish. Have you ever feared people couldn't love

you if they discovered something about you or something you have done? Have you ever tried to hide a part of yourself from others?

7. Evangeline wondered how she could get absolved from the sin of deceiving Westley into thinking she was mute. Have you ever struggled with guilt over something you've done? How did you, or how can you, overcome your guilt?

8. Why did Evangeline carve *"Absolve me"* and three crosses into the wall of the church? What do you do when you want to get God's attention?

9. Evangeline felt peace when she realized she didn't need a husband or a friend to take care of her; she only needed God. What thought gives you peace?

10. Westley was very upset with Evangeline for defying his order for her to stay in Glynval. Do you think he was right to ask her to stay behind? Did you understand why she did not stay behind? What would you have done?

11. Evangeline and Westley were both willing to sacrifice themselves for each other. How do husbands, wives, family members, or friends make sacrifices for each other in today's world?

12. In this story, what parallels or similarities did you see to "The Little Mermaid" fairy tale?

13. How did you feel about seeing familiar characters again from *The Merchant's Daughter*? Did their lives end up the way you imagined they would? In what ways?

Don't miss the Medieval Fairy Tale novels also available from Melanie Dickerson!

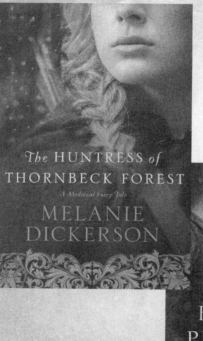

Available in print and e-book

The GOLDEN BRAID

The one who needs rescuing isn't always the one in the tower.

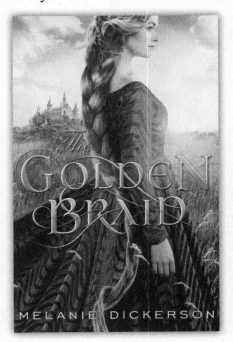

Rapunzel can throw a knife better than any man around. And her skills as an artist rival those of any artist she's met. But for a woman in medieval times, the one skill she most desires is the hardest one to obtain: the ability to read.

Available in print and e-book

THOMAS NELSON
Since 1798

Chapter One

*Late winter, 1413, the village of Ottelfelt,
Southwest of Hagenheim, the Holy Roman Empire*

"Rapunzel, I wish to marry you."

At that moment, Mother revealed herself from behind the well in the center of the village, her lips pressed tightly together.

The look Mother fixed on Wendel Gotekens was the one that always made Rapunzel's stomach churn.

Rapunzel shuffled backward on the rutted dirt road. "I am afraid I cannot marry you."

"Why not?" He leaned toward her, his wavy hair unusually tame and looking suspiciously like he rubbed it with grease. "I have as much land as the other villagers. I even have two goats and five chickens. Not many people in Ottelfelt have both goats and chickens."

She silently repeated the words an old woman had once told her. *The truth is kinder than a lie.*

"I do not wish to marry you, Wendel." She had once seen him unleash his ill temper on one of his goats when it ran away from him.

That alone would have been enough to make her lose interest in him, if she had ever felt any.

He opened his mouth as if to protest further, but he became aware of Mother's presence and turned toward her.

"*Frau* Gothel, I—"

"I shall speak to you in a moment." Her mother's voice was icy. "Rapunzel, go home."

Rapunzel hesitated, but the look in Mother's eyes was so fierce, she turned and hurried down the dirt path toward their little house on the edge of the woods.

Aside from asking her to marry him, Wendel's biggest blunder had been letting Mother overhear him.

Rapunzel made it to their little wattle-and-daub structure and sat down, placing her head in her hands, muffling her voice. "Father God, please don't let Mother's sharp tongue flay Wendel too brutally."

Mother came through the door only a minute or two later. She looked around their one-room home, then began mumbling under her breath.

"There is nothing to be upset about, Mother," Rapunzel said. "I will not marry him, and I told him I wouldn't."

Her mother had that frantic look in her eyes and didn't seem to be listening. Unpleasant things often happened when Mother got that look. But she simply snatched her broom and went about sweeping the room, muttering unintelligibly.

Rapunzel was the oldest unmarried maiden she knew, except for the poor half-witted girl in the village where they'd lived several years ago. That poor girl drooled and could barely speak a dozen words. The girl's mother had insisted her daughter was a fairy changeling and would someday be an angel who would come back to earth to punish anyone who mistreated her.

Mother suddenly put down her broom. "Tomorrow is a market

day in Keiterhafen. Perhaps I can sell some healing herbs." She began searching through her dried herbs on the shelf attached to the wall. "If I take this feverfew and yarrow root to sell, I won't have any left over," she mumbled.

"If you let me stay home, I can gather more for you."

Her mother stopped what she was doing and stared at her. "Are you sure you will be safe without me? That Wendel Gotekens—"

"Of course, Mother. I have my knife."

"Very well."

The next morning Mother left before the sun was up to make the two-hour walk to Keiterhafen. Rapunzel arose a bit later and went to pick some feverfew and yarrow root in the forest around their little village of Ottelfelt. After several hours of gathering and exploring the small stream in the woods, she had filled two leather bags, which she hung from the belt around her waist. *This should put Mother in a better mood.*

Just as Rapunzel reentered the village on her way back home, three boys were standing beside the lord's stable.

"Rapunzel! Come over here!"

The boys were all a few years younger than she was.

"What do you want?" Rapunzel yelled back.

"Show us that knife trick again."

"It's not a trick." She started toward them. "It is a skill, and you will never learn it if you do not practice."

Rapunzel pulled her knife out of her kirtle pocket as she reached them. The boys stood back as she took her stance, lifted the knife, and threw it at the wooden building. The knife point struck the wood and held fast, the handle sticking out perfectly horizontal.

One boy gasped while another whistled.

"Practice, boys."

Rapunzel yanked her knife out of the wall and continued down the dusty path. She had learned the skill of knife throwing in one of the villages where she and Mother had lived.

Boys and old people were quick to accept her, an outsider, better than girls her own age, and she tried to learn whatever she could from them. An old woman once taught her to mix brightly colored paints using things easily found in the forest, which Rapunzel then used to paint flowers and vines and butterflies on the houses where she and Mother lived. An older man taught her how to tie several types of knots for different tasks. But the one skill she wanted to learn the most had been the hardest to find a teacher for.

She walked past the stone manor house, with the lord's larger house just behind it and the courtyard in front of it. On the other side of the road were the mill, the bakery, and the butcher's shop. And surrounding everything was the thick forest that grew everywhere man had not purposely cleared.

Endlein, one of the village girls, was drawing water from the well several feet away. She glanced up and waved Rapunzel over.

Rapunzel and her mother were still considered strangers in Ottelfelt as they had only been there since Michaelmas, about half a year. She hesitated before walking over.

Endlein fixed her eyes on Rapunzel as she drew near. "So, Rapunzel. Do you have something to tell me? Some news of great import?" She waggled her brows with a smug grin, pushing a strand of brown hair out of her eyes.

"No. I have no news."

"Surely you have something you want to say about Wendel Gotekens."

"I don't know what you mean."

Endlein lifted one corner of her mouth. "Perhaps you do not know."

"Know what?"

"That your mother has told Wendel he cannot ever marry you because the two of you are going away from Ottelfelt."

Rapunzel's stomach turned a somersault like the contortionists she had seen at the Keiterhafen fair.

She should have guessed Mother would decide to leave now that a young man had not only shown interest in her but had declared his wish to marry her. The same thing happened in the last two villages where they had lived.

Rapunzel turned toward home.

"Leaving without saying farewell?" Endlein called after her.

"I am not entirely sure we are leaving," Rapunzel called back. "Perhaps Mother will change her mind and we shall stay."

She hurried down the road, not even turning her head to greet anyone, even though the baker's wife stopped to stare and so did the alewife. She continued to the little wattle-and-daub cottage that was half hidden from the road by thick trees and bushes. The front door was closed, even though it was a warm day for late winter.

Rapunzel caught sight of the colorful vines and flowers she had only just finished painting on the white plaster walls and sighed. Oh well. She could simply paint more on their next house.

Pushing the door open, Rapunzel stopped. Her mother was placing their folded coverlet into the trunk.

"So it is true? We are leaving again?"

"Why do you say 'again'? We've never left here before." She had that airy tone she used when she couldn't look Rapunzel in the eye.

"But why? Only because Wendel said he wanted to marry me? I told you I would not marry him even if you approved of him."

"You don't know what you would do if he should say the right thing to you." Her tone had turned peevish as she began to place their two cups, two bowls, pot, and pan into the trunk.

"Mother."

"I know you, Rapunzel. You are quick to feel sorry for anyone and everyone." She straightened and waved her hand about, staring at the wall as though she were talking to it. "What if Wendel cried and begged? You might tell him you would marry him. He might beg you to show him your love. You might . . . you might do something you would later regret."

"I would not." Rapunzel's breath was coming fast now, her face hot. It wasn't the first time Mother had accused her of such a thing.

"You don't want to marry a poor, wretched farmer like that Wendel, do you? Who will always be dirty and have to scratch out his existence from the ground? Someone as beautiful as you? Men notice you, as well they might. But none of them are worthy of you . . . none of them." It was as if she had forgotten she was speaking to Rapunzel and was carrying on to herself.

"Mother, you don't have to worry that I will marry someone unworthy." Rapunzel could hardly imagine marrying anyone. One had to be allowed to talk to a man before she could marry him, and talking to men was something her mother had always discouraged. Vehemently.

Mother did not respond, so Rapunzel went to fold her clothes and pack her few belongings.

As she gathered her things, she felt no great sadness at the prospect of leaving Ottelfelt. She always had trouble making friends with girls near her own age, and here she had never lost her status as an outsider. But the real reason she felt no regret was because of what she wanted so very badly, and it was not something she could get in tiny Ottelfelt.

Rapunzel was at least nineteen years old, and she could stay in Ottelfelt without her mother if she wanted to. However, it would be difficult and dangerous—unheard of—unless she was married, since she had no other family. But if they went to a large town, there would certainly be many people who knew how to read and might be willing to teach her.

"Mother, you promised someday you would find someone who could teach me to read. Might we go to a large town where there is a proper priest who knows Latin, a place where there might dwell someone who can teach me to read and write?" She held her breath, watching her mother, whose back was turned as she wrapped her fragile dried herbs in cloths.

Finally, her mother answered softly, "I saw someone in Keiterhafen this morning, someone who . . . needs my help with . . . something."

Rapunzel stopped in the middle of folding her clothes, waiting for Mother to clarify the strange comment.

"And now we will be going to meet him in Hagenheim."

Her heart leapt. Hagenheim was a great town, the largest around.

She tried not to sound eager as she asked, "Isn't that where you lived a long time ago, when Great-Grandmother was still alive?"

"Yes, my darling. Your great-grandmother was the most renowned midwife in the town of Hagenheim—in the entire region." She paused. "Someone I once knew will soon be back in Hagenheim after a long stay in England."

"I don't remember you saying you knew anyone who went to England. Is it a family member?"

Her mother turned to Rapunzel with a brittle smile. "No, not a family member. And I have never mentioned this person before. I do not wish to talk about it now."

The look on Mother's face kept Rapunzel from asking any more questions. Mother had never had friends, and she had never shown any interest in marrying. Although she could marry if she wished.

She was still slim and beautiful, with her long, dark hair, which had very little gray.

Later, as Rapunzel finished getting her things ready to tie onto their ox in the morning, she hummed a little song she'd made up. Mother enjoyed hearing her songs, but only when no one else was around.

When night fell, Rapunzel sang her song as Mother finished braiding Rapunzel's long blond hair. Mother smiled in her slow, secretive way. "My precious, talented girl."

Rapunzel embraced her and crawled under the coverlet of their little straw bed.

The next day Rapunzel trudged beside her mother down the road, which was nothing more than two ruts that the ox carts had worn deep in the mud that had then dried and become as hard as stone. She led their ox, Moll, down the center between the ruts, careful to avoid stepping in the horse and ox dung. Their laying hens clucked nervously from the baskets that were strapped to Moll's back.

Night began to fall. Rapunzel lifted her hand to her face and rubbed the scar on her palm against her cheek absentmindedly. She'd had the scar, which ran from the base of her thumb to the other side of her hand, for as long as she could remember. The skin over it was smooth and pale, like a long crescent moon.

"How much farther to Hagenheim, Mother?"

"At least two more days."

Rapunzel didn't mention what she was thinking: that a band of robbers could easily be hiding in the trees at the side of the road. It was not safe for two women to be traveling alone, although they had never been attacked in all the times they had moved from one village to the next.

They had also never traveled so far. They normally only journeyed a few hours.

When the moon was up and shining brightly, and they had not encountered any other travelers for at least an hour, Mother said, "We will stop here for the night."

Rapunzel guided the ox off the road and among the dark trees.

They made a small fire and prepared a dinner of toasted bread, cheese, and fried eggs.

After making sure the ox and hens had food, and after putting out their fire, Rapunzel and Mother lay close together, wrapped in their blankets. Rapunzel sang softly until Mother began to snore.

The next day was uneventful and the unusually warm weather continued. The sun shone down on Rapunzel's head and shoulders as she plodded along at the speed of the ox and to the sound of the chickens' clucking and squawking. Occasionally she amused herself and Mother with her songs, but she always stopped singing when someone came within listening distance. Her mother had warned her not to let strangers hear her beautiful voice or see her golden, ankle-length hair, which Rapunzel kept covered with a scarf and sometimes a stiff wimple. But Mother had never explained why. Perhaps she just didn't want Rapunzel attracting attention to herself for the same reason she didn't want her singing or speaking to men, young, old, or in-between.

On the second day of their journey, two travelers caught up with them, leading two donkeys that pulled a cart loaded and covered by burlap, with one of the men riding on the tallest lump on the back of the cart. As they passed by to Rapunzel's right, the man leading the donkeys smiled. "Pardon me, but would you know how close we are to Hagenheim town?"

"We should reach it by tomorrow night." Rapunzel noticed a big scar on the side of his face. "You may reach it sooner since you are moving faster."

"Thank you, kind maiden." He nodded.

Mother turned to stare hard at something just behind them. The second man stared pointedly at their bundles and baskets tied to Moll's back. When the man's eyes darted to hers, the hair on the back of her neck stood up at the look in his eyes and the strange smile on his face.

"A good day to you." He spoke politely, and they moved ahead until they rounded a shady bend in the road and disappeared.

She sighed in relief, until her mother said in her irritable tone, "Don't speak to strangers, Rapunzel. You know it is dangerous."

"He only asked a simple question. Besides, he didn't look dangerous."

"Dangerous men are the ones who take care not to look dangerous."

Clouds encroached on the sun, sending a shadow creeping over her shoulder. As they entered the double shadow of the trees that hung over the curve in the road, the cart that had passed them a few moments before sat idle several feet ahead. Its two owners were nowhere in sight.

Rapunzel felt a sensation like bugs crawling over her skin. She put her hand on her belt, where she usually kept her knife, but it was not there. She must have left it in their food bag when she put everything away after their midday meal. Should she stop? Or speed up?

Before she could decide, she heard footsteps running up behind her. She spun around just as the man who had smiled at her earlier reached his hands toward her. And he was still smiling.

The story continues in *The Golden Braid* by Melanie Dickerson.

About the Author

Jodie Westfall Photography

*Melanie Dickerson is a two-time Christy Award final-*ist and author of *The Healer's Apprentice*, winner of the National Readers' Choice Award for Best First Book in 2010, and *The Merchant's Daughter*, winner of the 2012 Carol Award. She spends her time writing romantic medieval stories at her home near Huntsville, Alabama, where she lives with her husband and two daughters.

Website: www.MelanieDickerson.com

Twitter: @melanieauthor

Facebook: MelanieDickersonBooks